Brought to Light
More Stories of Forgotten Women

Brought to Light

MORE STORIES OF FORGOTTEN WOMEN

Edited by Bernadette Rule

Seraphim
EDITIONS

The publisher gratefully acknowledges the financial assistance of the Canada Council for the Arts and the Ontario Arts Council.

Library and Archives Canada Cataloguing in Publication

    Brought to light : more stories of forgotten women / edited by Bernadette Rule.

Includes bibliographical references.
ISBN 978-1-927079-36-2 (paperback)

    1. Creative nonfiction, Canadian (English). 2. Short stories, Canadian (English). 3. Canadian fiction (English)–21st century. 4. Women–Fiction.
I. Rule, Bernadette, 1951-, editor

PS8323.W65B76 2015   C813'.01083522   C2015-905239-4

Editor: Bernadette Rule
Design and Typography: Julie McNeill, McNeill Design Arts

Published in 2015 by
Seraphim Editions
4456 Park Street
Niagara Falls, ON
Canada L2E 2P6

Printed and bound in Canada

For Maureen Whyte,
who has given a voice to so many writers
through her beautiful publishing company,
Seraphim Editions.

CONTENTS

FOREWORD

In 2012, Seraphim Editions published *In the Wings: Stories of Forgotten Women,* which was born out of a class I taught for the McMaster Writing Certificate Program. In that class, which was called Writing Women Characters, the final assignment was to think of a famous man, then research a woman connected to him and write her into a story – remember her. The story was to be written in the genre of creative non-fiction, true to the facts, but using the tools of fiction. *In the Wings* inspired requests for more such stories, which is how *Brought to Light: More Stories of Forgotten Women* came to be. That first anthology, like this one, was expanded to include women who made a name for themselves unconnected to famous men, but who have been forgotten or misremembered. This collection follows the same guidelines.

Handled carefully, I believe creative non-fiction is a very powerful approach to understanding a person's life. As Virginia Woolf put it: "Let the biographer print fully, completely, accurately, the known facts without comment; then let him [sic] write the life as fiction." It is a recipe for mind-expansion, for toppling barriers.

I and the other writers of *Brought to Light* are extremely grateful to Maureen Whyte of the aptly named Seraphim Editions for this book. We are also grateful to Julie McNeill, our book designer, Trudi and George Down of The Book Band for their help with promotion and sales, and to Donna Yates for the title of the collection. Here, from writers across Canada, are stories of women as varied as Michelangelo's wet nurse and the last Mi'kmaq shaman of Newfoundland. We are so used to seeing the world through the point of view of powerful men that many people aren't even aware of how limited a view that is. However, as the brilliant Irish writer Nuala O'Faolain says, "The view is always clearer from the edge of empire." Here are stories from the edge of the human empire. Read them and weep, laugh, grow.

Bernadette Rule

A MOTHER'S LONGING

MICHELANGELO'S MOTHER FRANCESCA & HIS WETNURSE

Michelle Ward-Kantor

Italy – 1475
Francesca – Caprese, Chiusi

Francesca lay, remembering the long ride on horseback, up twisting roads to this remote town some five months ago. Although it was September, the air had cooled off as they climbed higher into the Casentino mountains. She had been terrified at the steepness of the trail, praying they would arrive safely and thinking of the child she carried in her belly. She wondered, too, about the health of her first-born son, who was still in the care of a wet nurse.

And then the horse had stumbled. She remembered slipping, remembered trying to hold on to the horse's warm belly, remembered her terror when she continued to slip and felt her shoulder hit the ground. She could smell the earth, hear the scrabbling of the horse's hooves as it tried to right itself, and when it did, it carried on, up the steep trail, pulling her with it. She heard the shouts of the others and finally the horse was brought to a halt.

It was her husband, she found out later, who had gotten to the horse's head, even on that narrow trail, and forced him to stop. It had taken all of five minutes, she was told, but it hadn't seemed that way. It had felt like eternity, and all the time she had prayed for her unborn child. She herself had some bruises, and a terrible ache in her shoulder and back for weeks after the fall.

She worried that a doctor could not possibly get to this remote location for the birth of her son. Yet in the early, dark hours of a cold day in March, with the help of the servant-girls and a local midwife, Francesca had laboured, the pain making her scream and cry out. When she reached for her son, his body still damp from the womb, he looked, by some intervention of God, to be unharmed. His cheeks were pink, his cries as hearty as those of her firstborn. She said a silent prayer of thanks and wondered at the miracle that had prevented her head and belly from being hit by the horse's hooves.

These memories ran through her mind as she listened to the church bells, ringing out sweetly from the church of San Giovanni, where her son was being baptized. What a special day, she thought. She wished she could tell her son that her absence at his baptism was because she needed to rest. And today the town was in winter's grip, made worse by an icy wind.

She heard the door sometime later, and voices.

"Francesca, we are back!" Vincenza, one of the servant girls, stood in the doorway, the baby in her arms. "Oh, but it is cold! We kept your son very warm, and, bless him, he is asleep now. He was so good, just a little cry when the water was poured over his head."

She placed him in the cradle beside Francesca's bedside. Although many women slept with their newborn children beside them, Francesca did not want to risk lying on her baby and suffocating him. Many families now had cradles to avoid a tragedy.

"Several of the townspeople were there. They send their very good wishes. Is there anything you need?"

Francesca shook her head. "No Vincenza, thank you."

Francesca watched her baby's sleeping form from her bed. She took in his curved lashes, his smooth skin, his tiny nose and mouth. She reached out to caress his silky head. Michelangelo didn't stir.

She lay back and fell asleep, and awoke later to his cries. Another of the servant girls came in, gathered him from the cradle and placed him in Francesca's arms. Francesca helped him latch himself, and as he nursed, she stroked the tiny hand lying across her breast. She savoured the scent of him, sadness engulfing her at the thought of turning him over to a wet nurse.

"My term here as *podesta* is almost finished," her husband announced at dinner the following week. "We'll be returning to Florence at the close of this month."

Francesca stopped eating. Her heart sped up at the thought of returning down those same steep roads with her newborn son. Although she missed Florence, she felt tears form at the corners of her eyes.

"Oh, Ludovico, I don't know if we can manage the return down that trail. And the reports of the plague, they scare me so."

"*Amore mio,* you know how worried I was about bringing you to this remote place, all that way on horseback, and you with child." Her husband reached across the table to grasp her hand. "I understand reports of the plague are few. After all, it has been many years since the outbreak. As for our journey down, we will go very slowly. I make my promise to you that all will be well."

Maria – Settignano

Maria lay silently, staring at the wall, at the cross where Jesus hung. She wondered why he had abandoned her, why he had abandoned her son. The tears fell silently down her flushed cheeks and her body shook.

"Forgive me, son of God. I am ashamed. But please. I am broken inside."

She wept then, remembering the pain that had engulfed her body hour after hour after hour, until time had merged into one unending moment of torment. One that didn't end when night fell or when dawn approached. She thought of the ravaging from the inside out, remembered the screams and how they had spoken excitedly, "The head, give me your hand! Feel your baby's head!"

They gave him to her after the birth and she stared at the tiny body, his dark, damp hair, his tiny perfect nose, his full lips, his lovely soft cheeks. He wailed and she put him to her nipple. He attached himself clumsily, and Maria, remembering her first child, helped his tiny mouth open wide enough to encircle the whole nipple. She knew that a bad latch caused terrible pain.

After a few unsuccessful tries, she had him latched properly, and she closed her eyes with fatigue. She knew it would take a few days for her milk to come in, but for now, her son would get the nourishment he needed with the foremilk that came first. Some thought this milk was no good, but Maria knew better.

As she nursed, she listened to the hammering and chiseling going on outside her window. Her husband and father were training a new apprentice and although they often worked at the site where they were building, today they were in the lodge. Maria knew they were teaching the apprentice what each tool was for. He would have to learn this before moving on to the work itself.

She knew the importance of the quarries to her family's well-being, yet she didn't like the thought of her baby breathing in the dust that always hung in the air in the village. The quarries were filled with *pietra serena,* a grey, clay-type rock that was easy to work with, and had been used for centuries for important buildings in the city.

Maria had the joy of taking care of her son for several weeks; yet one morning he did not cry to be fed. She went to his cradle and saw that his eyes were closed, his face flushed. He was hot to the touch and when she bent and put her ear to his chest, she heard him struggling to breathe. A doctor was summoned but within hours, her baby took no more breaths. His eyes remained closed in a long, forever sleep.

She had two other children to look after, yet in her grief, Maria pleaded with the figure on the cross. "It should have been me. You should have taken me."

The ache in her breasts over the next few days heightened the terrible sadness she felt. Just the thought of her son was enough to make her engorged breasts leak. Around the time she was instructed by the physician to bind herself to stop milk production, her husband came to her. He put his arm around her shoulder as she stood in the kitchen, steeping leaves for a cup of tea.

"I know you are grieved, Maria, as I am." He turned her to face him and stroked her cheek. "Yet I must tell you there is a family from Florence, the family who owns the small farm where Giovanni and his wife live. They have a son, not yet one month old." He paused. "They would like to enter into a contract with you. It seems word has traveled about the death of our son."

Maria stood quietly while her husband gave her this news. Her two other children were playing nearby and she glanced at them, remembering the first time she had offered her services as a *balia*. This had meant sending her own children away to nurse.

"You know I would not turn away an opportunity to offer my services and bring income to our family."

Her husband was a good man. He did not beat her. She knew he would not force her into this contract. She thought of her own good friend, Vanni Castellani, who just this last six months had nursed the daughter of a rich merchant. Vanni's own daughter had died four days after birth.

"When will the child arrive?"

"He will come tomorrow afternoon." Her husband paused. " The child needs you, Maria. Perhaps he will ease your pain somewhat."

"I will do my best." Her voice became strained. "But I cannot replace my son."

The next day, the child arrived with a man and a servant, who held the babe in her arms. "He is called Michelangelo," said the man. "I am Ludovico."

He gave to Maria's husband four woolen swaddling cloths, eleven linen swaddling cloths, two linens, six bands, a cradle-*aruccio*, a mattress and a small quilt. Maria was grateful to see the cradle. This past three months she had heard of a death by overlaying of a two-week old infant in this very village. Likely the *balia* was too tired to use the cradle, if she had even been given one.

The servant girl took Maria aside. "His mother would like you to know that he seems to prefer nursing on the right side. She loves him very much, and she thanks you for looking after him."

Maria gazed at the girl. "Tell his mother I understand how it feels to miss your son. My own died just three days ago. I will look after him well."

The servant smiled and seemed relieved. "Thank you."

In the first weeks, Maria compared Michelangelo to the son she had lost, but as the days became weeks and then months, she found it happening less and less. She nurtured the child as well as she could, given that she had two others to care for, meals to prepare and chickens to tend.

She also kept the books and records for her husband's craft as a stonemason. Growing up in a family of stonemasons, Maria knew the names of all the tools needed for the trade. She had also proven herself better with the abacus than her brothers, and as she grew older, she was given the job of recording sums in her father's record books, how many *lire* and *florins* were spent each month and the totals at the end of each year. Her husband was proud that his wife was able to keep accurate records. She knew some men would not let their wives manage the books of their trade.

As the months went by, Maria grew to love Michelangelo. She knew the time would come when she would have to return him to his family, yet that didn't make her care for him any less than her own children. With her other duties there were times she felt she couldn't give the children as much attention as they needed. She felt then that perhaps she was a bad mother and nurse.

Francesca – Florence and Facciano

The Buonarroti family had been settled in Florence for several months and had welcomed their first-born, Lionardo, back into their home. At first, he seemed unhappy and Francesca thought perhaps he needed time to adjust to new surroundings, and to being without his wet nurse.

Several months after their son's return, her husband accepted a posting in Facciano, as keeper of the castle there. This was another remote place, north of the small village in Caprese. Francesca was not happy to be leaving again. She wondered how Lionardo would adjust to yet another unfamiliar home.

Still, she was grateful that her husband had employment. While the farm in Settignano gave them a small monthly income, it was not enough to live on indefinitely. With these things in mind, she tried not to complain in the days leading up to their departure.

"After all, it might be easier to make a journey when I am not with child," she told her husband.

Some belongings were packed and soon they traveled north-east to Romagna. Francesca was glad for the company of two servants and her son, as this castle was as remote as the mountain-top in Caprese. She wondered how Michelangelo was faring. She missed his smooth skin, his scent, just as she had missed Lionardo when he was put out to nurse.

During the days in the castle, she busied herself helping to manage the household, the grain stores, wood, wine, tableware and servants. She tried to be attentive to two-year old Lionardo, yet he often screamed "No" when she asked him to do something and many times refused to eat his food. She hoped he would adjust to his surroundings and to her, but his behaviour made her anxious.

She thought about Michelangelo and wondered if the physicians and priests were right when they said maternal nursing was of the utmost importance. Her own physician once told her how the mother's milk helped shape the body and mind of the child.

She had even heard that the late preacher San Bernardino said that women fell into sin when they put their babies out to nurse. She knew that women of lesser means sometimes suckled their own, but she had not heard of any of her friends doing such a thing. And what of becoming pregnant and having the milk sullied? It was not possible to nurse while pregnant without consequences..

She knew her husband understood the importance of finding a wet nurse of good character, since character was transferred through the milk. Still, one evening at dinner, after being in the castle several weeks, she asked him, "How did Michelangelo's wet-nurse seem? What character does she possess?"

Her husband frowned. "You doubt my choice, Francesca? You know how difficult it is to find a good wet nurse. It is not something I take lightly. These are my sons! Perhaps you are feeling lonely here and becoming prone to letting your mind wander?"

Francesca knew her husband was right and she vowed not to think about it again. In four months, the contract had ended and the family returned to Florence, where they rented a small dwelling. By now, Francesca was carrying their third child.

Now that she was settled once again in Florence, her thoughts turned to the writing of a will. She knew that pregnancy and child-birth were dangerous times for a woman. She had briefly thought of it with her first two pregnancies, but she had been distracted with moving, resettling and fatigue. She would have liked to have left her dowry to her sons if this birth went badly, and lamented the fact that her husband had used most of the money to pay off his taxes. She knew, however, that it was the only way he would have been allowed to accept government posts.

"*Amore mio,*" her husband said one evening as they discussed how many *florins* would be available for food that month after paying rent. "I have done my best for you and for our sons. This place is not where we would have lived, had the family home not been lost those thirty years ago. But we will make do here."

Not far from where they lived was the Stinche, a debtor's prison that occupied one city block and was surrounded by a moat.

"Many a Florentine has been jailed for not paying their debts," her husband continued. "We must never let expenditure exceed income in this family."

In their small home, they also made room for Ludovico's mother, his brother and his brother's wife. It was crowded, but Francesca was glad to be surrounded by family after months of living in remote villages.

Soon after the family settled in Florence, Ludovico traveled to Settignano to bring Michelangelo home, a boy who now knew how to walk and had mastered many words.

"Our son is healthy and was given good care," he told Francesca when he returned. "You needn't have worried about Maria's character." He laughed. "She showed me some drawings he had done, in black chalk. He loves to draw."

"He seems unhappy," Francesca told her husband during the first few weeks of his return. "He calls for 'Rea' sometimes, although I tell him she is not here and I am his mother. I try to hug him but he seems unsure of me. I think he prefers his brother to me."

"Well, it's not a bad thing for brothers to be friends." He kissed his wife and patted her growing belly. "And let him draw if that's what he likes. It will keep him happy. We'll take him out to the pageant this weekend. He must get used to living here, after all."

As Francesca's belly grew with the impending birth of her third child, she became tired and irritable. She could not get comfortable at night and was tired during the day. Her back ached terribly and the pain in her shoulder, which had bothered her since the fall from the horse, was getting worse. Sometimes she spoke harshly to her sons as they played. She felt guilty, yet once the words had left her mouth, they could not be taken back. She thought perhaps she was becoming a bad mother.

Her husband was sometimes gone for hours. She worried that he had taken a mistress because she could not satisfy his needs. When they had been away in remote villages, she thought there was little chance of that.

Her son Buonarroto was born following a prolonged labour and Francesca was exhausted when he finally arrived. But he was in good health and she was thankful. The lying-in period was much longer than with her first two sons. Even though she was again saddened at the thought of his leaving, she was somewhat relieved when he was taken to his wet nurse.

While she rested, Enza Fireni came to visit. "Francesca! What a joy to see you again." She had brought a lovely birth tray, a *desco da parto* laden with jars of chicken soup and sweetmeats. "Some *zuppa* to help you recover," she said as they hugged each other. "And the tray is from Petro di Giovanni's workshop! I missed the birth of your second son so I wanted to get you something special for this baby. How is his health? And how have you been, moving around these past years, living away from Florence?"

Francesca confessed she had been lonely sometimes. She told her friend of her fall in Caprese and her worries about Michelangelo and Lionardo. "I envy those who can afford to bring a wet-nurse into their home. I think I don't know my boys as I should, and they do not know me."

"Yes, Francesca. That would be nice, but not very practical. And you know as well as I that people in our position could not dream of that!" She took Francesca's hands. "My sons also had to adjust when they came home. They will be fine, Francesca. You need not worry so!"

Francesca hugged her friend again and turned to admire the *desco da parto*. It was painted with several images of Cupid, as well as Aristotle and Phyllis and Samson and Delilah.

"My cousin from Tuscany wrote me this last month," said Enza, "and told me how fashionable these trays are now. These pictures are to make you think good thoughts so you produce strong, healthy boys in future!"

"This is lovely. Thank-you, dear Enza. I will hang this tray on the wall and think of Buonarroto while he is away. He won't be gone for long, as we cannot spend too many *florins* now."

Later that year, Francesca was at home with Buonarroto. There was some commotion in the streets outside. Francesca heard yelling and wondered when Michelangelo and Lionardo, who were out with their father, would return. Just a few weeks before one of the ruling Medici brothers had been assassinated during Mass at the Cathedral of Florence. The other brother had escaped with stab wounds. It soon became known that the Pazzi family were responsible and they and their co-conspirators were caught and executed, among them the archbishop of Pisa.

Francesca had seen the bodies of some of the men hanging from the windows of the *palazzo communale*. One of her friends had told her of a body that was dropped to the ground so the poor could steal the clothes from it. She preferred not to go outside now as the unrest made her uneasy. The commotion today made her anxious and immediately upon the return of her husband and sons she hurried to meet them.

"What happened today? There were many yelling out in the streets!"

Her sons began talking excitedly. "I saw a man. He was torn apart!" said Michelangelo. His eyes were wide. "On Papa's shoulders!"

"What do you mean to tell me?" she asked her husband. "What has he seen? A man torn apart?" She crossed her arms and the pitch of her voice increased. "You permitted our three-year old son to see this?" She reached out to take Michelangelo but he shrank from her and stood behind his father's legs.

"Do not worry, *il mio dolce figlio*. Your mother is just relieved that we are home." He bent down to his son, and put an arm around his small frame. He looked up at his wife. "He was on my shoulders. I turned away when I saw what they were doing. It was the body of Jacopo de' Pazzi. They were tearing at it and beating it." Her husband shook his head. "The people are angry, but this is not the way to behave."

Francesca comforted Michelangelo that night when he awoke from a nightmare. Her husband slept soundly and never woke if the children cried. It was she who heard every whimper.

"Will they do this to Papa?" he asked her.

"Jacopo de' Pazzi was a bad man. Your papa is a good man." She hugged her son. "That will never happen to your papa."

In the following year, the family welcomed their fourth child. He was called Giovan Simone. The three boys welcomed their new brother, although they were quickly ushered out of the room by their grandmother, who told them their mother needed to rest.

Less than two years later, Francesca delivered her fifth child. She had felt bilious through much of this pregnancy and it proved to be the most difficult birth she had had. As the hours dragged on through her painful labour, she became too tired to even cry out.

Sigismondo made his entrance into the world many, many hours after his mother's labour started and by then Francesca had lost a lot of blood. By the second day, she was running a dangerously high fever. Michelangelo and Buonarroto came to her bedside. Of her four boys, these two sons were most likely to be together, laughing and playing. She was glad of their friendship and, though she felt terribly weak, she held each one close.

"*Mamma*, you are very hot," said Buonarroto, his brow furrowed in concern.

Ludovico was standing by the bedside, watching over his wife. "Fetch your mamma a cool cloth," he said to his sons. "Hurry now."

"My two sweet boys," she murmured as Bunonarroto laid the cloth on her forehead. "Always remember how I love you, even when I feel unwell and cannot tend you. Bring your brothers to me."

She fell in and out of sleep that afternoon. Her thoughts came in bits and pieces: a night spent with her husband; Michelangelo's unhappiness after the time with his wet nurse; an illness that left Buonarroto weak for days and how she worried; how stubborn Giovan Simone could be; the way Lionardo laughed at something silly and made her smile; her best friend Enza; and her fifth child, whose crying she could hear through a foggy haze. Would she ever hold him?

A doctor was summoned, but by the time he arrived that evening, Francesca had closed her eyes. She never woke again.

Maria – Settignano

In the days following Michelangelo's departure, Maria busied herself with her children, keeping her husband happy, doing the necessary farm-work and bookkeeping duties. The months and years passed and her own children gave her much to smile and worry about.

Sometimes she found herself remembering both the baby she had lost and little Michelangelo. These two small bits of her heart had been permanently dislodged. Word eventually traveled to her that Michelangelo's mother had died, and Maria sent out a silent prayer for her soul and for the soul of the small boy she had loved as her own.

Author's Note

While deciding on a woman to write about for this anthology, one who had been forgotten in the history books, I began to wonder about the mother of Michelangelo. Biographers often speak of the lack of maternal warmth and circumstances that prevented his mother from looking after him. I discovered that he, like so many other children of his time, had been sent to a wet nurse.

Michelangelo was born to Francesca, daughter of Neri di Miniata del Sera and Ludovico Buonarroti (Lodovico in some references). Francesca was married in 1472, when she was sixteen. A fall from her horse when she was pregnant with Michelangelo, is documented, and it was rumoured by some that she gave birth by the side of the road the night she fell. During the nine years she was married, she had five sons. A major role of Renaissance women was to deliver children, and boys were the sex of choice. Clearly, Francesca "did her duty" as a Florentine wife.

Francesca died in 1481, at age twenty-six, likely from complications after the birth of her fifth son. Michelangelo was barely six years old, and according to biographers, he never spoke of her loss. While Michelangelo made no mention of his mother, he did remember his wet nurse.

> *Caro Giorgio, if I have any intelligence at all, it has come from being born in the pure air of your native Arezzo, just as also I imbibed from the milk of my nurse the mallets and chisels I use for carving my figures.* – Michelangelo, from *Young Michelangelo* by John T. Spike.

The wet nurse made an impression on Michelangelo, although she made none on historians, as I found no mention of her name. What is acknowledged is that she lived in Settignano, a village not far from Florence. Both her father and husband were stonemasons.

"A Mother's Longing" is an attempt to explore reasons for the lack of maternal warmth often suggested by biographers. I also felt the need to shine a light on the two women most responsible for shaping the first six years of the life of one of the greatest artists the world has ever known.

For further information on the women in Michelangelo's young life, refer to *Michelangelo: A Tormented Life,* translated and edited by Allen Cameron. For more information on women in renaissance times, I recommend *Women of the Renaissance,* by Margaret L. King.

A TURTLE LAYING EGGS IN THE SAND

Tecumseh's mother, Methoataske

Jean Rae Baxter

Standing on the bank of the Tallapoosa River, Methoataske watches the canoes draw near, cutting through the steel-blue water. She knows that Tecumseh is in one of those canoes. She has not seen him since he was ten years old. That was thirty-four winters ago.

Her son is not coming to see her. He may not know that she is still alive. He may not care. Tecumseh is a man on a mission, and that is why he is coming here. His purpose is to rally all the nations against the white settlers. Many tribes have gone to war at his signal. He is a great chief. His greatness does not surprise his mother. She knew it from the moment of his birth.

"Will I recognize him?" she asks herself. There are twelve canoes, two warriors in each. She squints to see if she can distinguish one face from another. Not yet. They are still too far away.

This will be his first visit to the village where his mother was born and to which she long ago returned. It is a small village, upstream from the bend in the Tallapoosa where it sweeps down from the north to turn west and join the Coosa River to form the Alabama.

Her people, the Muskogee Creeks, are not wanderers. Until her sixteenth summer, she had never been more than half-a-day's journey from her home. If a young Shawnee warrior named Puckeshinwa had not shown up at that particular time, she would have married a Muskogee man and never left the Tallapoosa River.

Puckeshinwa had appeared just when she was ripe for marriage, and she found the good-looking stranger more exciting than the Muskogee boys she had known all her life. The Shawnees were a wandering people. Puckeshinwa had been born in Florida, he told her. He gave her a silver brooch and promised that if she would marry him, he would settle down and make his home with her on the winding, gently flowing Tallapoosa.

For three years he kept his word. But their first child, Chiksika, had scarcely been born when word came down the Tallapoosa that the Shawnees were on the move, migrating to the Ohio country. The urge came over him to live again with his people.

Puckeshinwa fashioned a dugout canoe from a great log, and that spring he and Methoataske and their baby began the long journey. They moved and moved again, travelling in summer but wintering over in villages along the way. They did not hurry. By the time they finally reached the land of the Shawnees, she had presented him with two more children, their son Sawaseekau and their eldest daughter Tecumapease.

Methoataske's fingers stroke the silver brooch that was Puckeshinwa's gift. It is all that she has to remember him by.

Now the canoes have landed. The Shawnee warriors climb from their canoes. All of them wear war paint, streaks of red semi-circles under each eye. Each warrior's hair is plaited in three braids hanging down his back; their temples are shaved. They are naked from the waist up, and each has a large red dot painted on the centre of his chest. Methoataske has no doubt which warrior is her son. She recognizes him at once. He looks so like his father that her heart gives a jolt. He is a handsome man: tall, broad-shouldered, slim and muscular. Her mind runs wild with memories.

◯

She and Puckeshinwa and their first three children had settled down in Old Piqua, a village that straggled along the bluffs of the Mad River in Ohio. A fourth child, a daughter, was born.

Tecumseh came next.

Although it was forty-four years ago, she clearly remembers the night of his birth. Her labour had been long, but she knew enough to rest in the spaces between pains. Relaxing on the mat in the birthing lodge while the holy woman rubbed her back, Methoataske listened to the sounds of the summer night. Crickets chirped. Frogs croaked. Outside the birthing lodge, Puckeshinwa waited.

He had always been at hand to welcome each new child. For this she was grateful, though it was mostly luck that he never chanced to be away on a war party or hunting trip. His nearness kept her from crying out the way some women did. To make her husband proud of her, she held her pain inside, directing it downward to add its force to the great push that would be needed at the end. For half the night she had been waiting for that push.

Then it came, suddenly and with a force that seemed to come from the sky above. Her belly shifted, and she felt the firm roundness push from between her legs, then the fleshy gate opened, and the gush of water rushed the child's head out into the world on a wave. One more push, and the holy woman caught the baby in her hands.

Methoataske, exhausted, stared up at the roof poles and waited to be told.

"You have a son," the holy woman said.

Still attached to the cord that connected him to somewhere inside his mother, the baby squalled out his first breath of life.

Outside the birthing lodge, her husband heard the cry. At the same instant a blazing star raced across the sky. Puckeshinwa understood the sign. He belonged to the Scioto clan, and that clan has a guardian spirit. It's a star they call The Panther. When he saw that shooting star, he knew that the child was born for greatness. Tecumseh means "Panther in the Sky." Right from birth, that was his name. No need to earn another.

Not like me, Methoataske thinks. *I earned my name.* Methoataske. In Shawnee the name means "A turtle that lays her eggs in the sand." She had given Puckeshinwa eight children, five sons and three daughters. Yes, she had earned her name.

After Tecumseh she gave birth to another daughter, Nehaaemo, and to a son, Kumskaukau. No she-turtle laying her eggs in the sand ever worked as hard as Methoataske did during those years. Breeding and feeding. Field work, too. She and the other women planted corn in the rich river bottom below the rolling hills. They had no metal tools, just ploughs made from the shoulder blades of buffalo and hoes from tortoise shells. Methoataske was too busy to think about her old life back on the Tallapoosa River. She was happy in her marriage and proud of her growing family.

O

The head sachem of the Creeks steps forward to meet the Shawnee delegation. Tecumseh presents him with a wampum belt. The crowd surges away from the river, but Mathotaske does not move. *What do I want from Tecumseh?* she asks herself. *Understanding? Forgiveness?* A mother who abandons her children has no right to expect either.

When she looks around, she sees that the delegation has gone with the sachems into the great lodge at the centre of the village. They will be there for a long time, passing the calumet from hand to hand until it is burned out. Methoataske sits down on the river bank and gives herself completely to her memories.

O

She was pregnant with her eighth child when she had her first vision. She knows that the child then in her womb has grown up to become famous for his visions. Today, people call him The Prophet. Like her, he sees things that no one else can see. That is the one thing they have in common. Is it a gift or a curse? She isn't sure.

Her first vision came while she was standing by the cooking fire stirring a pot of cornmeal mush. She often fell into a dream while pushing the long wooden spoon around and around. This time her dream turned into something more, as if eyes inside her head suddenly opened. She saw a man covered with blood lying motionless beside a trail, and she heard a voice from the sky above. "Your husband will die soon. Tell him to prepare."

So she told him. Puckeshinwa listened gravely, for although she was a woman, he knew she was no fool. At that time the Shawnees were getting ready to go on the warpath. They were joining with Delaware and Wyandotte warriors in a war against white settlers called Virginians. This warpath would lead them far away.

Before he left, Puckeshinwa told Chiksika, their eldest son, that it would fall to him to bring up his younger brothers to be skilful hunters and brave warriors.

The battle was a bloody one. Many warriors died. But Puckeshinwa returned unharmed. Methoataske rejoiced when he came back to her, happy beyond words that her vision had been wrong.

Her happiness did not last long. Mere days after the war party returned, Puckeshinwa was hunting alone. She had expected him home by sundown. When he did not return to their lodge, she set out to find him. Leaving her youngest children in her daughter Tecumapease's care, she took Tecumseh with her. Although he had only six winters, he could already follow a trail. They found Puckeshinwa lying beside a path in the forest. He was still alive.

His buckskin shirt was soaked with blood, and she saw the hole where the bullet had entered. She cut his shirt away and stopped the blood. But he had lost too much.

"What happened?" she asked.

"Some white men ... were hunting." He stopped speaking, waited for strength to continue. "They ordered me ... to be ... their guide." He had just enough strength to finish. "I said, 'No.' So ... they shot me."

"You will be avenged," she told him as he drew his last breath. She pressed her hands to his wound. Raising them, sticky with Puckeshinwa's blood, she smeared Tecumseh's smooth cheeks, painting them red, the colour for war. Then she took Tecumseh's small hand in her bloody hand and lifted it toward the sky. "Do you swear that the people who did this will be your foes forever?"

Staring at her wide-eyed, Tecumseh nodded. "I swear it."

Then she pulled Puckeshinwa's tomahawk from his belt, for his killers had left that, taking only his rifle. Using the tomahawk as a hatchet, she chopped two branches from a spruce tree and tied them together with sinew cord from her husband's pouch. She lashed them in such a way that the cut ends formed poles that she could hold, one under each arm, the way a travois is rigged for a dog or horse to pull a load. Interweaving the side branches, she made a crude litter. Tecumseh walking behind, she dragged Puckeshinwa's body home.

She took his body to her lodge and sat beside it through the night. In the morning she dressed him in his deerskin shirt. Warriors came to paint his face. They placed his body in a boat-like bier made of heavy bark. By his side were his tomahawk, his war club, his bow and a quiver filled with arrows, a bag of parched corn finely ground, and strips of dried meat. These were the things he would need for his journey to the Land without Trouble. When all was ready, Puckeshinwa's body was carried outside the village for the burial.

When that was done, Methoataske went into her lodge and lay down. She spoke to no one, not even to her children. If her eldest daughter Tecumapease had not been there, the little ones would have gone hungry. A child herself, she cooked their food, dressed them and told them stories. She brought food and drink to Methoataske, which she accepted because she lacked the will to refuse. This was in the eighth moon of her pregnancy.

When her time came, she had no husband waiting outside the birthing lodge to hear the baby's first cries. And cry he did. He was born yelling. Everyone in the village heard him.

"You have a son," the holy woman said. She laid the baby on Methoataske's chest. Methoataske raised her head to look at him. He was ugly, his skin red and wrinkled and his arms and legs thin as sticks. She felt nothing for him, no desire to hold him or take him to her breast. She turned her face away.

They gave him the name Lolawauchika – Big Mouth – because he was always making a noise. He shrieked and wailed. At night the others in their lodge pulled up their blankets to cover their ears. Methoataske made herself deaf to his cries. It was left to Tecumapease to try to console him. "What's wrong? What's wrong?" She pleaded with the baby, but of course he could not put his anguish into words.

As he emerged from infancy, it seemed impossible that he would ever be much of a warrior. He was awkward, under-sized, and backward in every way. The other children did not want him to join in their games. His oldest brother Chiksika despised him. Even tender-hearted Tecumapease had little patience with his tantrums. Tecumseh alone, of all her children, had any use for the youngest child.

Methoataske shakes her head, thinking about it. Who would have believed that someday Lolawauchika's fame would spread through all the nations? He is The Prophet. His new name is Tenskwatawa – The Open Door. Thousands believe that he offers the only way for the native people to save themselves.

O

Lolawauchika had reached the age of four when the Invisible Spirits spoke to Methoataske for the second time.' She had gone with Tecumseh to visit Puckeshinwa's grave. Tecumseh always went with her, for they shared the memory of Puckeshinwa's death. As on every visit, the boy renewed his pledge. She led him, as she did each time, in the reaffirmation of his vow.

"Do you promise to avenge your father's death?"

"I promise."

"Do you swear to bring destruction and death to the settlers?"

"I swear it." Tecumseh turned his face to her. "Three more winters will pass before I become a warrior. I can't bear to wait so long for my revenge."

"Those winters will pass quickly."

Not quickly enough, she thought. More settlers arrived every year. From spring until fall they kept on coming. Their huge riverboats moved west along the Ohio River. They brought their families, their livestock, their furniture, even their ploughs. When they saw a spot they liked, they went ashore, dismantling the boat for lumber to build their first house, acting as if this land belonged to them.

That night she sat in silence outside her lodge. She looked up at the stars, the same stars that were shining down on the little Muskogee town on banks of the Tallapoosa. Was the same thing happening in the south as in the country of the Ohio? She imagined land-hungry settlers landing on the banks of the Tallapoosa, building their cabins, cutting down trees, driving away the wild animals, erecting fences, ploughing up the bones of her ancestors. Was there no way they could be stopped?

Then the vision came to her that would change her life. She heard a voice: "Go back to your people. Warn them of the danger ahead. Tell them that no one tribe can stand alone against the settlers. Only by joining together can they save their lands. This is the message you must take to your people, and not just to the Muskogee Creeks but also to the Chickasaw and Choctaw people you will meet along the way."

"How can I leave this village?" she asked. "I have eight children."

"Go in secret," the voice commanded. "Otherwise, the Shawnees will not let you leave."

○

Slowly Methoataske rises to her feet, brushes grass from her tunic, and turns her back on the river. Her legs ache from sitting so long on the damp earth. People are coming together in the square in front of the great lodge. Tonight there will be a feast. Already women are arriving with food prepared at their own cooking fires. Nobody pays attention to Methoataske as she walks to her lodge.

It is a hut made of logs and poles, where she lives with her widowed sister, Akcawhko. Methoataske sits down upon her mat of woven grasses. Until the feasting ends, this is where she will stay. Afterwards, she will ask Akcawhko to tell her what Tecumseh talked about. She hopes that her sister will be close enough to hear him speak.

Listening to the distant sounds of feasting, Methoataske drifts off to sleep. It is dark when Akcawhko comes into the lodge. Methoataske is instantly wide awake. She props herself on one elbow. "What happened? Tell me everything."

"You should have come," Akcawhko scolds. "You could have seen and heard for yourself. Why did you stay away?"

Why indeed? Shame. Fear. Perhaps both. But her sister is right. "Maybe tomorrow," she says. "But tonight, please be kind. Tell me what you have learned about him. His wife. His children."

"He has a son called Pugeshashenwa," says Akcawhko. "Long ago Tecumseh sent away his wife."

"Why did he send her away?"

"Some foolish quarrel. He admits that family life is not for him. His sister Tecumapease raised the boy."

Methoataske laughed. "Tecumapease raised Tecumseh. Why not raise his son?"

"Tecumseh barely mentioned his son. All evening he talked about his brother The Prophet."

"From the start there was a strong bond between them," says Methoataske. "I never understood it."

"He said that his brother is his inspiration. 'Tenskwatawa dreams the dreams,' Tecumseh said. 'I'm the one who carries them into action.' Then he told us about The Prophet's first vision."

"Tell me," says Methoataske. "I have heard many times about those visions but never knew how they began."

"He had fallen into a trance," says Akcawhko. "In his trance he saw himself walking along a trail in the forest. He came to a fork in the path and did not know which way to go. After hesitating, he walked a short way along one path. It led him to a scene of terrible misery. Children were starving. Men and women lay about on the ground in a drunken stupor. The stink of disease and death filled the air. Quickly he turned back, and then set out along the other path.

"He came to a peaceful village. Women were tending the fires, cooking food in big clay pots. Children were playing. He saw men return from the hunt, bringing fresh meat. They carried bows and wore quivers of arrows on their backs. There was feasting and laughter. It was like the happy days before the white man came. As he stood watching, he heard a voice. 'Return to the old ways,' it said. 'No rum. No rifles. No iron pots. Live the way the Great Spirit meant you to live. Then the Great Spirit will help you in your struggle.' When he woke, he told Tecumseh his dream.

"Tecumseh thought long about his brother's vision. Finally he said, 'My mission is to stop the settlers from taking over our land. Your mission is to teach our people how to live. It will take both if we are to survive."

"Many years ago," said Methostaske, "I came home with a message for our people. They were not ready to listen. But perhaps I helped to prepare the way."

Akcawhko lies down on her sleeping mat. She yawns. "Tomorrow Tecumseh will make a speech. You must come to hear it. But now it's late. I want to sleep."

In moments her regular breathing tells Methoataske that she is asleep. But Methoataske cannot sleep. Her sister is right. She should not hide. She should come to hear Tecumseh speak. More than that, she must summon her courage to walk up to him and call him Son. But what if he then says to her, *Woman, you are not my mother. You ceased to be my mother when you abandoned your children.*

She could not bear to hear such words. Yet they are true. She remembers how she secretly packed a basket with food and how in the middle of the night she rose from her sleeping mat and went outside, just as anyone might do if she needed to relieve herself. The basket, a blanket and a knife were all that she took with her. She put them into one of the canoes resting on the riverbank. Silently she waded into the shallows. When the water reached her knees, she climbed into the canoe and picked up her paddle. A fish broke the surface of the water a little way downstream. Apart from the light splash of her paddle, there was no other sound. The river ran straight under the moon.

After that first night, she travelled by day. She paddled her canoe down the Mississippi, stopping at Chickasaw and Choctaw villages along the way. She told the people she met that her husband had been killed by settlers and that she had a message for all to hear. Whenever people gathered to hear her, the Invisible Spirits put words into her mouth. She warned what would happened if settlers were allowed to live among them. People listened politely but shook their heads. They were at peace with the white men, they said, and wished to remain so.

After two moons she reached her village on the Tallapoosa. When she told her people how Puckeshinwa had died, they comforted her and listened to her message. The chief sachem told her, "What you say is true. The tribes will have to unite before we can stop the settlers from taking over our land. But we have no leader strong and fierce enough to lift the tribes from their lethargy. We are too fond of presents and of rum."

Years went by. Methoataske grew old telling her story.

Then word came that such a leader had appeared among the Shawnees. The news travelled from village to village along the waterways. Soon everyone knew Tecumseh's name.

○

In the morning Methoataske goes with her sister to hear Tecumseh's speech. They sit on the ground on the women's side. Methoataske is just a bent old woman, almost invisible as she takes her place. She keeps her face lowered, although it is hardly necessary. Since

Tecumseh hasn't seen his mother for thirty-four years, he is unlikely to recognize her now.

When her son emerges from the great lodge holding the eagle feather in his hand, her heart swells with pride. He addresses the crowd in Creek, the language he learned from her, although he speaks it with a Shawnee accent. He has a strong voice that matches his pride and self-assurance, a kind of arrogance. As he speaks, the dream of a great mission burns in his eyes.

"We must go back to the old ways," he tells the people. "We must not listen to traitors who tell us that it is prudent to sell our lands and learn to be farmers. Planting crops is women's work. For a warrior, farming is one step up from slavery. It is unthinkable that a warrior should live surrounded by fences and tied to a flock of chickens."

Men and women grunt their approval and murmur, "It is so."

He thanks the Muskogee war chiefs and the sachems for agreeing to join the Shawnees and the other tribes in their struggle. "United, we will be a storm that brings destruction and death to the people who steal our land. Our feet will be as swift as forked lightning, our arms as strong as the thunderbolt. We will be a fire spreading over the hills and valleys, consuming the race of dark souls."

When he finishes his speech, he tells the crowd that he and his warriors will leave the next morning.

Akcawhko nudges Methoataske. "If you're going to speak to him, you must do it now."

"I will speak to him," says Methoataske. "I'll do it tomorrow before he leaves."

In the morning her courage fails, but Akcawhko will not let her change her mind. She forces Methoataske to dress in her best tunic of white doeskin, with its long fringes and its bands of bright bead-work. She braids Methoataske's hair, weaving in red ribbons. Finally, she pins on the front of the tunic the silver brooch that Puckeshinwa had given his bride so many winters ago. She takes her sister by the hand and leads her from the lodge, ignoring her whimpers of, "No ... No ..."

When they reach the riverbank, the canoes are being loaded for departure. Akcawhko propels Methoataske to the spot where Tecumseh is standing. There is no way he can fail to see her, or the silver brooch. He stares at his mother, puzzled at first. Then a light shines in his eyes.

It is too late for speaking. He lifts his arm, saluting her with a gesture that is at the same time both greeting and farewell.

The canoes are ready. Standing on the bank, she watches them depart. When they disappear around a bend, the crowd disperses. She does not move.

As the sun slants its arrows through the clouds, a vision comes to her. She sees a river, not a gently flowing river like the Tallapoosa, but a river flowing fast at the bottom of a wooded ravine. She sees the trees in all their colours: the red of the sumac, the yellow of the birch, the crimson of the maple, the copper of the oak. She sees a burning mill and a broken bridge. There are soldiers in blue uniforms and soldiers in red, warriors in war paint, and bearded men with rifles. There are men on horseback charging through the woods.

She sees Tecumseh rallying his warriors. He wears a silver medallion at his neck and a single feather in his hair. Guns roar. She feels the jolt as a bullet slams into his chest. He staggers, recovers. Blood pours from his mouth, but he keeps on firing until he falls.

That is not the end of her vision. The fighting stops. The sun goes down. She sees two warriors bear Tecumseh's body away. They disappear into the night.

Darkness covers everything. She feels it spread, swallowing rivers and villages, creeping west over hills and valleys all the way to the Mississippi and beyond. It overwhelms the great plains and the roaming herds of buffalo. It seems that the very stars are extinguished, so vast is the darkness that smothers all the land.

Author's Note

Tecumseh's mother first came to my attention while I was research-ing material for my historical novel *The White Oneida*. It was she who inspired Tecumseh with his dream of uniting the native people to resist white expansion. The murder of her husband by white settlers left her with an understandable hatred of white society. Less under-standable is the fact that she abandoned her children when the young-est was only four years old, returning to her home village in Alabama. It is a matter of historical record that Tecumseh visited this village one year before his death at the Battle of the Thames in 1813. My story recounts Tecumseh's visit from her point of view and in the context of both their lives.

SOPHIA

SOPHIA POOLEY, A SLAVE WHOSE OWNERS INCLUDED JOSPEPH BRANT

Jane Mulkewich

I never expected to live this long. I am now more than ninety years old, and everyone I know is younger than me. I think back over all the things I have seen in my life, and I reckon I am one of the strong ones, to live through everything I have lived through. Yes, I have aching in my bones, and I can't work the way I used to, but I still walk and I can still walk to visit my neighbours and they help me a good deal. Sometimes I wonder how much longer I have to live, but I don't let myself think about that much. I have never been one to give up on life easily.

Sometimes I wonder if my mother lived to be an old woman like me. I like to think she did, but I never saw her again since I was a girl. I believe she gave me strength, and she made sure I knew where I came from. I will never forget her; her name was Dinah. My father's name was Oliver Burthen. They were slaves, so of course they worked very hard from morning light to end of day, and me and my sister had to fend for ourselves quite a bit, but our mother taught us to stay out of master's way so nobody would bother us. We were only seven and five, so small, but our mother had already warned us about staying away from white men, and what they would do to girls like us. As long as we stayed out of sight, we had time to play. My sister and I used to play in the garden, down amongst the currant bushes, and we thought we were safe there. We knew every square inch of that garden. It was in Fishkill, New York State. I guess my mother made sure that we knew the name of the place, though we had never been anywhere else. That was our world.

Often we helped our mother in the kitchen, and we would see master's family and all their comings and goings. I knew to stay away from the young men, my master's sons-in-law. I was taught that they would want sex from us, but I didn't know they would try to sell us for money. I didn't know the value of money then. I don't think my parents ever knew what happened to us, and that was always the thought that made me saddest. I wish I could have seen my mother just one more time.

My master's sons-in-law, Daniel Outwaters and Simon Knox, came into the garden where my sister and I were playing among the currant bushes, tied their handkerchiefs over our mouths, carried us to a vessel, put us in the hold, and sailed up the river.*

I know that Fishkill was twelve miles from North River, the one they call Hudson River, because I remember Mr. Outwaters and Mr. Knox complaining about how far they had to carry us. They were mean and stupid men. They were trying to cheat our master without him knowing, and I don't know if he ever found out what they did. They kept us tied up in the hold of that boat all the way up the river, and we couldn't see anything. They never brought us out to see the sunshine until we got off of the boat. My sister and I had each other but we were scared and hungry and hurting, and calling for our mother. I don't know if the men had a plan of where to take us, but they took us away from the white towns and into Indian country. Indians weren't buying slaves, so that's why I don't think Mr. Outwaters and Mr. Knox knew what to do with us. When we were taken out of the boat, we had to walk. Oh we walked until our legs ached, and one of the men might sling us roughly across his shoulders. I had never walked so far or so long. We passed Indian settlements, and we learned the names of the people. There were Onondagas, Senecas and Oneidas. I had never seen any villages like that before, and I remember staring at the people and the way they dressed, and they stared at us. There were no other black people there. I remember when we came to the Genesee river, and the men started talking about taking us to Canada, where there were more white people who might need some slaves.

I was stolen from my parents when I was seven years old, and brought to Canada; that was long before the American Revolution. There were hardly any white people in Canada then – nothing here but Indians and wild beasts ... I guess I was the first colored girl brought into Canada. The white men sold us at Niagara to old Indian Brant, the king.

When we got to Niagara, we saw a few other black people, because some of the white folks already had slaves. The people were living in crowded makeshift housing around the Fort, and nobody was interested in two small slave girls like us, who were skin and bones. We saw some Indians there, mostly Mohawks, like Joseph Brant and his family. Brant was there for the winter, but in the summer he was away fighting. He had already made a name for himself as king, fighting in the Mohawk valley and all around New York State. He had already been married twice, and had two children by his first wife. They were Isaac and Christina. I met them there that winter; Isaac was about the same height as me, and I think about the same age. Brant sent Isaac and Christina back to the Mohawk valley to be looked after in the Indian village. I wasn't old enough to do a grown woman's work around the house, but I guess Brant needed someone to do the work, and nobody else was much interested in us. He bought both me and my sister from Mr. Outwaters and Mr. Knox, and those two men left us without a backwards glance.

His mother was a squaw – I saw her when I came to this country. She was an old body; her hair was quite white. I saw Brant's sister Molly, too. Molly had been living with an Englishman in New York State. His name was William Johnson, and she had his children. Johnson sent Brant to an English school. After Johnson died, Molly came to Fort Niagara with her family and all the slaves from Johnson's estate. Brant left the fighting and came to winter at Niagara, and that's when he bought me and my sister. We were the first slaves he owned.

He kept my sister and me at Niagara at first. My sister never regained her strength after that long march through Indian country. She had taken poorly and none of the squaws at Niagara could save her. Oh how I wished for our mother then. I held her when she died, and I was glad she was not suffering anymore. I wouldn't let anyone see me cry. I didn't want anyone to think I was weak. They took her tiny body away and I don't know what they did with her. When she died I was truly alone in the world.

I got used to being on my own, and I got used to moving around a lot. Brant and his people moved from Niagara to establish homes in villages along the Grand River. Brant was always on the go, going about here and there, and he had different houses too. *Brant lived part of the time at Mohawk, part at Ancaster, part at Preston, then called Lower Block: the Upper Block was at Snyder's Mills.* It was much later that Brant built that big house on the lake by Burlington Bay. In every house Brant ever had, he lived in style, with proper furniture and good food, even if some of the people around us were living in poorer conditions. I learned to work hard, and I always had food to eat. I stayed quiet like my mother had taught me. And yes, Brant expected me to satisfy all his needs, and sometimes took me to his bed. There was nothing I could say about that.

Brant was a good looking man – quite portly ... When Brant went among the English, he wore the English dress – when he was among the Indians, he wore the Indian dress, – broadcloth leggings, blanket, moccasins, fur cap. He had his ears slit with a long loop at the edge, and in these he hung long silver ornaments. He wore a silver half-moon on his breast with the king's name on it, and broad silver bracelets on his arms.

I grew to care for Joseph Brant, but I always wondered about how much he cared for me. He was not rough with me, but he did not give me my freedom. After the American Revolution, Brant returned all the white captives from the war. That was the law, he said. He kept only us slaves. I remember meeting some of the white captives. One of them was Mary Sitts; she came with the Mississaugas to the Lake to see Brant in the "hungry year", and Brant had her returned to the English. Another one was Margaret Clyne. After she was returned to her people, she married Rousseaux, who was an Indian interpreter for the government. The wedding was at Brant's home; it was a big crowd and a lot of work for us to feed all of those people. I also heard that Brant had given Margaret Rousseaux some land for her children. Brant acted kindly towards me, but he never gave me any land.

While I lived with old Brant we caught the deer. It was at Dundas at the outlet. We would let the hounds loose, and when we heard them bark we would run for the canoe – Peggy, and Mary, and Katy, Brant's daughters and I. Brant's sons, Joseph and Jacob, would wait on the shore to kill the deer when we fetched him in. The babies, John and Elizabeth, were too young to help. *I had a tomahawk, and would hit the deer on the head – then the squaws would take it by the horns and paddle ashore. The boys would bleed and skin the deer and take the meat to the house. Sometimes white people in the neighbor-hood, John Chisholm and Bill Chisholm, would come and say 'twas their hounds, and they must have the meat.* But we would not give it up. John later became the first toll collector for Burlington, and Bill became the founder of Oakville.

Brant's third wife, my mistress, was a barbarous creature. She was a pretty squaw: her father was an English colonel, George Croghan. *She could talk English, but she would not. She would tell me in Indian to do things, and then hit me with any thing that came to hand, because I did not understand her. I have a scar on my head from a wound she gave me with a hatchet; and this long scar over my eye, is where she cut me with a knife.*

I tried to keep out of her way. She didn't like to talk to me anyway. She would give orders, that was all. And I didn't need ordering about, I knew what to do. And I did everything. The secret was that I didn't mind doing it. I liked to wash clothes, up to my elbows in the soapy water. I liked to hoe the weeds from the emerging rows of cornstalks, to be out in the sunshine and feel the cool breeze from the lake.

It happened one day when I was putting some of her clothes away in the bedroom that she shared with him. She had a cedar chest, and in that were some fine linen dresses that I had not seen her wear in years. I was fingering the lace on the hem of one of the dresses when she came in the room. She shrieked something in Mohawk, and picked up the candlestick from the dressing table and hurled it at my head. It hit hard, and I shrieked even louder than her. My head was throbbing and it felt like there was noise everywhere, from the blood pulsating in my ears, to the wailing coming up from my belly, to the clatter of running feet as two of the youngest children came running to the door of the room, and the unceasing unintelligible tirade coming out of their mother's mouth.

Holding my head in one hand, I used my other hand to push myself up from the floor, and hurled myself out of the bedroom, pushing past my mistress Catherine. I swept up baby Elizabeth under one arm to keep her safe, and fled to the kitchen. I was setting the baby down in the kitchen when Catherine burst into the room. She grabbed a knife that I had been using earlier that day cutting up squash. Then I was cornered. I crouched down close to Elizabeth and watched Catherine now as she paused, knife in hand, enjoying this moment. She switched to English to be sure that I understood every word she said.

"You will stay away from him. When he gets back, he does not want to see your face. I will make sure he will not want to see your face."

And she came at me with the knife.

I was scared for the baby so I left Elizabeth there in the corner and darted for the door, hoping to lure Catherine out after me. I had my left arm up to protect my head which was still throbbing from the attack with the candle-stick. She slashed at me, and I felt the sharp pain along my arm and dropped my arm and then she came in again with the knife and slashed my forehead. I swear she would have put my eye out if I had not half-fallen and half-lunged forward and grabbed at the knife with both hands until it clattered to the floor amidst the sounds of all the shrieking, coming from her, from me, and from the children. She didn't stay to see where all the blood was coming from – she turned on her heel and left.

I gingerly took my hands away from my face and blinked my eyes and tore a piece of cloth from the bottom of my skirt to wipe the blood from my forehead.

I spoke to the space where she had been standing, and said, "I was his before you was."

And Elizabeth pulled herself to her feet and toddled over to me and threw her arms around me.

Brant was very angry, when he came home, at what she had done, and punished her as if she had been a child. Said he, "You know I adopted her as one of the family, and now you are trying to put all the work on her."

I am glad that he said that. I still remember he said that after all these years, but I know that he wanted me to do the work so that she wouldn't have to work so hard. They had seven babies together, and when those babies were all grown up, that's when he sold me.

I was sold by Brant to an Englishman in Ancaster, for one hundred dollars,– his name was Samuel Hatt, and I lived with him seven years.

Brant told me that he got one hundred dollars for me. I had mixed feelings to know how much I was worth. It was good to know that I was still worth something, but I knew that other slaves had sold for more money than that. On the other hand, how I wished that I could have one hundred dollars for my own self to spend any way I wanted to. One hundred dollars seemed like an impossible sum of money.

Hatt was looking for slaves; Hatt got married and his wife Margaret was my new mistress. They got married just before Brant died.

Nobody was buying much slaves then because some of the men were getting their freedom by fighting in the war. Those coloured men fought with John Brant. John, the youngest of Brant's sons, was favoured by Catherine. She gave him the title of chief, passed on through her mother's line. He was only 18 when he led the troop of

Indians and coloured men fighting at Queenston Heights. I was living with the Hatt family by then. Samuel Hatt was on the battle-field too; he was a Captain or a Major in the war. *I was seven miles from Stoney Creek at the time of the battle – the cannonade made every thing shake well.*

The war ended in 1814. *Then the white people said I was free, and put me up to running away. He did not stop me – he said he could not take the law into his own hands.*

Do you know it has been more than forty years now that I have been a free woman? Oh my, but the years have gone by. Lots of us black folks came to live here. The white folks called it the Queen's Bush; I just call it the bush. We still had to work just as hard as we used to work when we were slaves, but now we were working for ourselves, building homesteads and growing our own food. Those of us who made it this far were the survivors, who knew how to get things done. Some of these folks came all the way from plantations in the South, and I have heard so many of their stories. I never knew that plantation life. That's what first attracted me to Robert Pooley. He was a talker, and I used to like to listen to his stories. He knew how to run a farm, too. We got married and I thought we would stay together and get old together, but like I said, he was a talker, and I guess he had other ideas. He found a white woman to listen to his stories, and they ran off together. It caused a great sensation. People used to send me back news about how he was doing, and so they let me know when he died. I still keep his name and people know me as Sophia Pooley.

I still think about Joseph Brant a lot. Not many black folks lived with the Indians the way I did. *Brant had two colored men for slaves: one of them was the father of John Patten, who lives over yonder, the other called himself Simon Ganseville. There was but one other Indian that I knew, who owned a slave.* There was Molly Brant who owned slaves, as well as another Mohawk woman named Sarah Ainse in the Windsor area, but I didn't know her.

I learned so many things from the black people I have met here in the bush. They told me about the year the stars fell. We saw it that night, of course. It was in November and it was cold, and those stars were falling down all around us all night long. Down in the United States, the white slave-owners thought it was Judgment Day, and started calling all the slaves together to tell them who their mothers and fathers were, and who they'd been sold to and where. Thinking about the year the stars fell, I was always glad that I knew my parents and I knew their names. I just wish I could have seen them again.

I still think about Catharine Brant too. Word got back to me here in the bush when she died. *Brant's wife survived him until the year the stars fell. She hid a crock of gold before she died, and I never heard of its being found.* I never had any money or gold in my own name. If I knew where that crock of gold was, I would go find it.

Author's Note

It was about twenty years ago (in the mid-90s) that I came across the story of Sophia Pooley, published in "The Narratives of Fugitive Slaves in Canada" in 1856. I have used some of her words from that narrative directly, and those words are indicated in italics.*

Sophia's story was different from the rest as it was about someone who lived in slavery in Canada, rather than someone who fled to freedom in Canada. It also caught my attention because she was brought here by Joseph Brant, an Aboriginal man, before "Canada was filling up with white people". As an anti-racism advocate, I found the story compelling because it reminds people that slavery did exist in Canada here for a time, and it shows black history in this area has roots at least as long as the history of settlers with European roots.

Also, I became fascinated with the customs and the laws around slavery as well as the tradition of Aboriginal people (the Iroquois in particular) taking captives and adopting them into their families. My own ancestor, Michael Shaw, was "captured" and/or "adopted" by the Iroquois. He was born in 1763, and family tradition has it that he was kidnapped at age seven and returned at age fourteen. Michael later joined Butler's Rangers in the Mohawk Valley, and may have even met Joseph Brant. Michael was my great-great-great-great-great-grandfather, so a seventh generation ancestor, and there are teachings in the Aboriginal community about the significance of seven generations. I wonder if it is no coincidence that about seven generations after the time this land was first colonized by white settlers, we are seeing a shift in the relationship between Aboriginal and non-Aboriginal people in Canada.

The owners of Sophia have not been forgotten; the namesakes of Joseph Brant include the town of Brantford and Joseph Brant Hospital in Burlington (located where his house once was). Samuel Hatt's name is on a historical plaque located on the Niagara River Parkway, in Niagara-on-the-Lake, describing his role in the War of 1812. Hatt later moved to Chambly, Quebec, and there is a street named after him in that town. There is also Hatt Street in Dundas,

Ontario, named after his family, which is the street I now live on. So there are all these namesakes for Sophia's owners, whereas the story of Sophia is largely forgotten.

Sophia told her story as an old woman, over the age of 90, and perhaps there are details, particularly dates, that she has mis-remembered. I have worked hard to corroborate her life story with other historical records. It is particularly difficult because of the lack of detailed records from that period of history. There remains much that we do not know. There is no evidence that Sophia had children, but we do know that there are descendants of Joseph Brant in the black community. For more on this, see the "Responses for Resistance" by Joyce Brown, which tells of her ancestry, and specifically of being descended from Joseph Brant, in: "*...but where are you really from?" Stories of Identity and Assimilation in Canada*, edited by Hazelle Palmer (Sister Vision, Black Women and Women of Colour Press, Toronto, 1997). It is said that a black man, John Morey, married one of Brant's daughters, possibly Elizabeth (which would have been before Elizabeth married a white man, William Kerr). I believe that had Sophia had children, she would not have omitted to mention them when she told her life story.

What we do know is that slave-owners commonly sexually exploited female slaves, and in my view, a sexual relationship between Joseph Brant and Sophia would explain Catharine Brant's violent treatment of Sophia.

The "year the stars fell" was the Leonid Meteor Shower of November 12, 1833. The meteor storm of 1833 was exceptionally intense, and because of developments in scientific knowledge at the time, the Leonids of 1833 marked a major upturn in the development of the scientific study of meteors, and as can be seen by Sophia's story, it also marked a major moment in the cultural history of the black community.

THE CRIMINAL LIFE OF CATHARINE COFFIN

ABOLITIONIST AND UNDERGROUND RAILROAD ACTIVIST

Carol Leigh Wehking

S he didn't look like a criminal. Kneeling on the floor beside the cedar chest, sorting carefully through its contents, she did not seem felonious. You could not tell from her sober Quaker dress, her demure Quaker bonnet, her modest manners, her steady grey eyes, or her sweet and composed face that a criminal mastermind was at work inside her head. Breaking the law regularly, consciously, and intrepidly was Catharine Coffin's way of life.

In the chest, Catharine found a soft green woollen dress, removed it, and set it aside. A grey knitted shawl came next, then linens and a petticoat, trousers, a shirt, and – near the bottom – Catharine found the blue and green blanket she had hoped was still there.

"I did not think that had been given away yet," she murmured to herself as she began to return other items to the trunk.

Scrambling quickly to her feet, Catharine carried the bundle of clothing into the kitchen. Eliza was up now, and, perched on a wooden stool, was helping their servant Martha scrub potatoes for supper, though her child still slept peacefully in his nest on the rocker bench.

"Here thee is, my dear," Catharine said to Eliza. "I believe that we can make these things fit thee very well."

Eliza turned from the bowl of murky water where she was scrubbing. "Oh!" she said softly when she saw what Catharine placed on the table. Eliza quickly dried her hands on her apron and reached to touch the soft wool. "Oh," she said again, and her eyes filled with tears, as they had so many times since her arrival at the Coffins' home.

"Oh, Mistress Coffin... "

"Katie," Catharine corrected.

"Aunt Katie," Eliza whispered shyly, "these are so beautiful! They are much too fine... "

"To be hidden in a trunk," Catharine finished for her. "I agree; the dress and shawl will look well on thee. And thy child will be warm as a coddled egg in the blanket."

Eliza picked up the dress and held it against her body, looking up with questioning eyes. "It shall be hemmed and altered to fit," Catharine assured her. Eliza placed her golden brown hand on the white linens.

"Are these also for me?" she queried.

"Yes, my dear. These are worn beneath the dress. Thee will find it more comfortable that way. And warmer, too."

Eliza sat down on the cradle rocker with the clothing in her lap. Overwhelmed by the fineness of the garments and the generosity of her host, her tears slid silently down her cheeks for a few moments. Then she brushed them away with the corner of her apron, and looked up with shining eyes. "Thank you," she said, "thank you from my heart!"

"Thee is welcome from mine!" Catharine replied. "Now try these on, my dear, so we can see how to make them fit thee."

Potatoes were left to Martha's willing hands while Eliza tried on the clothing and Catharine pinned the seams, basted the hem, and tailored the dress to the other woman's shape, as if they were two sisters enjoying an evening at home. Then came the men's clothing, also made ready to fit Eliza.

Eliza stood on the chair in trousers and shirt, abashed at her masculine appearance. "I will never pass as a boy with my hair," she said.

Martha glanced up and laughed, "Thee has far too lovely a face to be a man, too. Perhaps thy hair can be made into a beard!"

Catharine's head went up with a jerk. "Martha! What an idea! Thee is inspired! Of course we can fashion that. What a complete disguise that will be! All thee will need is a wife," she said, turning again to Eliza.

At that moment Jesse came through the door. Stamping the snow from his boots, he looked up at the sudden silence greeting him in place of his mother's usual cheerful words.

"What?" he said. He looked down at himself to see whether he had accidentally brought something unacceptable in from the barn. He looked up again, and caught a meaningful twinkle in his mother's eye. "What is thee cooking up, Mother?" he said suspiciously.

"Son," she said, "how would thee like to be married?"

"Mother! I am only thirteen years old!" he cried.

"But just the right size to make a lovely wife," his mother retorted.

"Wife! Mother! Has thee abandoned thy sense?"

"Not at all, my dear, only look at thy handsome husband!"

Jesse now took in Eliza, standing in man's clothing on the wooden chair. Realization dawned on his face, and he grinned widely. "Thee *has* taken leave of thy sense, Mother – but I am willing to give thee the medicine thee needs!" He snatched up Eliza's discarded apron and threw it over his head, clutching the ties under his chin. "Oh, husband!" he chirped in a falsetto, "when do we travel forth? I do hope we can wait for drier weather, so that my petticoats need not be dampened!" He minced forward and lowered his eyes demurely at Eliza's side, causing her to laugh so uproariously that the baby woke and stirred.

"Oh, Harry," she said softly, jumping lightly down and running to her child's side. "Quiet now, little love, shhh..." and she sat down on the rocker and began to sing softly as she rocked back and forth, her hand making gentle circles on the little boy's back.

Everyone in the kitchen went immediately silent, and Martha got on with the potato scrubbing. Catharine picked up the pile of clothing, and Jesse pulled the apron from his head.

"It's as well that she should be off her feet," he whispered to Martha on his way by her; "I think they have not yet healed very well."

Eliza's feet were still bound in bandages from the freezing they had suffered only a week ago. The rest of her had recovered miraculously well, considering her ordeal. But her spirits were still as fragile as glass, and tears came easily for any reason, good or bad.

○

Only one week earlier, Eliza had been a slave on the Davis plantation in Kentucky. She was the mother of but one surviving child, who was all the more precious for that. She had been prized as a slave for her beauty and her light skin, for both her mother and her father had been sired by masters on slave women. Her light complexion also made her desirable as a commodity. She decided on her own to make an attempt at escape, after she had discovered that Davis, who had suffered some pecuniary vexations, was about to sell her south, away from her family, doubtless for a very favourable price. Knowing that either way she could lose both husband and child, she took the young boy with her in the hope that he might grow up free from the bonds that turned herself and all her people into chattels.

That, or die in the attempt.

In the deepest hour of night, when the darkness was like a velvet cloak over the plantation and all were asleep in both the big house and the slaves' quarters, she had lifted her sleeping two-year-old into her arms, wrapped a long shawl around him to bind him against her, and, with a last brief fond look at her sleeping husband, slipped from the cabin like a shadow. All night, she walked until she could walk no more, rested, and walked again, until at dawn she at last reached the Ohio river, ten miles north of the plantation, where she planned to cross to the free state of Ohio. To her despair, she found that the river was not the solid ice she expected, but rather had begun to break up, and was flowing slowly in sluggish chunks – not a safe passage at all, but a perilous obstacle course.

Exhausted with exertion, terror, and disappointment, she had been taken in by a white family who lived in a cabin on the riverbank. These people gave her food, warmed her, and let her rest through the day. Eliza knew that her disappearance from the Davis place would be discovered that morning, and that she was not safe resting here. The slave catchers would be on her trail, and since this was the most direct path to the river, they were not likely to be long in coming.

Indeed, at dusk she was barely waking from sleep when she was sure that she heard hoofbeats in the distance. Alert in an instant, she sat up and listened carefully. There was no mistake, horses were approaching at an alarming speed. She gathered the sleeping child into her arms and darted out the back door of the cabin, and at that very moment she heard the horses being reigned in at the front. Down the sloping bank she scrambled, but the horsemen had caught sight of her.

With the three men crashing through the brush only a few yards behind her, she hesitated not a moment at the edge of the dark icy water flowing past. She used the momentum she had from rushing down the slope to make a desperate leap onto an ice floe. It tipped crazily under her weight, but she stepped to its other edge, and jumped to the next floe without an instant's delay. It dipped and began to turn, but she went on to the next and the next. In her rush to outrun the slave catchers, she had left the cabin without her boots, and her feet were soon cut and bleeding. Each floe was marked with red as she jumped onto it and leapt off again. Her pursuers stood in consternation on the southern bank, believing she would surely fall in, and drown or freeze. Fascinated, they watched her progress.

Halfway across the river, one of the floes tipped more wildly under her weight than the others, and dipped below the water, sliding her into the black iciness. Somehow she tossed the boy onto the floe as she went into the water, and then, clawing, scrabbling, she pulled herself onto it, picked up the child, and jumped to the next floe, and the next and the next, until at last, as if by force of will or grace of God, but not by any seeming likelihood or probability, she reached the far shore. There, out of the darkness, a hand reached down and pulled her onto the bank and safety.

"Any woman who crossed that river carrying her baby has won her freedom," said the voice of Chance Shaw. ("*Every* person *deserves* freedom," Catharine had said when she heard this part of the story.) The slave catchers on the Kentucky shore were dumfounded by her escape, but none of the men looked at the prospect of pursuing her across the river on the flowing crush of broken ice as worth the risk. Chance Shaw helped her to find the house of John and Jean Rankin, where she was warmed and given food. The Rankins, however, felt as Eliza did, that it was still too dangerous for Eliza and the baby to stay there in Ripley, and so once she and the child were in dry clothing and had eaten, they were hurried on to another safe house farther from the river.

The next night they were taken from station to station, as the safe houses were called, until they reached Newport and the relative safety of the Coffins' home. At least in Indiana, it was not legal to search a home without a warrant, which for abolitionists usually meant that a fugitive would have time to be hidden properly before anyone could enter the home.

Eliza and her little son were recovering their strength under Catharine's tender ministrations. Nutritious food, proper clothing, sound sleep, and, most important, a sense of safety which Catharine's calm produced, had brought both of them to a place of far greater physical and spiritual well-being than they had known since Eliza had discovered her master's plans to sell her.

Her feet, however, though bathed and bandaged carefully each day by Catharine herself, were healing more slowly. The bruises were diminishing and the cuts closing, but it was still unclear whether all her toes would recover from the frostbite. She padded gingerly about the house on her thick bandages. Catharine had no intention of letting

Eliza travel onward until her feet could be safely laced into the boots the Rankins had provided for her.

O

The following Wednesday, Catharine's sewing circle met. After lunch, Catharine and Martha set chairs in a circle on the rug in the parlour and prepared the lemonade and cakes.

At the stroke of one o'clock, Esther and Rebecca arrived with their sewing baskets over their arms, their shawls wrapped closely against the chilly March breeze.

"Here are the two dresses I took home to finish, Katie," Rebecca said, after they were indoors. "I left the hems to complete when we see who it is will wear them." The dresses were dark blue, of a soft lightweight woollen material, with Rebecca's beautiful fine stitching. Catharine placed them in the cedar trunk under the side window.

Martha was just opening the door to Frances, who took five knitted shawls from her basket. These, too, were added to the cedar chest. As each woman arrived, she added to the collection of finished garments: men's clothing, women's clothing, children's clothing. Warm things against the weather, for further north it was colder still.

When they were settled and all of them sewing or knitting, Prudence spoke quietly: "Katie, I am glad to understand that thee and Levi will be forwarding that parcel of dry goods as soon as thee can."

"Now?" asked Hannah. "Right here beneath our feet?"

"No," Catharine replied, "not hidden in the false cellar this time. There is no present danger."

Hannah's breath came shakily. Though she hated slavery with all her heart, and worked tirelessly to clothe the freedom seekers, the thought of being actually physically involved with the illegal activities of hiding and transporting them was more than her timid heart could contemplate. She was quite terrified to think that there was a fugitive in the house while she was there herself.

Amanda, also afraid, not so much of the stress of secrecy, but of the punishment if caught, observed, "I do not know how thee does it, Katie. Thee never seems to be nervous or anxious or out of countenance in any way. How can thee and Levi face the constant peril with such calm?"

"As Levi says, we feel it is always safe to do right."

Sarah, ever a plain speaker, voiced a different concern: "But how, Katie, can thee have them in thy house – in thy *beds*? They all have been wandering through forest and swamp, and come to thee and Levi filthy and stinking – and covered in vermin for all thee knows. How can thee bear them in thy home?"

"I give them baths if there is time," Catharine answered simply. "I give them the clean clothes that we make here every week. And if I have not time to offer them an opportunity to be more refined in their person, I hope they will find that chance along the way. They have gone through unimaginable tribulations by the time they reach me. If they are not dainty in their grooming, they are not to blame. They are welcome in my home and welcome to whatever aid I may be blessed to give them."

"But Katie, their skins are *brown*! How can thee ever think of that as clean?"

"Sarah," Catharine retorted in a mild voice, but with flashing eyes, "thy dress is brown – how can thee ever think of *it* as clean?"

Sarah opened her mouth in astonishment, but found no words.

"They are God's children, as we are," Catharine continued, "no different from me for their skin colour than thee and I are for our hair colour. I will hear no more such narrow talk in my house. Thee should be ashamed!"

Sarah's cheeks coloured, but she made no further comment. The other women bent their heads to their sewing, and conversation was abandoned for a time. Soon they were chatting again, about less weighty matters, and the hours flew by with the speed of their needles.

When the Sewing Circle departed, there was another pile of fresh clothing to add to the cedar chest.

Clothing never stayed in the chest for long.

O

Three nights later, a stealthy knock upon the back door was followed by the code phrase, "A friend of a Friend," and Catharine and Levi opened their door to a party of four frightened freedom seekers. They were cold and hungry, but they also felt sure that they were closely followed, so instead of being given food first, they were quietly ushered into the space between the false walls in Martha's room, where there was room enough for ten more had there been such a need. Quickly going up the stairs, Catharine wakened Eliza, and together they pulled the bed away from the wall, giving access to the low door that the bed head concealed, which gave into the eaves of the house. Eliza wrapped herself and the child in a blanket, crawled into the space, and pulled the door shut. Jesse, awake now, helped his mother reposition the bed, then helped her to make it up again.

"Back into bed with thee now, my dear," Catharine whispered. "This is just an ordinary night, after all; no need for children to be up." Jesse understood; he gave his mother a quick embrace and disappeared into the room from which he had emerged.

Scarcely had Catharine rejoined Levi in the kitchen when there came a heavy, insistent knock. Levi and Catharine held hands in the dark, and tiptoed back toward the stairs. Catharine went halfway up the flight, and Levi turned, paused again, and then went to the door.

"Who knocks at this dark hour?" he called through the door in a voice that sounded still half asleep.

"Open the door! We have a warrant!" cried a rough voice from the other side.

Levi opened the door a small crack. "Let me see it," he said, and a hand thrust a paper through the opening. Few slave-catchers could produce the warrant required by Indiana law to search a private home. Levi closed the door, lit a candle, examined the paper, and then reluctantly opened the door. This was a legal warrant, and he had no choice but to admit them. Catharine, listening from the stairs, was glad that her guests were well hidden.

As the two men entered the kitchen in a clatter of boots, Catharine descended the stairs, clutching a shawl about her and saying, "Pray keep thy voices low, as my children are asleep."

"It is not your children we seek, but we believe you have some runaways arrived not an half an hour since," the better-dressed of the two men said, as he moved boldly into the room. "Fetch a lamp," he commanded.

"Thee is not an invited guest in my home," Catharine answered mildly but firmly. "If thee desires to have a light, surely thee thought to bring a lamp of thy own."

The man looked about, and, seeing the glint of a glass lamp chimney on the mantlepiece, seized the lamp, strode to the table where Levi's candle stood, and fumbled with a spill from the fire until the lamp's wick cast its steady glow about the room.

"Since you are here, may we offer you a cup of tea, Friends?" Catharine enquired. By this time Martha had appeared at the door to her room in her night cap and shawl, also feigning to be newly wakened.

Ignoring this civil offer, the first man, who appeared to be the speaker for both, demanded, "Where does this door lead to?"

"That is our servant's room," Catharine answered, "and thee can see that thy clamour has disturbed our Martha from her sleep."

He pushed past Martha and entered her room. It was, like the rest of the house, simply furnished. There was no furniture behind or under which a person could hide. A quick glance around with the lamp assured the man that no-one was in the room.

Likewise the other ground-floor rooms provided no hiding places, and soon the men were stamping up the stairs. As they opened one door and then another, sleepy white faces either slumbered on or looked up blearily as the doors opened. Six children, all white. No-one under the beds or in the shadows beside the bureaus. The men descended to the cellar, where they also found nothing. From the kitchen above, Catharine and Levi could hear the men grumbling to one another: "I'm certain they entered the house." "Couldn't have just vanished." "No place else to hide."

At last the two men departed, and the door was closed and bolted behind them. Catharine sank onto a chair. Levi sat opposite her. But for the candle's flicker, there was no movement in the room. Catharine leaned forward and blew the candle out. She and Levi and Martha sat quietly in the darkness. When twenty long minutes had ticked past, Catharine spoke softly. "I think they will not return this night," she said. "We must release our guests from their accommodations."

Martha went instantly to her room, where she slid away the false panel and let out the four people who had stood silently between the walls for over an hour. Levi went upstairs to release Eliza and the boy, while Catharine began to make tea and heat the potatoes and chicken left from supper, to feed the newcomers, doing all by touch and by the faint glow of moonlight that gave the room some shape.

"The danger is great," Levi said to his wife when he was downstairs again. "I have bid Eliza to ready herself and the child for travel. Jesse is up and dressing himself for his part. We must forward all the freight by morning, or risk another search."

Catharine nodded, and left the food preparation to Martha while she went to find good clothing for the four new fugitives. From the bottom of the cedar chest, she also drew out a muslin parcel in which was wrapped the false beard she had created from Eliza's hair, which now Eliza would wear upon her face.

Jesse came downstairs, awkward in a dress and shawl, carrying Eliza's sleeping child in his arms.

Levi and Catharine discussed the situation as the four newcomers ate, and decided that everyone should prepare for the journey ahead, and then have a few hours' rest before leaving in the grey light before sunrise. When the newcomers were wrapped in blankets and curled before the banked fire, Martha and Catharine prepared food for the journey, and Jesse and his father sat in silent vigil, eyes closed, heads bowed, but alert to any sound.

There were no further visits from the slave catchers, but it was not possible to know who might be watching the house still, so after the moon had set and the night was at its deepest before the coming dawn thinned the cover of dark, the four newest fugitives were taken one by one to the barn, where they crawled into the shallow space below the false bottom of Levi's specially constructed wagon. Levi gave them blankets, and passed the cloth sack of food to them before shutting the end of the wagon and piling sacks of goods into it. Jesse, in bonnet and shawl and carrying the baby, and Eliza, in her man's clothing and her false beard, came out of the house and climbed onto the seat. Levi hitched the horse to the wagon, and when the eastern sky began to show the first signs of growing pale, he swung open the heavy barn door.

"Thee must appear to be the driver if we are stopped," Jesse said quietly to Eliza. "Is thee able to do that?" Eliza nodded without a great deal of confidence, then more strongly. Jesse picked up the reins, nodded gravely to his father, and drove out of the barn into the deep grey of early dawn with only a soft swirl of new snowflakes to mark their departure. The next "station" was ten miles distant. Jesse would leave the six people there, change into his own clothing, and drive back alone.

Levi returned in almost-darkness to the house, where Catharine, also without light, waited for him. She had sent Martha to bed.

"All being as planned, Jesse should be home again not long after midday," Levi commented.

"Let us pray that the journey succeeds without incident," Catharine answered.

It had been a long night with little sleep. Levi took his wife's hands in his own and kissed them. "Dearest Katie," he said tenderly, "my partner in all. These people go on their way having had comfort, and been given new hope by thee. We have 'fed the hungry and clothed the naked' as we are bidden, and now we must try to rest ourselves for our day to come."

They moved as one in the lessening darkness and started up the stairs. As they reached the third step, they heard a knock upon the door.

Author's Note

Only a few years after its restoration as a historical museum, in 1976, while I was attending a Quaker gathering in Richmond, I visited the Levi and Catharine Coffin home in Fountain City, Indiana. I had for a long time been very interested in the Underground Railroad and its passengers, and those who helped them on their perilous way. Levi Coffin was often referred to as the "President of the Underground Railroad". His and Catharine's home was referred to as "Grand Central Station". The community of Newport, as Fountain City was then called, was largely Quaker and sympathetic to the Coffins' work.

Though Levi was the public face of the Coffins' work for the Underground Railroad, and the one who gets most of the "press", he and Catharine clearly worked as a team, and he gives her credit in his book *Reminiscences of Levi Coffin*. Without her "on the ground" to tend to the individual needs of their guests, Levi's ingenious strategies would have been far less successful. The freedom-seekers needed food and clothing as well as transportation, particularly as they were going north into a climate foreign to their experience. Catharine led a team of women who were abolitionists and supported the idea of slaves finding freedom, many of whom were either against breaking the law, or too timid to do so, or could not risk it for other reasons. However, they were willing to make clothing and food for the fugitives.

This is of course a fictional account, and departs from fact in two points. First, the Coffin home in Indiana was never actually searched. (Many safe houses were, however, and the Coffins were prepared for such a possibility at any time.) Second, the trap door in the living room is a feature of a different home; however, the hiding places between walls and under the eaves were designed and built into the Coffin home.

THE TWENTY-EIGHT DAYS

ELIZABETH WARNER CHRYSLER, A WIDOW OF THE BLOODY ASSIZES

Barb Rebelo

Rainham Township, Nanticoke, Ontario
December 4, 1813

Bitter wind sprang up beneath a pale moon. Ragged cloud cover sailed across its face, parting to reveal the road, where a horse-drawn wagon full of Norfolk Militia rolled to a stop beneath the creaking branches of an ancient tree a few hundred yards from Adam Chryslers' homestead.

The soldiers peered through the murk toward the cabin. Their leader, Colonel Henry Bostwick raised a hand for silence. A lantern bobbed in Chryslers' rear yard, then the light pinched out. Bostwick motioned for his men to advance; in moments they'd leapt from the wagon. Now they crouched and sped across the hard-packed snow to the door, rifles at the ready.

My name is Elizabeth Warner. I was a daughter to a prominent, daunting father, and the wife of a notorious and complex man. Silenced for years, I will now tell you of events long suppressed because of shame and despair.

I was born the eldest daughter to Christian and Charity Warner, from Schoharie, New York. We came to Upper Canada when I was a year old, and settled in the Niagara region of St. Davids, as my father had served during the American Revolution with Butler's Rangers, a British provincial regiment of Loyalists. After they disbanded, those that had served were granted land in the Niagara Region of Upper Canada. Father, a vigorous personality with forceful religious beliefs, became a lay-preacher and, with his thunderous voice, delivered Methodist services in the Warner Meeting House.

In the spring of my fifteenth year, I accompanied Father to Four-Mile-Creek, the farms of William and Adam Chrysler, brothers near St. Davids. Tethered to our wagon was a cow, a horse, and two goats which the Chrysler's had purchased. Upon our arrival in the barn-yard, a young man strode from a shed to lead the animals to the stables. The brothers introduced him to Father as their hired hand and nephew. Twenty-three-year-old Adam Chrysler had come from New York when he was eighteen.

Feeling Adam's eyes rest on me, I stole a glance at him from beneath my bonnet. He was of medium height with a husky build, thick dark hair and a face browned by the sun. But it was his gaze upon me that stirred my heart – sorrowful hazel eyes that warmed in admiration, then suddenly hardened like flint and looked away when his uncle spoke to him.

Father observed this; he saw all. He finished his business, and on the way home he admonished me for giving young Adam my attention; for some time he'd had a much older man in mind for my hand, but I had no interest in becoming the wife of a widowed farmer with three children. I said as much, and it was then that my father told me that young Adam's father Baltus had been executed under murky circumstances early in the Revolutionary War, and that while his uncles were respectable Loyalists, I was to have nothing to do with him. Instead, I was to set my mind on the plans he had for me.

But I was rebellious, in fact I yearned for glimpses of Adam around the village, unable to forget the way he'd looked at me. It wasn't long before he called at our home asking permission to walk out with me. Father of course voiced strong objections, and arguments prevailed in our home all of spring and summer. Mother, seeing the love in our eyes, urged Father to yield, for she saw my devotion to Adam.

Father relented, on condition that Adam and I attend our meeting-house on Sundays, where our wedding banns were read. We married before my sixteenth birthday.

We had nothing of our own, but lived with and worked for Adam's uncles. A few months later, together with Reverend Dunn who married us, we went to the Executive Council Office of Niagara, where I petitioned the Government for our own land. We were hopeful it would be granted when I came of age, as I was allowed to state that my father had served with the Military for the Crown.

The wait began. A year later, while we were still with Adam's uncles, our eldest daughter Elizabeth was born. Two more years passed and our son Baltus arrived, followed by the births of Charity, Mary, and Roger. I had come of age the year Charity was born, and we still had no land of our own. Adam worked hard, but I could see how discouraged he was.

It was now 1806. That year, in addition to his 400 acres in Niagara, Father was granted 182 acres of land in the Township of Walpole, near Nanticoke by Lake Erie. This land needed to be farmed, and Father came to us, suggesting that we clear a section, build our cabin, and begin sharecropping.

My spirits lifted with this opportunity, but when I hugged Adam, he stiffened in my arms. I had not anticipated his wounded pride and bitterness. He stalked away from us. I wanted to follow him, but thought it best to let him consider the offer alone; I turned to Father and tried to explain. He silenced me, understanding the situation. We could give him an answer when we were ready.

Adam finally agreed, with reluctance, and much persuasion on my part. I asked him for at least five years. Who knew, we might after all receive our own property in the meantime. And perhaps we could put away a little money from our share of the crops. It wasn't much, but it was a home for our growing family.

Adam's uncles gifted us with a horse and wagon, a cow, two sheep, a goat and chickens. And they, along with my brothers Peter and Michael, helped us clear a patch on the land to build a cabin and till our garden. Our lives were busy indeed, as Adam still worked for his uncles. At times he'd be in St. Davids for days, then they'd come and clear more small sections of land in preparation for crops.

My sisters Catherine and Margaret were now old enough to help mind our youngsters, while I worked in the fields with Adam. We were poor and the work was hard; at times our crops failed and animals sickened and died, causing Adam's face to darken with bitterness. The longer we were married, the more I sensed that he begrudged his past and the terrible way his father had died. Did he feel cheated? I witnessed him suffer imagined slights from remarks about us working Father's lands. Worse yet, because we felt such heavy obligation to Father, we had to endure his religious and judgmental reprimands.

At these times, Adam was a stranger to me. I didn't know how to soothe him, so I'd wait for his storms to pass until he was himself once more. That was his way, rather mysterious and brooding, and I loved him the more, helping him to forget by challenging his dark moods with passion. From 1806 to 1810, four more wee babes arrived, a son and three daughters. In all, I had given Adam nine children by the time rumours of war threatened.

○

It was early summer, 1812, when Father rode up our lane with news from the British Post at Fort George, Niagara. American armies threatened the border strongholds, including Queenston, right by our doorstep. War was declared between the United States and Upper Canada.

Adam and I were raising our children and crops, and cared little for political issues. We were no different than our Loyalist settler friends, who had been lured by the promise of cheap land. Neighbouring farmers arrived at our cabin, echoing our sentiments in vigorous talk with Adam out in the barnyard: this war was a nuisance, an interruption of our lives and a threat to our autumn harvests. Indoors, while quilting, my women friends and I overheard our husbands' hints of uncertain loyalties, and that they did not want to fight.

We women took our sewing outside under the fresh green shade of maples and listened, taking heart when some of our men said they believed the war would be over by Christmas – that we were defended by a skilled British military presence, and an alliance with the displaced American Indians. But Adam argued this, pointing out reasons for American outrage. They'd had enough of the Royal Navy boarding their ships and impressing their men into service. British blockades had seized over 400 American ships, ruining their export trade of cotton and tobacco. No, Adam maintained, it could be a long war.

During the summer of 1812, militias were hastily summoning citizens and farmers. Father's old regiment, Butler's Rangers, was raised again and renamed the Lincoln Militia. Uncle Adam and William rode over one evening and advised that Adam join up with them before he was conscripted. He reluctantly did so, becoming a private with the Lincoln 2nd. They were drilled three times a month and called upon as needed. Adam and others were placed on the flanks, and after engagements and skirmishes, were sent home to tend crops. That autumn ripened into scarlet-and-gold, pungent with the aroma of threshed hay. It was the last decent crop we had, brought in with the help of two men Adam knew, Isaac Pettit and John Johnston.

As 1813 began, Adam was away from home more and more. With only fifteen-year-old Elizabeth and eleven-year-old Baltus and myself to work in the fields, by that autumn harvest, we lost what little we had. The animals were starving and there was little milk for the children. Adam would go hunting with the local men and come home with rabbits and deer meat. Young Baltus begged to go and learn to hunt. Adam agreed, as if he sensed we would have to depend on Baltus in the near future.

It was at this time that I felt my husband begin to reject me. He'd become almost a stranger to us, his manner ever more cold and distant. When I asked him what was amiss, he told me he was trying to find food and money. He'd met some men who were heading up a farmer's aid committee to help settlers like us, in dire need of food and supplies. Adam hated being questioned. His vexation toward me rose along with his voice: Couldn't I see there was no sympathy or help from the government? That they had their own headaches keeping the Natives fed, happy, and on their side, on meagre stores intended for their own ships? And no Loyalist opposition – no outlet for any political disagreement? *Tell* me, Elizabeth, how else are families to survive unless we take matters in hand?

I knew not of these things. I made no reply, but left him to his ways, and tried to harden my heart. I'd not felt as cowed since I was a young girl silenced into submission by Father's roaring voice.

By now, with British retreats from Niagara and Burlington, and with a vast American army advancing, Adam believed the tide had turned and that the Americans had all but won the war. As far as he and his friends were concerned, if and when the Americans discovered the British were moving toward Kingston and Montreal, it would be over.

By October, his talk distressed me; dark suspicions were circulating our township, vague remarks about disloyalty and fearsome punishments. One morning, when Adam took Baltus out hunting for deer, our friends Isaac and John, the men who had helped with our harvest the previous year, stopped at our cabin for a moment with a parcel for Adam. I gathered courage and spoke with them briefly. They knew nothing of the farmer's aid committee. After they left, I went to the barn where Adam and Baltus were gutting the deer they'd shot. When I asked Adam why Isaac and John weren't part of the group, he became so angry he hurled his deer knife into a wooden joist, thrust me outside and shut the door in my face.

Later, he and Baltus came into the cabin and told me they'd hung the deer meat to dry. He went about stuffing some bread into his rucksack. Without explanation or a good-bye, he left. Because he'd become so miserable and distant, I was relieved he'd taken the tension with him.

He didn't come home until the dawn of the 13th that month, when I awoke to see him standing at the foot of our bed without his coat, a thin and ragged scarecrow, eyes sunken, his hair and beard matted. He took up a blanket and his rifle, and went to the barn for the night, with no account for his absence, other than to say if anyone came looking for him, I hadn't seen him.

He didn't pause to notice my tears of anguish. Where had he been, and what had he done?

O

My fears were well-founded, for next day, a knock came at the door. Two women in heavy cloaks slipped inside. One grasped my hands and sat me down; the other sent the children into the next room and drew the curtain. In low voices, they told me that the previous night, Nanticoke Militia had raided and arrested one of their husbands and fourteen other men at John Dunham's cabin near Nanticoke. And that a couple of men had escaped – where was Adam?

Stunned, I couldn't catch my breath. Young Baltus slipped into the room, and putting his arms around me, bade the women leave, that we knew nothing, and that it was better we knew nothing. One woman began to cry; she said the Militia were herding the prisoners off to York Gaol with no explanation, and that in the village there were already whispered suspicions of treason. The women left us, uttering, "May God help your man."

Are the words "fear and secrecy" apt in describing our next days together as a family? Adam fixed a hiding spot in our root cellar under the cabin floor. He admitted he'd been at Dunham's cabin that night. They'd gathered to divide money some had received from revealing British movements, and to make further plans to provide for starving local farmers and their families. What did it matter now that the British had all but abandoned the Niagara frontier, the Americans at their backs? I asked him gently if he had informed. He shrugged and looked away, then faced me once more. To my shock, he said that night at Dunham's cabin, he'd had a split second to escape by smashing a glass pane with his musket and vaulting out of the window. He'd not had time to snatch his coat he'd left at Dunham's, so it was a matter of time before the Militia came for him. Softening toward me, he described an idea he'd had to send us to his brother Richard across the border but, being so out of touch with people and events, he doubted we could cross the Niagara River without help.

During this time, the children, eager to help their father, watched the roads and fields for strangers approaching. Then Adam prepared us for winter food in the Indian ways his uncles had taught him during his youth in Schoharie. He sent Baltus and Elizabeth to the swamp with pitchforks to dig up duck potato, cattails and bulrushes for their potato-like roots, and dried fluff to use as tinder and torch. Then he sent them to the woods for balsam fir branches and willow leaves. These, he explained, were medicinal in teas for colds and pain relief. The younger children and I scoured our meadows, collecting asters and thistles to be dried and crushed for flour. Adam ground the dried deer meat to powder, and afterward, we mixed this with melted fat, adding dried sumac berries to make pemmican. Adam showed the children how to form the mixture into balls, then we all sewed them into little hide pouches for storage. The pemmican, he explained, was the best way he knew to extend what meat we had into nourishing food for the harsh winter. Watching his face soften while teaching the children, my heart filled with love for him.

The night of December 4th, I sent Baltus to the shed with the lantern to bring in some kindling. Busy kneading bread, I suddenly realized he'd been gone longer than necessary; at the window, I saw lantern light disappear into the barn. He couldn't stay away from his father or his project, for Adam had struck upon a plan to build planks beneath our wagon to conceal himself and have Isaac drive us across the border.

Then the light re-emerged from the barn, and Adam and Baltus entered the woodshed. The light went out, but I could see them come out by the moonlight, arms filled with sticks and fire-logs. They came inside, stamping snow from their feet, and dumped the wood into the bin.

At that moment, the front door was kicked in. Men swarmed inside, soldiers of the Norfolk Militia pointing rifles at Adam. Everything happened quickly – I remember Baltus' shriek as he rushed at the men, and me, helpless with bread dough all over my hands. They seized Adam, pinned his arms behind his back, then threw him to the floor, rifles pointed at his head. They arrested him, their barking orders overriding our children's wails of terror. They watched their father twist and struggle in vain as they took him from our home.

O

Our December days passed in despair amid furious snowstorms. Father came with the sleigh, bringing provisions and news of Adam. He'd been sent to York Gaol along with the others on suspicion of treason. I pleaded with Father to help him, hoping that his renowned position in the community and past service with Butler's Rangers might aid Adam's fate. Father raged in his thunderous voice: to think that after all he'd done for us, Adam may have taken part in a conspiracy. I then endured remarks that I could have made a much better marriage. In no state to bear this, I hushed his voice, reminding him of the children's presence.

At my mention of the children, he quietened, but I was taken aback when he next urged me to allow our two youngest children to stay with him and Mother until we learned more. I wanted my children with me, privately thinking of the food preparations we'd made in the past weeks. I felt if I told him, he might believe Adam guilty. Therefore I kept silent, with Father reminding me that he was the only one providing for us now, with Adam's uncles away in service, and with the harsh winter deepening, he couldn't be certain he'd be able to travel to bring us replenishments.

Then war events forced my hand, for a few days later, on December 10th, during a blizzard, the Americans burnt the town of Newark to the ground, forcing women, children and old men out into the harsh winter elements. Father, enraged, sent word that he was coming for our two youngest children, and that there were many displaced families roaming the countryside seeking refuge and food. I was, therefore, to have my little daughters, four-year-old Rebecca and three-year-old Christiana packed in readiness.

O

Those of us left in our family kissed the little ones and waved goodbye, for how long we knew not. Forlorn, we sat around the table and joined hands in prayer for their safe journey to their grandparents' home. When they'd all bowed their heads, I glanced upon each of them with sorrow in my heart for our situation. Our eldest, Elizabeth, appeared much older; indeed she had a beau by now. Baltus, only eleven, already wore the hardened look of a young man who'd seen too much. Charity, ten, and Mary, nine, had work-hardened hands and expressions too solemn for little girls. Next was Roger, eight, pitifully eager to please, fearful lest he too be taken away. Lastly, Catharine, six, and John, five, unaware that their childhood was gone.

Now we were eight, I thought, facing a harsh and uncertain future. My eye faltered at the sight of two little stools belonging to Rebecca and Christiana that someone had pushed into the corner.

O

It was now February. *A New Year has begun, and may it bring good fortune to our family*, I remember praying, for the charges against Adam and others were yet unclear, and the children and I still had hope. Seven men, including Adam, were still confined in York Gaol, and made appeal to the Governor as follows:

> To His Excellency Governor Drummond, Commander in Chief of His Britannic Majesty's Forces in Upper Canada:
>
> The Petition of Your humble petitioners hereby humbly sheweth that they are confined in York Gaol, that were

taken from their homes by Militia guards under the command of colonel Henry Baustwick about the 1st of December last past & brought to this gaol where we have remained in close confinement ever since without being informed for what cause our families which are numerous Small Children residing in the County of Norfolk Upper Canada, our families in Suffering Conditions for want of our presence & Assistance we humbly pray to have our cases examined into and if any crime or crimes should be immediately found that is bailable, we are willing to give Sufficient bail & where no crimes has been committed we pray to be released from imprisonment as your excellency must see fit. In Duty Bound We Shall ever pray.

York Gaol February 7, 1814[1]

Joseph Fowler

Adam Chrysler

Griffis Colver

Isaac Pettit

Wm. Carpenter

Datis Linsey

Wadsworth Philips

The appeal to the Governor had no effect. By May, we learned that their trials were for treason, and would be held in Ancaster's Union Hotel, which the British possessed temporarily as a hospital. The General agreed to turn it over as a short-term courthouse for the inquests.

On 23rd May, the Court opened. I travelled to Ancaster with Father and Adam's uncles to hear the Bills for High Treason read against Adam and the nineteen other accused that were in custody, and against the near-fifty men not yet apprehended. A copy of this indictment was delivered to each of the accused in the presence of eyewitnesses, and then the court adjourned for a week. I was wild with fear, and begged to see Adam. It was not possible, I was told, and Father had to wrench me away.

In the following days at home, once I regained my nerves, I paused to consider the names of those whom I had heard accused at the Court – some of them good men of our acquaintance: Noah Payne Hopkins, John Johnston, a friend who had helped us with harvest along with young Isaac Pettit, one of the men who, with Adam, had made appeal from the York Gaol. The other name on the appeal was Dayton Lindsey, whom I had only heard Adam mention and who was therefore a stranger to me. The rest Adam had never spoken of: Aaron Stevens, George Peacock Jr., Isaiah Brink, and Benjamin Simmons.

My mind clouded in confusion. What had Adam done along with these men? How could I eat, sleep and live with my husband and not suspect or indeed attempt to confront him with my fears before it was too late? Although at that time I knew with certainty that High Treason by English Law meant death, I did not grasp by what manner.

Father arranged for us to stay with friends in Ancaster during the trials, while my brother Peter oversaw the children at home. We were having trouble with Baltus. Heartbroken, he had twice struck out on his own for Ancaster, and I could no longer restrain him. The day we left for the trials, Elizabeth and the youngsters kissed us good-bye, while at the cabin door, Peter had a firm hold on the weeping Baltus to keep him from running after us. I will forever have that scene in my memory.

The Ancaster Assizes began the next day in a nightmarish atmosphere – people crowded and lunged at the building; hecklers cried out, throwing stones. Inside, in stern and deathly silence, from 7th June until the 21st, all were tried and sentenced, although at this time I can only bear to speak of Adam's fate. I was not allowed to testify on his behalf; spouses cannot by law.

Adam was tried 16th June before Judge Campbell, and from the witness testimony of Captain William Francis, was found guilty of participation along with others, of capturing Francis, along with six of his cattle, and leaving them in Buffalo; of informing to the enemy for benefit and raiding farms along the Lake Erie shore. Judge Campbell considered Adam's conduct "worse than that of his comrades" after

Adam muttered words incomprehensible to the court, but which I caught and understood later.

I begged Father to help save Adam, and on 18th June, he and nine respectable men, including Adam's uncle, and two Captains, a 1st Lieutenant and a gunner with Adam's 2nd Lincoln Militia[2], appealed on his behalf:

... in consideration of the long tried Loyalty and known respectability of his connexions and relative as well as the deplorable state in which a family consisting of a wife and seven children must inevitably be involved when deprived of its Head and Chief Support ...[3]

The petition failed, for Adam and fourteen others were found guilty of High Treason on the final day of the Assizes, and sentenced while they stood on the dock with the public looking on.

That each of you are to be taken to the place from whence you came and from thence you are to be drawn on hurdles to the place of execution, whence you are to be hanged by the neck, but not until you are dead, for you must be cut down while alive and your entrails taken out and burned before your faces, your head then to be cut off and your bodies divided into four quarters and your heads and quarters to be at the King's disposal. And may God have mercy on your souls.[4]

○

It is twilight, July 20, 1814. I am sitting beneath our maple tree, remembering Adam's muttered words at the trial. I have always known in my heart how bitter he was about the execution of his Loyalist father, accused as a traitor early in the American Revolution. Adam believed, probably rightly, that he was also punished by being denied his own land. I imagine now that Adam's part in the abduction of Captain William Frances stemmed from his opinion that men like Frances might have done more to save his father. While Adam wouldn't have proof of this, so young at the time of his father's death, these things preyed on his mind, and he became swept up in events along with his comrades.

Tears blind my eyes while I search the road for a glimpse of Father's wagon, on his return from Burlington Heights, where Adam and the others were hanged to death today.

I did not go – I could not watch.

Epilogue

The day following Adam's trial and death verdict, despite a tremendous emotional toll, Elizabeth Warner came forward and testified on behalf of John Johnston and young Isaac Pettit before Justice Scott. It was suggested from evidence that Pettit had taken some part with the marauders, but he had refused to accompany them and had been branded as a coward. He was found guilty, but later sent to Kingston Gaol, where he died March 16, 1815, of Gaol Fever. Johnston was also saved from hanging, and was sent to Kingston Gaol. He survived and received a pardon on the condition of abandoning the province and all other British possessions for life. He was sent to the United States.

Of the fifteen men sentenced to death, eight were hanged, and the rest sent to Kingston Gaol. While the executions were not as horrific as the judge ordered, they were terrible enough. A twelve-year-old boy witnessed the hangings and described the scene to a Hamilton newspaper, later written in an account:

At Burlington Heights, on July 20, the sentences are carried out after a fashion. A rude gallows with eight nooses await the victims, who are driven in two wagons to the scene. Once the nooses are adjusted, the wagons are driven off, leaving the prisoners to strangle. Their contortions are such that a heavy brace comes loose and falls, striking one of the dying men on the head, and mercifully putting an end to his struggles. Later all eight heads are chopped off and publicly exhibited.[5]

In October 1814, Captain William Francis was killed in retaliation for his testimony during the 28 days of the Bloody Assizes, Ancaster, against Adam Chrysler, Isaiah Brink, Isaac Pettit, John

Dunham, Garrett Null and John Johnston. The Dickson gang, friends and relatives of the condemned men, came to Francis' home, drew him to his upstairs bedroom window, shot him in the head and then burned down his house.

Adam and Elizabeth's two youngest children remained with and were raised by her parents, Christian and Charity Warner.

Her eldest child, fifteen-year-old Elizabeth, married Benjamin Stewart Jr. later that year, and the rest of her children were separated and lost contact with one another. It is speculated that the older ones were indentured out as farm labourers, and that Elizabeth was obliged to vacate her father's property as, according to his 1824 will, he left the land to his eldest son Matthew.

Elizabeth Warner later married her daughter's father-in-law, Benjamin Stewart Sr.

Footnotes

1   Canada, Upper Canada Sundries, *Civil Secretary's Correspondence Traitors and Treason, War of 1812* RGS. A1. Vol. 16, 6731

2   David F. Hemmings, *War of 1812 Lincoln Militia*, 2012, 30 Mar. 2015 http://www.niagarahistoricalmuseum/media/01.LincolnMilitia-warof1812.pdf

3   Canada, Upper Canada Sundries, RGS. A1. Vol. 16, 6731

4   Pierre Berton, *Flames Across the Border.* (Toronto: McClelland and Stewart Limited, 1981) 298

5   Berton, *Flames Across.* 299

Author's Note

The Twenty-Eight Days is Elizabeth Warner's story, a work of creative non-fiction, set amid the turmoil of the War of 1812. Elizabeth Warner and her husband Adam Chrysler were my great-grandparents of six generations ago.

I discovered Adam Chrysler's fate when I was a teenager, helping my Chrysler cousin do ancestral research in Norfolk County. And several years ago while attending writing classes, I met Sandra Lloyd, whose grandfather six generations ago was Peter Warner – Elizabeth's brother.

Since then, through extensive reading, study of timelines and events, and information generously shared by Sandra Lloyd, I have attempted to reconstruct Elizabeth Warner's story in her own voice.

MRS. WAIT, WAITING

MARIA WAIT, WIFE OF 1838 REBEL, BENJAMIN WAIT

Katharine O'Flynn

On an August day in the year 1838, Maria Wait watched from the spectators' gallery of the Niagara courthouse as the judge placed a flat black cap on his wig and addressed the prisoner in the dock. "Benjamin Wait, you have been found guilty of high treason and are hereby sentenced to be taken from this place to the place whence you came, and there remain until the twenty-fifth day of August when you shall be drawn upon a hurdle to the place of execution and hanged by the neck until you are dead and your body shall be quartered. May the Lord have mercy on your soul."

Maria's husband stood straight and tall through his sentencing. Anger was evident in his features, but no fear. Maria took courage from him to choke back her tears and still her trembling hands. She too could be brave.

The judge addressed the next prisoner. "Samuel Chandler, you have been found guilty of high treason and are hereby sentenced to be taken from this place …"

On the bench beside Maria, Sarah, the eldest of Chandler's ten children, gave a strangled cry.

Maria reached out to the young woman. "Courage," she whispered. "While there is life there is yet hope."

One by one fourteen other prisoners were found guilty and sentenced and led from the courtroom. Most walked with heads down;

some wept. Only Maria's Benjamin walked proud. He did not look like a man condemned to death.

That was because he didn't believe in the sentences, as Maria discovered as soon as she'd managed to bribe her way into the prison to talk with him through the grating of his cell door. "They only mean to intimidate us," he told her. "They wouldn't dare execute us. The whole country would rise in arms against them if they followed such a barbarous course. Our cause is just and its righteousness shall prevail."

The cause of which he spoke was much-needed reform of the corrupt government of Upper Canada, dominated at this time by a closely-linked coterie of wealthy families known as the Family Compact. The Compact used their positions of power to impose laws and taxes that favoured and enriched them at the expense of the poor, they ignored any laws passed by the elected assembly that did not suit them, and they packed public offices and judicial services with their supporters to enforce their tyrannical rule.

Benjamin and the other prisoners had first fought against the Compact's oppression with words: with arguments, petitions and newspaper editorials, through questions and memorials to elected members of the parliamentary assembly. Their questions and arguments had gone unanswered, their pleas ignored. Only then did the reformers turn to armed rebellion. Perhaps because they were men more used to words than to war, the campaign of the Niagara rebels had been short-lived and ineffective. They fought one not very fierce battle in which no one on either side was killed.

Yet for this act of treason their leader, James Morreau, had been tried and summarily executed. "The government has had its revenge, alas for poor Morreau," Benjamin explained to Maria. "They will let the rest of us off with prison sentences."

Maria squeezed her fingers through the grating and seized hold of her husband's jacket to pull him close to try to make him understand his peril. "Benjamin, you have been sentenced to death. They will hang you, as they hanged Morreau, and in two weeks' time."

Benjamin stroked her clutching fingers. "So they say. They do not mean it. Now," he changed the subject, "tell me, how is our little one? You will kiss her for me and tell her her papa will soon be back to rock her again."

Was he feigning unconcern for her sake? Maria wondered. Or did he really believe what he said? "Our little one is fine. Which she will not be when she is left destitute of a father's love and support." Maria let go of his coat, wriggled her hand back through the grate.

"Come now, my dear," Benjamin spoke as if he were soothing a frightened child. "You hardly understand what is here involved, I believe."

At that moment the jailer appeared to say that the interview was over and hustled Maria away. "Sleep well, and don't worry about that farce in the courtroom this afternoon," Benjamin called after her.

Maria could not sleep well. She nursed her baby and paced up and down in the room she had rented close to the jail. What could she do to save her husband and the others? There was no use appealing to the judge who had passed sentence; he was firmly on the side of the Family Compact. Nor was the governor of Upper Canada, Sir George Arthur – widely known as "the bloody fiend" – likely to show mercy. Certain clergymen and members of the elected assembly might speak against the executions, but did they have enough influence to deter the Compact? Maria doubted it.

The best course of action, she decided, would be to appeal to the supreme power in the land, the new Governor General, Lord Durham. He had pardoned some of the patriots of Lower Canada. Surely then be would pardon the Upper Canadians as well.

Next morning she brought a basket of scones and preserves to the jail for her husband's breakfast. She passed them to him through the barred window of his cell. Benjamin ate with good appetite and, as he ate, Maria announced her plan. She would travel to Quebec City and appeal to Lord Durham in person.

"Nonsense!" was Benjamin's instant judgment. "It's an impractical plan for any man to consider, and absurd for a woman with a suckling babe to care for."

"I shall leave the baby in the care of Mrs. Smith." The separation from her child would be painful, but it would have to be. She couldn't carry the infant with her on the long and arduous journey.

Benjamin licked his fingers and peered at his wife, who suddenly looked more fierce and formidable than he had ever seen her. "It's seven hundred miles or more to Quebec, through dangerous waters and over rough roads. You couldn't undertake such a journey alone."

"I have asked Miss Chandler to accompany me."

"What help could that young lady afford you?" Benjamin asked.

"I believe pity for her and her nine brothers and sisters will help win over even the coldest heart."

"Then let her go."

Maria was indignant. "I could not trust your life to the pleadings of anyone but myself, much less to an inexperienced girl of eighteen. Besides, as you yourself pointed out, it is unsafe for a woman to travel alone."

Benjamin tried another argument. "You have not enough money for the fare."

"Our friends will help us."

"You will go to our friends as a beggar? That hardly befits people of our standing."

"To save you and your fellow patriots, I would grovel in the dust with a begging bowl before the whole world," Maria answered.

Benjamin shook his head. "I can scarcely see you as a beggar. It seems to me you have greater facility in arguing and browbeating than in pleading. You, and Miss Chandler too, would do better to leave this matter in the hands of men who are used to dealing in public concerns. Letters and petitions are being drafted. These are sure to be more effective than an emotional appeal from two inexperienced women. Indeed the very fact of women interfering in affairs of state might prejudice our case."

"You will be dead and your mutilated remains burr
ters have any effect, no matter who writes them. I must &
on tomorrow's boat, to plead for you. Lord Durham is our .
only hope." Maria pushed another bundle of scones through th.
"These are for the others." Then she touched her fingers to her
and reached through to touch Benjamin's. "Pray for me," she sai.
"as I will for you," and she left.

O

The journey was not worse than expected. Maria and Miss Chandler
arrived safely in Quebec City and made their way directly to the residence of the Governor General. There his aide, Colonel Couper, told
them that his Excellency was indisposed, suffering from headache.
The two ladies were obliged to withdraw. They returned early the
next morning. The Governor's headache had not abated; he was seeing no one this morning, Colonel Couper informed them.

"I am sorry to hear it," Maria murmured. In fact she wasn't so
much sorry as frightened and angry. She suspected evasive tactics here.

The Colonel spoke with smooth assurance. "May I suggest that
you return later in the day – shall we say at four this afternoon?"

No! Maria wanted to answer. This is no time for delays and indis-
positions. I must see Lord Durham now. But she remembered what
Benjamin had said about browbeating and remained silent.

"In the meantime," Colonel Couper was saying, "I would be
pleased to carry your petition to the Governor and draw it to his
attention at the earliest opportunity."

Was this further evasion, or a genuine offer of help? Maria did
not know. Colonel Couper had a glib tongue, but kind eyes. He had
not dismissed them outright. She would give him the benefit of the
doubt. "Thank you." She handed over her petition, signed by every
man of importance she had been able to find. "We shall return at four
o'clock," she said. She made it sound like a warning.

○

Miss Chandler waited. Miss Chandler wept quietly. Maria's ached for her baby and her heart was sore with fear for her hus-'s peril, yet she shed no tears. Her resolve was strong and straight her backbone. She had undertaken the journey to Quebec to obtain a commutation of the death sentence and obtain it she would.

By a quarter before the appointed hour, the two women were back at the governor's residence. Colonel Couper met them with an apologetic mien. The Governor was still unable to meet them. This time the excuse was the pressing nature of other business matters which had precedence over their plea.

Nothing was more important than their petition. It was a matter of life and death. Maria took a deep breath. She fought back the urge to push this pale minion aside and force her way into the Governor's bedroom, or office, or dining room, wherever he was, and demand an immediate answer from the man himself. "The time has now arrived," she warned Colonel Couper, "when further delay would be adequate to a refusal of Lord Durham to grant a commutation. Should we receive no answer by the time our boat sails this evening, we must expect to return only to embrace the lifeless bodies of those we loved."

"I shall have his Lordship's reply sent down to the boat by special messenger," Couper offered.

This was kind, but not good enough. "With your permission, I prefer to wait here until Lord Durham is pleased to give his reply." Maria settled herself more firmly on the hard settee and signalled Miss Chandler to sit beside her. Colonel Couper bowed, and left.

Rightly was she called Mrs. Wait, Maria reflected grimly. Ever since Benjamin had joined the patriots, she had spent hours and days in anxious waiting, and was likely to spend many more before he was a free man. Unfortunately, waiting was not her strong point. She was a woman who liked to be doing.

The Colonel returned in a few minutes with w.
Maria sipped the restorative gratefully. She took it as a ge

And indeed within the hour Colonel Couper brought ge
"Lord Durham has ordered a stay of all executions until such
he can study the circumstances of the case. He conveys his decisi
this document," Couper handed a letter to Maria. "He has also se
a dispatch to advise Governor Arthur of the change." Maria snapped
the precious document into her reticule with profuse expressions of
gratitude, while Miss Chandler wept again, this time with joy.

"You may be fortunate enough to meet Sir Arthur on your journey, for he is at present in Montreal and bound for Kingston," Couper
said as he escorted the ladies to the door. Hardly would she call such
a meeting fortunate, Maria thought.

But later, safely on board the evening boat, she reconsidered.
Suppose no dispatch had been sent to Governor Arthur? It would not
be the first time a government official had lied about his intentions. Or
suppose the dispatch was sent, but failed to reach Arthur? Suppose it
reached him, but he pretended it didn't? That blackguard was capable
of any skullduggery.

She realized now that it was imperative for her to meet with
Arthur on this journey whether she wanted to or not, for the only
way to be sure he got the order and acted on it was to confront him
herself and present him with the document in the presence of witnesses. Here she had some remarkable luck. When she made inquiries
as to Arthur's present whereabouts, she learned that he was to board
this very boat at Coteau du Lac.

Scarcely had Sir Arthur set foot in his cabin before Maria was
at the door demanding an interview. Arthur, the scoundrel, made no
reference to having already received notice of the stay of execution
when Maria presented her copy of the order. Now he had no choice
but to open it and read. He flung the paper down in a fury. "I cannot
accede to this request and prevent the due course of the law upon such
offences," he shouted.

_t accede!" Maria echoed. "You cannot accede to a
_m the Governor General! I must write immediately to
_ of this." She held the high ground of superior author-
_ould afford to indulge just a little the contempt she felt for
_an. Sir Arthur huffed and bluffed, but in the end had to accept
order. As a precautionary measure, Maria sent a letter to Lord
_urham, telling him of the interview, and then took care to inform
Sir Arthur that she had done so, just in case he tried any further
subterfuge.

Relieved of anxiety, Maria and Miss Chandler arrived back in
Niagara on the twenty-second of August, three days before the execution had been scheduled to take place. They hurried to the jail to
rejoice with their loved ones, but to their dismay, they discovered a
scaffold being built in the prison yard. Maria at once informed the
jailer that the apparatus would not be required. His answer sent a
chill through her. "I have heard nothing of any commutation," he
said, "and until such time as I do, my duty is to proceed with preparations for the hangings."

"But I have the word of Lord Durham himself!" Maria exclaimed.
The jailer looked at her skeptically and refused to order a stop to the
sawing and hammering.

"Where is the sheriff?" Maria demanded then. It was he who
would have received the order. He must have neglected to pass it on.
He might well be one of the Family Compact toadies.

The sheriff was in Kingston. The jailer did not know when he
would return.

"No doubt he will arrive on tomorrow's boat with the new
order." Maria spoke confidently for the benefit of the jailer and Miss
Chandler, but she was worried as she hurried to Benjamin's window
with the news of the reprieve. That snake in the grass Arthur was up
to his tricks again. He should have sent the new order by special courier the moment their boat reached Prescott. It should have arrived in
Niagara a good twelve hours before she did.

Benjamin ignored Maria's worries in his elation at the news she brought. "You have done well, my dear. That you should brave such a journey and achieve success! I could scarcely have believed it. Verily you are a woman whose price is above rubies. You have saved us."

Maria kept glancing from her happy husband to the scaffold in the yard. "Arthur is a villain, through and through," she worried aloud. "What plan is he hatching against your release?"

Benjamin brushed aside her concern. "Even Arthur would not dare disobey the Governor General. He'd be arrested for treason himself, if he did."

Maria was not convinced. "I suspect he's up to something. I shall go to Toronto tomorrow and see what I can find out."

"Go back to Toronto! You've only just come from there!"

"I came away believing the Governor General's order would precede me. It didn't. That worries me."

"But you must get back to our little Augusta," Benjamin said. "The babe needs you."

Maria steeled her resolve and answered, "My heart aches for my baby, my breast weeps the milk that should nourish her, but she is not in danger of death, and you are. I shall go to Toronto."

The next morning Maria was pacing the deck of the Toronto boat, wondering what exactly she should do when she got there. Time was running out. Who could she call on to help her get the official word to the Niagara jailer? Would she find Sir Arthur himself there, stalling the order?

Upon landing she called first at the home of the chief justice of the colony, but he was not there. She tried the Attorney General next, and then, on his advice, went to the Parliament and accosted members of the executive council. They had had no word of a stay of execution for the Niagara traitors. "But if indeed Governor Arthur has received a command from Lord Durham," one of the members assured her, "he will certainly see that the order reaches Niagara in time, for Sir Arthur is an honourable man." He patted her hand. "Count on it, dear lady; the message will arrive this evening or tomorrow."

Maria could not count on any such thing, not when Governor Arthur was concerned. She stomped off to call on Bishop Mountain, who gave her tea and promised he would do what he could.

Frustrated at accomplishing so little, Maria caught the evening boat back to Niagara. There was no message from the Governor in the mail it carried. The jailer had heard nothing. In the jail yard, the gallows stood ready.

Another day passed and no message came. The execution was scheduled for one o'clock the following day.

That morning's boat was the last hope. It docked. Maria watched the passengers alight. An immigrant couple with a young child. A land agent in checkered trousers and a tall hat. Two soldiers who knew nothing of any government documents. A farmer with a cart of goods to sell. And no one else.

The clergyman who had been keeping watch with Maria, clasped her hand. "Go to your husband," he told her. "I shall keep watch here until the last hour has passed. And pray, Mrs. Wait, pray!"

Maria was allowed into her husband's cell to say farewell. The couple stood clasped together when the sound of shouting on the street below came to them. "Reprieve!" The pastor was running towards the jail, his black coattails flying, his long black legs pumping. The sheriff came panting behind him and a crowd followed the sheriff, all shouting, "Reprieve! Reprieve!"

The sheriff had received the order only the day before, in Kingston. Realizing travel by public conveyance would be too slow, he had commandeered the governor's private boat and sped to Niagara with all haste, for he was a man who did not like executions.

The patriots were saved! Maria joined in the celebration, and modestly accepted thanks for her role in the rescue, but her joy was mixed with misgivings. Governor Arthur had had to obey his superior but he'd taken his time, doubtless hoping the reprieve would arrive too late, but still allow him to prove that he had obeyed orders. He was an enemy, and a formidable one. And the patriots, for all their rejoicing, were not pardoned, only reprieved.

There was more work to be done. But for the present, she had to get back to her child.

O

Lord Durham's final decision was that the patriots should be neither executed nor pardoned. They were sentenced to transportation for life. Accordingly, on October 6th Benjamin and his fellow prisoners began the long, long journey to the end of the world, to Van Dieman's Land, the British penal colony off the coast of Australia. Handcuffed and shackled with iron fetters, the prisoners shuffled under heavy guard to the Niagara dock. Benjamin and Chandler rattled their chains at jeering onlookers and shouted their unrepentant opposition to the tyranny of the government that had made them prisoners.

A few weeks later Maria received a cheerful letter from her husband. The prisoners were now at Fort Henry, in Kingston. On the journey there they had suffered from hunger and cold and the chafing of "the Queen's ribands," as Benjamin called their fetters. But now they were installed in a large apartment with a good fire and the hateful irons had been removed. Prison food was plain but sufficient. The constraints of imprisonment offered many hours of leisure for study and for useful pursuits. The men busied themselves with small handcrafts. A literary society had been formed. Benjamin was to lecture on patriotism. Reverend Wixon expounded on the Psalms.

Maria read the letter and thought of the men, cold and hungry and cruelly fettered and now trying to make the best of their imprisonment. She would like to have heard that lecture on patriotism! What future hardships awaited these brave men, she wondered. Would they overwinter in the comparative comfort of Fort Henry? Or would they be sent to some less hospitable place?

She had better go and see how she could be of help, she decided. The journey would be as nothing to her now. She knew how to go about it. She gathered up contributions of food and warm clothing and money, and set out for Kingston.

Apart from distributing the few comforts she had brought, Maria could do little to help, and a few days after her arrival, the sheriff announced that the prisoners were to leave for England immediately on the second stage of their journey to Van Dieman's Land. Maria and Benjamin had only a few minutes to say their goodbyes.

Maria wept, but Benjamin was well pleased. In England, in English courts, far from the corrupt legislature and judiciary of Upper Canada, he was sure the patriots could not only win pardon for themselves, but at the same time draw the attention of the mother country to the oppression of the Canadian colonies. The British Parliament would see the justice of the patriots' demands. Changes would be made. "In a year's time we shall all be free men and back in a better-governed Canada," he told Maria, who clung to him fearing she might never see him again. As she watched the boat carrying the prisoners disappear over the horizon, Maria hoped her husband was right, but feared he might not be.

With no money and no means of support, she returned to Niagara to live on the charity of friends and family and wait for news. Once again she was Mrs. Wait, waiting.

The Atlantic sea routes were closed in winter. It was May before Maria heard from Benjamin. The sea journey to England had been a frightful ordeal, but they had arrived in Liverpool safely and conditions in the jail there were satisfactory. The story of Maria's heroic journey to the Governor General to save them from hanging had reached England before them and Benjamin was particularly sought out by visitors to tell the story. "You are a heroine here," he wrote.

Progress on their case for pardon was most encouraging. Lawyers, clergy and members of parliament sympathetic to the cause were working on their behalf. It had been discovered that the law prescribing transportation had never been ratified in Canada: their sentences, therefore, must be illegal. They would soon be set free, Benjamin believed.

But a second letter, dated in March, gave alarming news. Benjamin and eight others of the Niagara patriots were to sail for Van Dieman's Land.

Once again it was time for Maria to act, to do what she could to stop this travesty of justice. She began by writing letters to people of influence in the colonies and in the United States. Money and letters of introduction came in response. By late August, she was ready. Once again she made the heart-wrenching decision to leave her child behind. Once again she had to argue against those of her friends and family who said it was a brazen woman who would travel half way across the world without a husband's or father's protection, and a cruel mother who would leave her own child to another's care. "I am travelling with no husband at my side in order to be at his side," she answered. "As for the care of my child, I have prayed for guidance as to the best course for her and the Lord has sent a feeling of great calm to me which I take as a sign that no harm will come to her. It is my husband who is in danger. My duty is to go to him." Maria sailed from New York.

In London, she called on Lord Durham, who had once helped her, and was now back in England. She applied for an audience with the Queen and when that request was refused, she wrote again, asking her Majesty to issue pardons on the joyous occasion of her forthcoming marriage. The Queen replied that she regretted her "inability to remove the cause of your distress." Maria wrote to Governor Franklin of Van Dieman's Land. She organized prayer meetings. She called on Elizabeth Fry, the great prison reformer. She took teacher training at the Home and Colonial Infant School Society so that she would be able to earn a living as a teacher in Van Dieman's Land.

When she could think of no one more she could write to, interview, plead with, badger, pester or cajole in any way, she took a job as a governess and waited to see the results of her efforts.

Slowly, slowly those efforts were beginning to have effect. Discussions took place in committee rooms. Memorandums were sent. A correspondence was initiated with Sir John Franklin on the subject of the Canadian patriots in the colony he governed. The patriots of Upper Canada were granted better working conditions and early tickets of leave.

Maria, unaware of the progress being made, prepared to travel to Van Dieman's Land. She wanted an interview with Governor Franklin. She wanted to talk to the sheriff and the jailers there. She wanted to make sure that whoever was in charge knew that these Canadian prisoners were being held unjustly.

Then she heard about the formation of a new government in Canada, uniting the Upper and Lower provinces, giving the people fairer representation and breaking the stranglehold of the Family Compact. Maria changed her plans. Now was the time to take the struggle back to Canada, she decided. A more responsible administration might well be ready to pardon the rebels who had fought for the very principles this new government endorsed. Whereas a journey to Van Dieman's Land would certainly be long and dangerous, and perhaps futile as well, an appeal to the present government of Canada offered some hope of success. Maria returned to Canada.

There she wrote to the new Governor General, requesting an interview. He sent a brush-off reply. Maria wrote again. This time the reply expressed some sympathy for the rebels. Encouraged by the tone, she travelled to Kingston to circulate a petition among members of Parliament and gathered fifty signatures. She carried another petition through Niagara, winning widespread support for the patriots' pardon. Finally the Governor General consented to see her in person. He made no promises, but he did not say that pardons were impossible.

Once again Maria was at a standstill. She had done what she could. Once again it was time to wait. She found work teaching in Niagara Falls, New York to support herself and young Augusta while they waited.

In the spring of 1842 she received a letter from Rio de Janiero.

My dear Maria,

You will rejoice with me to learn that I am at last a free man, though not yet a pardoned one. Chandler and I, having last summer received our tickets of leave and growing impatient with the slow procedure of securing legal egress from the cursed isle of Van Dieman, determined on escape. Our plan, which I now recognize to have been a somewhat foolhardy venture, was yet, by God's grace, successful. I spare you the details of the dangers and privations we suffered. Suffice it to say, we offered profound and sincere thanks to our Maker when we at last reached this shore. We wait now for the first available passage to the Northern Hemisphere.

Trusting that you and the babe are in good health, and longing for a speedy reunion with you both, I am

Your loving husband,

Benjamin.

When in July of that year he arrived at the train station in Niagara, New York, Mrs. Wait was there, waiting for him.

Epilogue

It would be satisfying to finish this story with a happy ending, something like: Maria and Benjamin lived happily ever after, enjoying their life together under the rule of a more democratic Canadian government, for the establishment of which they had struggled and suffered. But that was not the way it was.

Less than a year after their reunion, Maria died giving birth to twins, and lies now in an unmarked grave. Benjamin remarried and became a lumber merchant in Michigan.

Author's Note

I found Mrs. Wait on the title page of a book published in 1843 entitled *Letters from Van Dieman's Land* and subtitled "Written during Four Years Imprisonment for Political Offences committed in Upper Canada" by Benjamin Wait. Mrs. Wait gets second billing in smaller print at the bottom of the page: "Embodying, also, letters descriptive of personal appeals in behalf of her husband, and his fellow prisoners, to the Earl of Durham, Her Majesty, and the United Legislature of the Canadas by Mrs. B. Wait."

Having read through all that, I thought I might as well go on and read the rest of the book!

Two things struck me as I read. First, the period of the Rebellion of 1838, the Family Compact, Lord Durham's Report and the winning of responsible government, was not at all so dull as school history classes I remembered made it out to be. The story of the struggle of the reformers against the flagrant abuse of power by the reigning oligarchy makes for fascinating and exciting reading. Second, I thought Benjamin Wait, and Canadian history too, should have given more credit to Maria Wait and her "personal appeals". Her first appeal saved Wait and his fellow rebels from hanging, and her later efforts were instrumental in shortening their sentences. Mrs. Wait was a strong-minded, brave, determined woman who let no obstacles stop her in her quest to gain fairer treatment for the reformers. I suspect that she may also have been something of a pain in the neck to those in authority as she pursued her pestering, pleading, chivvying campaign, always "confident in the rectitude of (her) course". Jack Cahill, in his book *Forgotten Patriots* calls her "a remarkable woman."

Daniel Heustis, one of the rebels Maria saved, paid her tribute in these words: "Her devoted and heroic services, embalmed in all our hearts, shall be handed down to other generations as a bright example of conjugal fidelity, and active philanthropy, worthy of an immortality of honour."

REMAINDERS

NORA SIDGWICK, MATHEMATICIAN & CO-FOUNDER OF THE SOCIETY FOR PSYCHICAL RESEARCH

B.D. Ferguson

December 27, 1875 Cambridge, England

The day my mother surely despaired of ever seeing has arrived: Henry Sidgwick has asked me to be his wife, and I have accepted. Moreover, I did so with all my heart, and not with a considered tabulation of numbers as my sister Evelyn has long predicted, only half in jest.

I imagine Evelyn will find it very odd that my "considered tabulation of numbers" should be part of what Mr. Sidgwick (or Henry, I suppose I may now call him) claims to admire in me. When I tell her Henry has no objection to my continuing as her husband's assistant, her bewilderment may double. She has scarcely begun to understand how much work her John faces, answerable as he is now to the House of Lords as well as the Royal Society and Trinity College. I see no reason to let marriage interfere with my mathematics, and I am pleased to find that both Henry and the new Lord Rayleigh agree.

Mother should have few objections. True, Henry Sidgwick has no barony to claim, but his ethics book was well received, and his dedication to Cambridge University, particularly the new women's college, should satisfy any fair-minded person. And Mother has already met Henry, as he has been such friends with my brother Arthur, regularly attending his philosophy meetings and séances. She still does not fully approve of the latter, as they don't entirely suit her Christian sensibilities, but as she has already accepted both Arthur's and my interests in spiritualism, Henry's should not be too great a mark against him. Why should welcoming my philosophical Henry be any stranger than welcoming Evelyn's mathematical John?

Regardless of anyone else, I should prefer our engagement best satisfies *us*. If that makes me selfish, only these pages will judge. Henry has a lively mind behind his kind face, and has evidently seen something of interest in me beyond my plain exterior. I have grown very fond of him in these last months.

I cannot say whether it was Mother's benevolent God or what one may call social physics that brought Henry and me together. Our circles have crossed and re-crossed one another through Arthur's séance sittings and John's mathematics, creating an intersecting space in our orbits that has deepened with each conversation. Even if, within our own spheres, I am drawn more to the numbers and Henry to the spirits, we meet in that intersecting space, and shall make our home there.

Let others think what they will.

February 6, 1880

Four years of marriage, yet still my husband can surprise me. He certainly did this afternoon, when he suggested I would make an excellent Vice Principal for Newnham College, under Mrs. Annie Clough.

"Vice Principal!" I repeated. "What on Earth makes you think so?"

"Nora, you are exactly the sort of influence these young ladies need. They are keen but new to this academic life, and vulnerable to the petty meanness of male students and administrators who perceive them as merely attractive distractions. They need a scholarly woman to emulate."

"I am no scholar, Henry. I certainly didn't attend Cambridge University." I admit to a dart of regret, that I was born too soon to do so.

"My dear, you don't need the robe – your brain and behaviour proclaim you to the world." I was ready to protest again, but he had already found a new tactic. "Although Mrs. Clough has been an excellent residence matron for us, her more complex role as Principal is, I think, not something for which she is naturally well-suited. Your steadying influence would be beneficial, both to her and to the lady students."

I hesitated, but he knew he'd found his mark. We have worked so hard to chisel out even this tiny place for women here. Some travelled for days to come to Cambridge, knowing that at Newnham they would have a place to stay and attend lectures, eagerly doing the same work as the male undergraduates – despite University laws that prohibit them claiming the degrees they earn. So maddeningly stubborn, these officials who have slowly and grudgingly ceded us lengths of the course until balking at that very last hurdle. It struck me that I might, as Vice Principal of a college within the University, apply my chisel to that hurdle from unexpected angles.

Henry chuckled, having divined my thought. "I'll leave you to consider it, then. Oh, and I won't be home for dinner. After my classes this afternoon, Guiney and I are attending an audience in town."

His voice held the same enthusiasm it did when he proposed the Vice Principalship. I have never seen anyone remain so optimistic despite an utter lack of result. Any sitting Henry goes to, no matter how renowned the medium, results in no revelations, no manifestations, no apparitions, nothing. Every time he comes home disappointed, I must resist remarking on the accumulation of fact, even as the likes of Edmund Gurney, Fred Myers and my brother feed Henry's hope for proof that some part of ourselves survives after death. My husband is like a newcomer to England who tosses a ha'penny coin into the air again and again, seeing only Victoria's head when it lands, yet remaining certain a different, reverse side exists. It baffles me.

Henry paused before the door. "Do you think you might ask Lord Rayleigh if he would share his Cavendish lectures with our Newnham students? We shall need more rigor in the sciences to be a truly modern college."

"I will, certainly – but do you think I would still have time to assist him, if I accept this new post?"

He chuckled again. "Somehow, Nora, I think you will find the time. Your need for numbers is as ingrained as his lordship's."

"And how many of our students would attend a physics lecture?" Henry's smile at my choice of words made me realize I'd made my decision about Newnham.

"A great many, I would imagine. After all, my dear Mrs. Sidgwick, you surely would have!" He bowed respectfully at me, but somewhat tarnished the effect with a wink of his eye before he left.

His faith in me is unshakeable. I find myself hoping, for his sake, that something truly marvellous appears for him at that sitting... though I suspect it won't, nor ever will.

January 5, 1883

The boys were here again, as they are almost weekly. I suppose it isn't respectful of me to use that name, but they can be so childlike in their enthusiasms. They enliven a house more usually filled with quiet scholarship.

This evening we had another "boy" in our midst: an American named William James, whom Mr. Gurney had recently met. How odd to hear those hollow vowels and startling r's in our drawing room. We all laughed to realize Mr. James, too, lectures at a university in Cambridge... Massachusetts! His is a new field, "experimental psychology", and he well-suited our company. It seems that interest in spiritualism is as widespread in America as it is here. Naturally, the boys started telling him about our Society, which continues to gain members at a gratifying rate. They assured him that the name – the Society for Psychical Research – was temporary and not much liked, though I suspect that, having now lasted eleven months, it will remain. Henry explained that our goal was to ascertain only *facts* through the investigation of mediums, apparition stories and other spiritualist claims. Mr. James expressed great interest, and asked intelligent questions.

Mr. Gurney was in cheerful form for his guest this evening, eager (as was I) to hear more about Mr. James' work, as it concerns the mysteries of the mind. Mr. Gurney and I share a growing interest in psychical phenomenon, quite separate from "spirits" knocking on tables or tootling a pipe from inside a cabinet. Those can be easily feigned, but how does a psychical sensitive, merely by holding a watch-chain for instance, suddenly know its history? Or another produce trance writings describing a dead stranger's childhood with uncanny accuracy? Mr. Gurney is compiling witness accounts, hoping to fill a book. They intrigue me, these indications that what remains after death is not a floating, gauzy body but *the mind* and its memories. If this proves true, how long does it endure? What force sustains it? And how are some people seemingly able to capture pieces of it to share with an audience?

I admit it daunts me a little, to think that one day our minds may no longer be private. Although it seems to me entirely plausible that the complexity of the mind should outlast the frailty of the body, on the whole I would prefer to keep my thoughts my own, and my secrets – small though they may be – to myself.

October 16, 1886

If Fred Myers intends to continually question my work for the Society's *Proceedings*, he should argue from firmer ground. Today he presented extracts from my latest report as if I weren't aware of my own words.

"'The indications of deception were palpable and sufficient'?" he read aloud. "Really, Mrs. Sidgwick, that seems unduly harsh."

"I disagree, Mr. Myers. I might instead have called Miss Wood an obvious charlatan, preying upon her audiences for financial gain.

Such a quick and furtive change of costume in the dark to play the 'ghost' for a roomful of clients twice a week must be wearisome to her, even at sixpence a head." I'm afraid the remembered dreariness of months of séances on the Society's behalf made my tone rather sharper than usual.

Mr. Myers clearly wanted to argue further, and, seeing that Mr. Gurney was sunk too deeply in one of his melancholy moods, he appealed to Henry. My husband merely shook his head, saying, "Miss Wood may have some genuine ability, Myers, but consider what happened in Blackburn. Whatever her motives, she has at least sometimes resorted to fraud, with unsubtle methods. Frankly, she's been caught out too often."

After the boys had left, Henry raised his brows at me. "You won't change your report, will you, no matter how others may argue? You remain unconvinced by manifestation phenomena?"

"Henry, I simply cannot believe in these 'ghosts'. Even discounting all the trickery we've witnessed, I have seen no manifestations, nor their residue, much less found any explanation as to why corporeal spirits would make such spectacles of themselves. Our energies would be far better spent investigating the minds and abilities of those who claim to perceive the spirits in quieter ways."

He nodded thoughtfully, though I saw regret in his eyes. "I'm afraid the Society's investigating members are too diverse in their interests, and too inconsistent in their credulity. We'll continue to see ourselves skewered in *Punch* if we cannot find some grounds on which to convince the public."

"We can only do so much, Henry, with the new hall at Newnham nearly completed and the University still dragging its heels," I said. "Arthur, John and most of the others likewise have responsibilities elsewhere. Mr. Gurney has made great progress toward explaining thought-transference simply because he devotes every waking hour. He and Mr. James may yet discover convincing answers there. As for Mr. Myers' collection of ghost stories..." – I couldn't suppress my sigh – "he is collecting only *tales*, often told third- or fourth-hand. With each retelling, they lose a percentage of their truth, if any existed to begin with."

"The ideal would be to find the originator, then. If we interviewed him soon after the event, we could judge the tale on its own merits or dismiss it out of hand."

"Even if we found him, the judging would be tedious. One would have to consider the health of the observer, the layout of the room, the weather conditions..."

"We could create an investigator's guide, Nora," he said. He rarely interrupts me, so I knew at once this was more than a whim. "Your reasoning would be of great help. Already you see where potential problems lie. With care, we could collect objective, convincing evidence, and avoid the will-o-the-wisp shades in the tales. It could be of enormous value!"

In the face of Henry's eagerness about this project – unformed as it may yet be – I could only agree to help in whatever way I could, and I earned several enthusiastic kisses for it. Perhaps, as we parted, I was myself intrigued by the possibility of objective data from the ethereal realm. It is difficult to find.

I only hope I can keep Henry and the boys away from those will-o-the-wisps he mentioned. They conjure too many nursery tales of flickering lights luring foolish men into the miry heart of the marsh.

(A strange and fanciful image, dredged from the deeps of my childhood! Truly, the brain's mysteries are more extraordinary than any table-knockings.)

June 29, 1888

I can hardly bear to write this, my heart is so heavy. Today we buried Edmund Gurney.

Fred Myers brought us the news on Sunday. He and Henry have been mute and staring with grief in the days since. My husband trembled on my arm throughout the service. The news will devastate poor Mr. James, who has become such a steadfast friend despite the ocean between us. Edmund (I cannot call him Mr. Gurney today) had spoken not ten days ago of inviting him back to England, and with such hopeful excitement in his voice...

Adding insult to injury is the lack of clarity from the inquest. It was hardly a revelation that Edmund carried chloroform to ease the pain of his neuralgia – he had done so for years. The idea that he should suddenly forget the safe dosage is at the far edge of reasonable doubt, and the idea that he should deliberately exceed that dosage is equally improbable. It is anathema to consider he might have let one of his black moods take him so far from the work he loved, and from his wife and daughter, and from us.

Already, some in our Society are speculating his spirit will return with tidings from beyond. I imagine there will be an upsurge in séance attendance in the coming weeks. If Edmund was right – as I myself suspect – and some minds persist beyond the body, then only the mind of Edmund Gurney has the answers we seek. He alone might reveal if this tragedy were accident or self-destruction. But I cannot bear the thought that, in grief, one of us might clutch at some vague and tattered message from a sixpence sensitive in a darkened parlor.

At the graveside today I wished for answers, but now I discover myself a hypocrite: I would much prefer that Edmund be granted the silence that comes with peace.

May 23, 1889

Nearly a full year has passed since Mr. Gurney's death, but he remains very much in our hearts and minds. Based upon his earlier work, the Society for Psychical Research intends to investigate the extraordinary experiences of ordinary citizens. We are calling it the Census of Hallucinations, to minimise any association with the ethereal realm in the mind of a non-believer. Our query – much re-written and argued! – shall be, "Have you ever, when believing yourself to be completely awake, had a vivid impression of seeing or being touched by a living being or an inanimate object, or of hearing a voice; which impression, so far as you could discover, was not due to any external physical cause?"

Several of our more literary members have grumbled about its clumsiness, but this is, I think, the best phrasing to exclude dreams, inhuman sounds, vague presentiments or anything later explained. More than four hundred S.P.R. census-takers across England are ready to begin, and each of them is to gather at least twenty-five responses, from healthy adults of any station.

Although our question does not say so, Henry and the others are especially seeking reports of "death-day apparitions": the unexpected appearance of someone which later proves to coincide with his or her passing. (I dislike poor Edmund's term, *death-wraith*, as it sounds like something from the most fantastic fiction. "Apparition" denotes a simple perceptive event.) They are a staple of fireside tales, though I am not certain how many we shall find in truth.

As a starting point, however, I have attempted to estimate the rates of such apparitions. Despite the stories, we must imagine the phenomenon is not a common one, and there are any number of unknowns about who might appear where, and to whom. I chose to approach the problem from the other side: the death itself. The Registrar General's office informs me that there is one death daily for every 19,000 people in England. *Ergo*, the possibility of one other person seeing an apparition of that death on that day is also one in 19,000. Stated differently: on any given day, for every 19,000 people in this country, only *one* might experience a death-apparition.

Mathematically, it is a highly unsatisfactory figure, though it rings true in its depiction of rarity. Perhaps we are too presumptuous, trying to apply statistical logic to the other world.

I am also a little concerned about the randomness of the census-taking itself. It heightens validity but leaves us at the mercy of the public – the earnest or the indignant, the thoughtful or the derisive, the elite or the illiterate, any of whom might just as well use it for hearth-kindling or propaganda in *Punch*. We should expect failures to respond as well as negative responses, but an equal possibility is false reports from impish wags. Even Henry admits that danger. Considering each response with due care will require significant time and energy.

I hope, after all this, that at least some reports are worthy of analysis.

March 2, 1892

Our preliminary census sortings have taken much longer than I had anticipated, as our other projects have continued to demand our attention. Henry's latest book was published last year, and his next work already begun. His teaching duties have not slackened, despite his serving on or chairing three separate educational boards as well. Newnham College grows apace, and the Principalship since Mrs. Clough's death has occupied much of my own time around my work with John, whose recent state-change studies demand precise mathematical modelling – perhaps that explains why I hadn't fully pondered the scale of what the S.P.R. had undertaken. Now that an astonishing 17,000 census responses have been returned, I appreciate it in full.

Fortunately, a broad examination of that mountain of responses has revealed that only 2,274 were answered in the affirmative. Henry and the others were so delighted with the number that I felt rather like a stern governess when I reminded them we had not yet eliminated those with disqualifying factors, such as dreaming or fever states.

"But perhaps such states open the subliminal self to thought-transference," Fred Myers protested. "Perhaps the dying mind is strong enough to..."

"The Census is not about thought-transference, Mr. Myers. We asked for hallucinations, and those alone are what we shall seek," I reminded him – gently, for I think we were both remembering Edmund Gurney then. How he would have delighted in this project! "For the same reason, we must eliminate any apparitions of the gravely ill or the elderly, who might reasonably be expected to pass at any time and would naturally occupy the thoughts of loved ones."

I felt obliged to repeat we should not *expect* anything at all and must remain as objective as possible while we consider very subjective reports. However, our sample of positive responses is far smaller than I should like, given the estimated incidence rate. "One in 19,000" waves in my mind like a warning flag on a ship's mast.

I shall keep that particular vision to myself.

July 20, 1892

The relative quiet on campus during the summer months has allowed us more time for the winnowing of the Census results, though weeks of sorting responses and creating a report of my own for later publication has left me little energy to write in these pages. Fortunately, we have had S.P.R. assistants to help us. Three months ago, when we had finally plucked out the dreamers, the feverish, &c., we had almost 1,700 reports remaining as possibilities.

Next to determine were timeliness and reliability, as I explained to our sorters. "Eliminate any report which came too long after the time of death, in the event the news may have arrived by more straightforward means – being perhaps overheard without realizing its importance. The hallucination must have taken place within, let us say, twelve hours of the recorded time of death. Further, it must have been reported to another person. Eliminate any that do not include at least one corroborative witness."

"Witnesses and time of death will require confirmation," Henry had noted. "That will take several weeks, at least."

"Yes," I had responded then, "but it will be our strongest evidence."

Those words are echoing in my mind now, as I look at the remaining pile of pages. And I cannot deny it is a pile, which in itself is striking, given that we were unlikely to find a single such incident. Instead we have *thirty-two* reports from across England, seemingly credible and reputable, of ordinary, healthy adults inexplicably seeing or hearing a loved one on the day of that person's untimely death.

Set against the estimated incidence of one in 19,000, a pile of thirty-two out of 1,700 positive responses is hundreds of times what it should be. Further, Mr. James reports the Americans have used the same process to sort their 7,000 initial census responses. They too have finished with a pile – one that is likewise hundreds of times what their incident rate predicted.

Henry is hoping to share a preliminary report at the Congress of Experimental Psychology in August; considerable work lies ahead of us. But it seems that, when it comes to connections between the living and the dead, something more than mere chance is at work.

We now have numbers on our side.

May 31, 1895

I'm afraid Henry's birthday was less than festive. Mr. Myers is still furious about the S.P.R. report on that Palladino woman, and is threatening to bring her to England for more thorough investigation, thereby alienating nearly all our American colleagues and half our English ones in a single stroke. John is immersed in his laboratory at Terling, and Henry and I been too occupied with Mr. Champneys, drawing up the plans for Newnham's library, to arrange any sort of celebration.

This evening, when I came into Henry's study with the few gifts I had gathered, I found him deep in thought. He half-smiled at me and held aloft what he'd been reading.

"The *British Medical Journal*. They've printed my response to their article about psychical research. I imagine they did so solely for impartiality's sake – there's a whiff of condescension about it." He sighed. "I should have asked you to respond, Nora. Of the two of us, you are the one who has served on a Royal Commission and has a handful of Royal Society papers to your name."

I chose not to remind him that co-authoring papers with John hardly amounts to publishing under my name alone. Henry has been outwardly determined but prone to private moments of despondency since the Census of Hallucinations report was published. Its mixed reception weighs more heavily on him during quiet evenings. "Nonsense. Your response was perfectly reasonable and addressed the errors in the original."

"Except they weren't errors, were they? The authors merely gave a slanted view and chose, perhaps, a few over-hasty words. No matter how illustrious our Society members or how diligent our work, we have yet to provide the definitive proof the public demands. The thinking public, especially, always wants more convincing."

I sat next to him. "As does the thinking researcher, surely?" He offered me another rueful smile as I continued. "Come now – science cannot dwell on what it does not have. It must use what it does have to test its hypotheses before it can seek what remains to be found. That requires evidence, the gathering of which can take years."

"It feels as if it has been a lifetime," he murmured. "Look at all that Lord Rayleigh has accomplished in that span. What have we to show for our labours?"

"Thousands of pages of investigative evidence, some promising theories, and public attention." I considered his mood a moment. "Here is a birthday tale for you, Henry. Some months ago, John was attempting to ascertain the precise atomic weight of nitrogen. To do so he conducted density experiments from which he could extrapolate what he sought. He made a set of measures based on nitrogen extracted from the atmosphere – we don't breathe purely oxygen, as you may recall – and then made a second set of measurements on nitrogen gained from the decomposition of ammonia through a system of..."

"Nora," Henry said, sounding pained. "I am fifty-seven today. I shall never need to decompose ammonia."

I couldn't help but smile. "He found the nitrogen from the atmosphere was heavier than the nitrogen from a chemical reaction. We re-examined the calculations, of course, yet the discrepancy remained. When John published his work, he suggested his atmospheric sample might have been somehow tainted. He invited others to reproduce the experiment in hopes of identifying the impurity and correcting the problem."

"And?"

"A man named Ramsey at University College made a suggestion, and together they've solved it. The 'impurity' is in fact a new form of gas, entirely inert in our atmosphere. The periodic table will have to be re-drawn to account for it. They're naming it *argon*, from the Greek."

Henry didn't look as enlightened as I had hoped, so I pressed on. "Do you not see? Proof of existence after death is not yet apparent to us, nor to anyone – we see only the faintest indications, though it may be all around us. We can only question those who claim to have the answers, filtering out any impurities to draw nearer to the truth. Someday, perhaps, we will determine the answer, and with it our understanding of the self and of life will need to be re-drawn, like the periodic table. Ours is no small task, Henry."

After a thoughtful silence, Henry took my hand and raised it to his lips, then looked up with the usual twinkle in his eye. "You've just compared psychical investigation to physics, my dear. The Royal Society would be scandalized."

"Some of them, perhaps. Others recognize that the world still holds some mysteries for us." I kissed the top of his head. How white his hair has become – I hadn't noticed before. "Happy birthday, Henry."

September 5, 1900

I shouldn't have come back to this house; I should have stayed with Evelyn and John. They told me so, but I felt sure I'd prefer familiar surroundings. Here now, though, it is far too quiet.

Henry's absence is like a hole in our home.

I am writing this in his study. His papers, like his chair and pipe, are awaiting his return. We had hoped he might convalesce at home after his surgery, but John and Evelyn insisted the country air at

Terling would be of more benefit. This time, however, even John's thinking was in error. Or perhaps it was merely wishful, as was ours.

A letter from Mr. James was here on my return. He is travelling on the Continent and heard the news of Henry's death. He wrote lovely things about him, and assured me that more people than I shall ever know mourn with me – for the loss of Henry, and for the loss of his work. "Everything seems left undone in this world," he said, and, looking around Henry's study, I can only agree.

Cambridge is stifling me; it is full of too much family and too many colleagues clamouring to offer sympathy. They mean well but do not realize they are piling up around me like the papers in this room, thin reminders without comfort. I am eager for a change of place.

Many of our young ladies have kept up correspondence with us after leaving Newnham, telling us eagerly about their achievements and adventures. Henry and I are – were – *are* as proud as if they were our own children, grown and thriving. A few are currently on an archeological dig in Egypt. Not knowing of Henry's illness, they wrote weeks ago to ask us to join them. The appeal of the journey is undeniable. Even if the invitation were extended out of politeness, I expect they can find space for their old Principal. Perhaps I can make myself useful with cataloguing or record-keeping.

Here in the study, a familiar aroma – Henry's distinct blend of tobacco, ink and paper – is more noticeable by the minute. Rationally, I know that the afternoon sun is warming the atmosphere, stirring the molecules to release old odours, but it is not science that brings tears to my eyes. Strange, how scent lingers. Strange too that I can almost hear Henry's step in the hall, his chuckle in our dressing room. Any moment now he may touch my hand, eager to share a new idea. His determination and cheer, his faith in me, and a hundred lively discussions with the boys echo from every corner.

I do not believe in ghosts.

It is the workings of the mind – and of the heart – that will keep Henry by my side.

Author's Note

When Nora Sidgwick returned from Egypt, she resumed her Principalship at Newnham, remaining until 1910. Along with her work for Lord Rayleigh, she also continued in the S.P.R., serving one year as its President, and later President-in-Honour. Late in her life, two English and two Scottish Universities awarded her honorary doctorates for her tireless work in education, particularly women's education, but Cambridge University was not one of them. She died in 1936, but Newnham College continues to thrive, as does the Society for Psychical Research. Although I have taken a few liberties with the timeline, all the S.P.R. and physics work mentioned here is well-documented; any errors in the explanations are mine alone. I am grateful for Deborah Blum's book, *Ghost Hunters: William James and the Search for Scientific Proof of Life after Death* (Penguin Press, 2006), for its engaging account of the S.P.R., which drew me to Nora and her boys.

THAT OTTAWA WINDOW

WILHELMINA GEDDES, IRISH STAINED GLASS ARTIST

Krista Foss

Maudsley Hospital, London Patient Admission Record
May 17th, 1925

Patient Name: Wilhelmina Geddes

Age: 38   **Sex:** Female

Admission: voluntary, uncertified

Intake Notes: Patient referred by Dr. Killarney of Downpatrick Asylum. Miss Geddes is an Irish stained-glass artist of some significant repute for a woman. Suffering from nervous exhaustion. Some hallucinatory episodes with persecutory ideations including sightings of comets, dying planets and large wolves. Patient expresses conflict and guilt over a desire to leave Ireland and her stained glass cooperative, especially the mother figure/socialite studio owner. She has severe anxiety, nervous exhaustion and erratic moods consistent with hysteria and melancholia, and trauma associated with the activities of Easter 1916 uprising. The patient is unmarried, and has never reproduced. Further, she is reticent to discuss sexual activity and desire. Raised a Methodist. Gynecological examination shows an infantile uterus, possible ovarian atrophy, which makes her a candidate for glandular treatments and thyroid shock therapy. Connections to stunted reproduction, repressed vital impulse and possible undetected "pubertal insanity" need investigation. Bromides, caffeine and high-frequency x-rays to head and neck have had some successes in patients with similar psychological profiles. Assigned to the caseload of Dr. Mary Barkas, as patient describes herself as "modern" and responds well to women in roles of authority – except notably some initial conflict with the ward sister over the storage of art supplies. Regression, re-socialization will be helpful in uncovering repressed anger toward father figure and redirection of sexual desire toward more acceptable domestic arrangements. Patient seeks accommodation to continue art practice and work on ongoing commissions: permission granted for patient to supplant the prescribed crafts room activities of rug-hooking and raffia weaving with self-directed sketching. Clinical record of pleurisy. Intermediate psychiatric case; prognosis promises full recovery.

Maudsley Hospital, London, September 1925

Ward Sister Report: Miss Geddes has a clear affect today. Seven hours of sleep. Moderate appetite. Requested her drawing material. Some agitation expressed over what she calls the "cartoon" for her Surrey window. Visited by American art journalist mid-morning. Miss Geddes informed about hospital policy regarding non-familial visitation. Further agitation. Dr. Barkas summoned; approved visit on verandah with private screen. Dr. Barkas requested nurse Fraser stand behind screen and record interview in short-hand for inclusion in case notes. The doctor has requested aural clues be recorded too: silences, abrupt change in tone or loudness. Informed Dr. Barkas this required extra staffing to address Nurse Fraser's absence from ward, monies which will be requisitioned from her budget. Waiting for superintendent's signature.

September 21, 1925, 2 pm

Transcript of patient, Wilhelmina Geddes (Case No. 637) in conversation with Sela Huntley-Woods, staff writer, *Modern Woman* magazine from Boston on the back verandah of Maudsley Hospital as recorded by Nurse Jessalyn Fraser

SHW: Good afternoon, Miss Geddes. Did you remember our appointment?

WG: Oh you came! I'd wondered if I dreamt you up! Yes of course I remember the magazine, the article, that lovely wool crepe wrap you had on the other day. Come sit. They've left us chairs and a little privacy. And there is the monumental wonder of afternoon sun. Thank you for your patience. The ward sister and I have locked horns ever since I arrived five months ago. I think she's a degeneration theorist that woman, takes a dim view of my Irish blood! Ha! Terrible creature. I'm getting better to spite her. Dr. Barkas says that many of the nurses are old-fashioned and don't approve of "modern" women, especially doctors such as herself. So we are in league, she and I, with the devil of feminine progress.

SHW: Well, that fits in brilliantly with the topic of my *Modern Woman* magazine piece. I'll just get myself organized here, so I can pay full attention.

WG: And modern is what you've come to discuss? Though I don't suppose your editors are so modern they'd approve of you conducting your interview at a mental hospital! The things we do as women. The things we understand that others don't. The things we forgive. (Pause. Audible sigh.)

So why me? I've only had one North American commission several years ago and don't expect another in my lifetime.

SHW: Yes, the Ottawa Window.

WG: You've seen it then? Dreariest capital in all the world I'm told.

SHW: Just pictures.

WG: Did I mention the Canadians gasped – the whole lot of them in that little church – they gasped when my window was unveiled! Thank goodness I wasn't there. Still I felt that gasp travel back over the ocean faster than any ship could carry it. It was painful to hear about.

I've imagined Canadians as a bleak stunted sort ever since, dull as their politics, and the few I've met here have done nothing to dispel me of that impression. Long-winded sorts – always ready to tell you the story of their lives, as if by not being in Canada they are suddenly interesting to us. The Australians too – they're the same. (laughter)

SHW: But the window is widely critically acclaimed, Miss Geddes. Seen as a breakthrough. Charles Connick, Boston's best stained glass artist said – excuse me I have it here somewhere – "Nowhere in modern glass is there a more striking example of a courageous adventure in the medium."

WG: It was so kind of him to say so. It saved me the full blow of that shuddering gasp. So tell me about this article of yours.

SHW: Our audience is made up of young, boundary-breaking women. Bobbed hair, fearless Jazz-Age gals – you know the type. Looking to Europe where there's a generation of painters, sculptors, craftswomen who've got acres more wisdom. My working title is this: "Lessons from a *Modern Woman* artist." So please feel free to talk to me as if I'm that younger artist and you're giving me some helpful hints for surviving and thriving. The editors want it to sound as if we're having a conversation with our readers.

WG: (laughs nervously.) Right then. A conversation. No tea? Oh, but then you American woman all drink coffee don't you?

Here's where I suppose some good old-fashioned Methodist upbringing comes in handy. My father was a serial sermonizer. Everything was about lessons. I dream in lessons and parables and terrifying examples. So let me speak as best I can in that language.

The first lesson would have to be: Start young, and if you can, be the eldest of your brood. Yes, put that down will you? I'm serious. Lovely handwriting you have dear, but can't you afford a larger notebook?

I think a woman is so easily thrown off anything really – and one of the worst things is to have siblings ahead of you, who take up all the money, get their father's attention, tire out the mother, set examples by which you will mark time forever. That's so typical in an Irish household.

My mother's people were British farmers, my father's Irish Methodists. Bibles sewn into their hips those people. We moved to Belfast when I was a wee slip of a thing, and my father became a successful building contractor. Fierce man. I was the first of four children, so mine were the only little hands he taught to draw a straight line. Too busy after that. I earned whatever dribbles of love my father could spare through draftsmanship, and in so doing, got his indulgence for my artwork. His attention was everything. He frightened me into wanting it. Moods ran through him like coal seams – as if the whole of him was always underground, engaged in the treachery of his own darkness.

He enrolled me in the Belfast School of Art – I was 15 and stayed for nearly eight years. He must have resigned himself to my spinsterhood by then – thought it best I have some trade for my keep. I drew from naked models, from still life settings; I copied the Masters. I went to suffragette meetings and acted in plays. My parents lost charge of my future, though they didn't know it.

That time! That time! I loved being alive. There was no turning back from that for me – there was no becoming a gentlewoman. My mother wrung her hands an angry pink those years. My father forced prayers on her. We never looked each other in the eyes. She knew I was free.

SHW: So let me get this straight. Your first piece of advice is to be born first.

WG: Yes! That's how every important piece of work begins – it begins as a child looking out on a beautiful countryside, humming a border ballad tune on an Ayrshire holiday, avoiding the dark moods of a parent because you've already had the best of them. Start young, and come out of the womb first if you can!

SHW: Well, it's certainly original. I'll have to discuss using that one with my editors. They're a hard-nosed set. What other advice would you give me – modern-woman-artist to modern-woman-artist?

WG: I would tell you that every work of art you make already contains within it a fragment of your greatest achievement. Does that make sense? You are building up to the art you will be known by, with every effort – and so that effort has to be cruelly beautiful, cruelly, cruelly hard on you.

SHW: I'm intrigued. Go on.

WG: When I was 23 I did a water-colour painting: "Cinderella Dressing the Ugly Sister." Sounds like a trifle doesn't it? I imagined myself becoming a book illustrator then. So it mattered to me. Very much. And I asked myself – what do I want people to notice? Not just some notion from their childhood of beauty and ugliness, but more: society and underclass, the British and Irish. My Cinderella had bright red curls, the sturdy flesh of a farm girl. The ugly sister; she's pale, chinless, bald as a member of the House of Lords, her dress a jaundiced cadmium. I wanted people to feel the ribbons in Cinderella's hands come right off the page, fluttering like a noose near the exposed neck of the sister, who also holds a ribbon, taut. Who will strangle whom?

SHW: Oh my!

WG: In the end, it was just a picture. But of course it was not. I spread myself on that page like a blue wash. It was the first work of mine that was sold.

SHW: Who bought it?

WG: None other than Sarah Purser. The painter. The formidable everywoman. The Irish Rasputin. My saviour and ruination. She saw it at the Arts and Crafts Society of Ireland Exhibit and wanted it immediately. There was a rare poetry in my line, she said.

(Silence)

WG: You don't know her?

SHW: No. Can't say I do. I'm from Boston, remember?

WG: You North Americans! Sarah Purser is a portrait artist: 39 years my senior and as hale and majestic as I am frail and unimposing. She's a story that one. Sarah had all of thirty pounds in her pocket when she went to Paris to study painting at the Julian Academy – became fast friends with Berthe Morisot and importantly, Constance Gore-Booth of the County Sligo Gore-Booths. Castle-born Constance, who came home from Paris with a Polish count as a husband and her own fiery politics. All Sarah returned with was Constance's friendship. But that opened doors. "I went through British society like the measles," Sarah famously quipped. And I suppose those words will follow her to the grave. She was a prolific painter in those days, and she used her earnings smartly, as an investor, as an advocate.

With her brother, she leased the Meslip House in Dublin; they held a salon called Second Tuesdays. That house was filled with Gaelic – revivalists, nationalists, republicans – and ruled over by women, larger-than-life Daughters-of-Erin. I was only 21 when Sarah first invited me. I can tell you, I have barely recovered. And it was a revelation, walking into a room where women were into their cups and yelling about Home Rule and rebellion, taking up all the space. Wild-eyed beauties like Maud Gonne and Countess Markievicz and Sarah – all of them so wonderful, so ferocious that the men in the corners quivered: William Butler Yeats in his "polite meaningless words" stage, his brother Jack the painter, John O'Leary and that sort.

I was not going to measure up to women who were used to imprisonment; who talked of spies and hermetic magic; who had sex in mausoleums to produce babies with reincarnated spirits; who would become parliamentarians; who had poets pining for them. They were all too much for me. I've suffered from pleurisy all my life: and I remember thinking I could not breathe among these women. They'd sucked all the air of the room. Still I was in awe.

SHW: Oh golly! I'm trying to keep up, Miss Geddes. So this Sarah buys your watercolor, and she's a colorful sort herself. But I'm missing where it leads. Why does that matter?

WG: It was 1910 when Sarah bought my watercolor: she was already a wealthy woman. She'd set up *An Túr Gloine* (Tower of Glass), an Irish stained glass cooperative. She was vehement that Irish churches must have windows made by Irish craftsmen – not imports. Among so many other things, she saw herself as a stained glass impresario – the one with an eye for the talent, the one who'd bring the commissions that would make a name for the cooperative. She was recruiting me.

SHW: So you joined En Ter Glinny, er Tower of Glass?

WG: (Laughter) *An Túr Gloine.* And no, not right away. I still had a year left at the Belfast School of Art. I did try my first stained glass panel after meeting Sarah. It was a hopelessly conventional depiction of Sir Walter Raleigh. But it was a window. It was glass. My fingers were scored with cuts from sharp edged pieces and stained with pigment. I'd bent and pinned leading. I'd thought about the angle of light coming through the panel before creating shadows in paint wash, and silver nitrate for yellow stain. It was so much more than painting. It was building something – I come from builders. Suddenly, I discovered my father's rigid logic in my own spine: I already understood the line of a building and the color of its stone, how the sun moved around it, what else was in it. And windows themselves are built things – lead supports, and pieces sewn together like a glass quilt; an alchemy of color and design and mathematics. And oh, the richness of glass – the very substances of the planets, fused from light and fire and silica.

SHW: So you joined the cooperative then?

WG: Oh you Americans are urgent! *An Túr Gloine* is fashioned after the Christopher Whall studio, which is true to the medieval roots of stained glass. *An Túr Gloine*'s manager, A. E. Child, found money for me to study with Whall: there were so many dusty, pneumatic men in his studio – old tradesman who resented my presence, hid the tools from me, barked at me about hovering too near the buckets of acid. I was all nerves. Dreaming blackly in my bedsit, breaking out in rashes every night. Yet there was nothing else for me after that. I was not going to be a simple book illustrator after all.

I returned to Dublin and made my first stained glass triptych for Sarah, to show her what I could do. Sarah imported all the best pot-metal, antique and slab glass from Hetley's in Soho. I was in heaven. And when I was done the *Life of St. Colman Macduagh* she said, *Yes, yes, yes, Willy.* She said, *More, more, more.* I joined the cooperative formally in 1912.

SHW: Would you say Sarah Purser was instrumental in the discovery of your artistic voice?

WG: Indeed. Sarah Purser had a speech for me when I arrived. She said, "Okay we're Irish here. Let William Morris pump out his hundred windows a year, with society artists contributing only the cartoons, while grizzled old men with knives do the cutting, and glaziers choose the color, and rough street boys paint the draperies. Not one of them considering the space they're in, the windows that will be beside them. We're something more here. We're the quality. So I'm glad you've had some first-class British training, but now your job is to lose the Britishness – take the skills, take the rigour, but be as Irish as possible in design, and line and color. Which means know what you like so you can be thoroughly, uniquely yourself."

She made a little sign for my studio space: Find out what speaks to you so you know how to speak.

SHW: Okay. I like that. Your work has been described as having, "a virile, almost alarming, strength ... even brutal at times." Were you considered one of the Tower's most modern artists right away?

WG: Well, I knew my Bible – there was nothing gentle or sentimental in it. And here's what I discovered about being modern – that often it means looking back rather than forward.

SHW: Sorry?

WG: The English and the French are the dominant forces in stained glass. But they're different. "Know them both. Steal from them both," Sarah said. "Be something new."

She insisted every stained glass artist had a duty to visit Chartres, Rouen, Paris. So in 1914, I went. And it was there that I finally understood why Christopher Whall was always barking at us, "Let the color sing." In France, I found the most modern windows of all: they were from the 13th century! Yes dear. I went back to go forward. I saw how red and blue are the truest, richest colors but you can't be a donkey about pictorial realism with them as your palette. Those archaic windows liberated me from wanting to be fully representational, "realistic." The medieval artists had understood that all along!

So my drawing went back in time too – back to Greek and gothic sculpture, back to Romanesque sketching – to find something leaner, bolder in the masculine face. It was all historically derived but everyone kept telling me how modern, how terribly modern I was.

"Wee Willy Geddes," Sarah would laugh, "the thoroughly modern woman. Making men even larger!"

"But they're Irish men at least," I'd protest.

"Yes of course! It's perfect. Harry Clarke's making all his men drip and lean and weep, and yours are Roman gods!"

SHW: Were you getting big commissions then?

WG: The war broke out. It only took a few months for everyone to realize it was going to be bloody. And there would be memorial windows. It sounds venal. But the truth is, as young men were dying, the diocesan officials were having meetings, setting out directives and policies for the inevitable commissions that would glorify their deaths. The window-makers were already vying for the jobs.

It made me queasy – as if we were eagerly polishing the keys to the charnel house. I had bad dreams in which the ruby flashing melted from all my windows into great rivulets of blood.

SHW: That is quite dark, Miss Geddes. Why not tell me how an Irishwoman lands a commission from an Ottawa church?

WG: Ah ha! The trick to snaring a good commission, Sarah once told me, was to know whose limousine was waiting with curtains drawn at the riverside entrance of Dublin's Hotel Shelbourne on a Sunday morning. Of course she didn't actually skulk. The guilty were happy enough to whisper in her ear in her own salon.

Sarah knew Lady Leslie, an American by the name of Leonie Jerome who'd married Sir John Leslie, a second baronet. It wasn't long before the new lady was keeping company with Prince Arthur, the Duke of Connaught. I'm telling you those Jerome women had a reputation for being as restless as panthers.

In 1911 the royal mum appointed the Duke as Canada's governor general. Suddenly, all of Lady Leslie's New York relatives were ailing. There were multiple crossings. The Canadians were said to be quite smitten with their new governor general and his family. But it was Lady Leslie who, under cover of darkness, kept the Duke at his most genial.

He was a breeches and plumage sort, always most comfortable around other soldiers I'm told, so all his personal staff could hum a few bars of *Pomp and Circumstance*. In 1914, they began leaving him to serve overseas. And many did not come back.

Sarah may have whispered "memorial window" to Lady Leslie, or the grand dame herself may have suggested it to the Duke, or the Duke may even have come up with the idea on his own. But there's no doubt *An Túr Gloine* got the commission because of a series of intimate Second Tuesday *tête à têtes* between Sarah and Lady Leslie. That Sarah was cut with shrewdness. I don't think the Duke ever entertained the idea that a woman would make his window; I am sure he imagined the cooperative was a workshop of withered leprechauns.

One day Sarah comes into the studio and says, "Oh Willy, I have a plum for you." I was short of breath before she'd even spit out "three-light east window at the church attached to the Canadian governor general's official residence."

Nobody, not even Lady Leslie, had seen St. Bartholomew's. But from descriptions and pictures it seemed to be nothing more than a country church, a Neo-Gothic runt. How was I supposed to design a window for it without knowing the building or the people?

Sarah got sharp. "You're not a school girl, Willy. We have the dimensions and you have an imagination last time I checked. It is wartime after all." So I started drawing. It was 1915.

SHW: Do you think there's a lesson here that's relevant for all modern women artists?

WG: Take all the opportunities, even ones you know you're not ready for, even ones you know will break you.

SHW: I'm sensing this wasn't an easy commission, Miss Geddes.

WG: No commission is easy, my dear. Every artist must fight to have her vision respected; sometimes those she must fight the most are other modern women!

There was much back and forth – Sarah to Lady Leslie, and Lady Leslie to I don't-know-who among the Duke's and St. Bart's crowd. I complained to Sarah about the meddling, worried that the Canadians wouldn't abide my style. She shrugged: "Show the world who you are, Willy. Let the naysayers be damned."

But an artist has demons. I was struggling with my health; there were days the planets were meddling, getting too close, threatening to crash into the studio, and interrupt it all, breath and work and the bloom of flowers. Some mornings I woke to a mania of great ideas, others to a frozen, frightened emptiness.

It felt as if Lady Leslie's little ermine-muffed hands were all over my design. I would dream of that over-distinguished mouth puckering, always puckering, trying to get me to make ridiculous additions. Lions! Oh there were some shrill words over the lions! I can tell you that much.

SHW: Forgive me. I don't recall. Are there lions in the final window?

WG: Absolutely not! I won that battle.

SHW: How did the design evolve?

WG: I proposed one fallen soldier with a broken spear – he would symbolize all the dead, because truthfully, we couldn't guess how many would die. I wanted him ascending into the heavens on winged horses, but that idea was promptly squashed. Though the Duke and his minions had lots to say about who should accompany the soldier into the afterlife; Saint Michael, Saint George, Arthurian heroes, French and English kings, Roman soldiers, so many damn angels: Gabriel, Raphael, Peace and Death. I started to feel as if my fallen soldier was in a receiving line. I said he might as well be shaking hands with the lot of them in that case. Sarah said I was getting chippy.

I fought hard against Joan of Arc. I didn't want a woman in the picture. Lady Leslie insisted. Sarah arched her eyebrows. "But there's a muscularity to this design," I told her. "The men stride like Assyrian kings toward each other across the bottom panels. A female figure breaks that momentum."

"So make her a king," Sarah said. And I did.

The actual commission wasn't confirmed until 1917 – it took two years to complete and I was working on memorial windows for churches in Belfast and Dublin at the same time.

So the war ended, several memorial windows were already leaded and ready for fitting, and I was exhausted, my dreams forevermore crowded with dead soldiers, saints and old kings and a red, red, red tide of blood.

SHW: But the window was a huge success was it not? The Ottawa Window is still talked about.

WG: People hailed, then it sailed, as they say. There was some splosh in Dublin and London about the work, and how an Irish woman got this grand commission in North America, and of course, how my art was so very modern.

Prince Arthur, the Duke of Connaught, lost ten of his personal staff to the war. But by the time the window was sent to Ottawa, he was nearly 70, no longer governor general and too frail to take the trip himself. They sent the Prince of Wales instead.

But not me. Lowly artists aren't meant for the hob-nobbery of Dukes and Princes. It was as if my window had been sentenced to purgatory. Or Ottawa. Same difference. (laughs) And in that cold country it merited nothing more than a gasp.

SHW: What do you make of the Canadian reaction?

WG: Nobody needed to decipher it for me; I never got another commission in North America.

But here's the thing: I learned that not everybody is going to love my work. In fact, there were times – and there will be again – when it feels as if more people hate it than love it.

(Pause)

I want to be loved. Of course, I do. I'm just not interested in making the art that will make me loved.

(Silence)

SHW: Oh, yes, how true. Well, you've been very generous with your time, Miss Geddes. Is there some final lesson, some final word of advice, for the modern woman artist you'd like to leave with me?

WG: Certainly, dear. I can only say this: keep working. Absorb the blows, battle your dying planets, the invading stars, the wolves whose hot breaths stain your curtains. Lay in bed for as long as you need, but only that long.

Perhaps the hardest lesson for every modern woman artist is finding out how much you're willing to give up – to leave – in order to keep working. Leave your senses? I certainly did. Lost my mind. But not my art. Never that.

You might not think it, but I will walk out of the Maudsley's doors soon, I suspect for good – I'm close to securing a studio space here in London – and I doubt I will ever go back home. I've had to go through an ugly rebirthing here. There's no returning to the Irish womb. Sarah's an old woman now. Ireland is too willing to spill its own blood. And I am quite through with fallen soldiers. But I will keep painting glass, and building windows and making sun pierce through pigment shadows and yellow stains in search of whatever truth there is in a moment of shifting light.

You see, among your set, a window appears to gather the past, to be stuck in time – embalmed in heraldic colors. But one need only look a second longer, to see beyond the glass, see right through it. That's where the art happens. The call and response between light and the subject's shadows. It's new; it's modern, at just the right angle.

(Pause)

Oh dear. My mind is spent. The sun has moved away from us, too. Shall we go in? I've left my drawings for the Surrey window out in the crafts room. That ward sister will get her meddling hands all over them!

3:15 pm. End of transcript.

Maudsley Hospital, London, November, 1925
Ward Sister Report: Miss Geddes is recommended for discharge. Nurse Fraser sent to crafts room to pack up numerous drawings, assorted sketching supplies. Dr. Barkas requested a celebration tea with lemon curd tarts, monies which will be requisitioned from her budget. Waiting for superintendent's signature.

Author's Note

I stumbled across the story of Irish artist Wilhelmina Geddes and the memorial window she created for Ottawa's St. Bartholomew's Anglican Church while doing research on the Arts and Crafts movement for my second novel. Geddes was a driven and prodigiously talented woman whose style was bold and often controversial. Surrounded by a dynamic group of fellow artists and activists, during a turbulent historical period, she overcame mental illness and physical frailty to make a name in a field dominated by men. Truly, she is one not to be forgotten.

Because this is creative non-fiction, I have taken many liberties: While Wilhelmina Geddes did stay at Maudsley Hospital in the time span mentioned, her interview with a Boston journalist is entirely my invention, including her antipathy toward the Ward Sister and Lady Leslie and feelings about her father. Dr. Barkas existed but I don't know that Geddes was her patient or that she would have asked a nurse to eaves drop on a conversation between a patient and visitor for case notes. The biographical snippets of Geddes' and Sarah Purser's life are factually correct, but other than a few phrases parsed from actual letters, the back and forth between the two is conjecture on my part, as is exactly how the commission for the Ottawa Window was obtained. (Lady Leslie is likely to have had a liaison with Prince Arthur and she was definitely among Sarah's Purser's circle.) There were battles over including lions and Joan of Arc in the Ottawa Window, and Geddes only won the former.

The writing of this piece relied heavily on publications by the Irish stained glass historian Nicola Gordon Bowe and York University art historian Shirely Anne Brown's article, "Wilhelmina Geddes' Ottawa Window" which appeared in *The Irish Arts Review* in 1994. The classic text, *Stained Glass*, by E. Liddal Armitage provided insight into the traditional stained glass process, and two articles by Edgar Jones about the history of treatments at London's Maudsley Hospital, as well as psychiatry case notes from its first two decades of operation were invaluable for the introduction.

Finally, I would like to thank the Ontario Arts Council for a Writers Reserve grant that helped fund the time to research and write this piece.

THE TOOTH CHARMER

LILLIAN MATTHEWS BURDEN, NEWFOUNDLAND'S LAST MI'KMAQ SHAMAN

Ethel Edey

1937

Knock, knock, knock. Marigold could hear the tapping on the front door from her upstairs bedroom. The knocking continued. She wanted to run down the stairs, but her mother had warned all the children never to open the door in the middle of the night. Now Marigold could hear her mother's footsteps quickly descending the stairs. The front door creaked open and the muffled sounds of voices floated up to her room. The footsteps proceeded to the kitchen.

Marigold wondered why she always seemed to be the only one, besides her mother, who woke up to the sound of the nighttime door-knocking. Her eight brothers and sisters slept soundly. She longed to sneak downstairs to see who was there and what her mother was doing. But, again, her mother had warned them all of dire consequences should they do this.

Wide awake now, Marigold strained to hear the kitchen conversation. First there was an unfamiliar male voice talking. Then, after a brief silence, she could hear her mother's voice – but it sounded different. Was she singing? Was she speaking in a different language? If only she could see and hear what was going on.

Just as Marigold was drifting back to sleep she heard the front door close and her mother's footsteps remounting the stairs. All was quiet again.

Next morning, in the confusion and busyness of nine children having breakfast and getting off to school, Marigold forgot all about the mystery of the night. By the next afternoon, however, the story of how Marigold's mother, Lillian Burden, had charmed away Mr. Fudge's terrible toothache had penetrated the three-hundred-soul hamlet of Woody Point. On the way home from school she met Mrs. Fudge.

"Yer ma is some angel, girl, charmin away Mr. Fudge's tootache. Da wurst ting ya can have in yer ead is nar toot."

Woody Point is a small outport on Bonne Bay in northwestern Newfoundland. The residences overlook the bay, which harbours floating icebergs in June. Beyond the hamlet's border is a thick forest leading to the surrounding mountains. The area is protected from the strong winds which buffet most of the island, but it often receives record-breaking snowfalls. In 1937 there were no roads in and out. There were no streetlights, and cattle, sheep and goats roamed freely throughout the town. Three or four times a year a doctor, a magistrate, and a member of the Newfoundland constabulary would pay a visit. If it was foggy or stormy, which it often was, the visit would be cancelled.

Marigold's family, the Burdens, lived in a beautiful, two-story, box-style, five-bedroom house on Burden Lane. It was one of the nicest houses in Woody Point, with a big parlour used only for visitors. The house had no electricity or indoor toilet. The children made a game of watching whales from the second story windows. They counted the seconds from the time they spotted a water spout until the large two-finned tail broke the surface of the water. The Burdens raised their own cattle, which provided milk for the children. The meat was bottled or kept frozen under the snow in winter. Staples like flour and sugar came by boat. The sea and the many fresh water ponds provided fish that could be eaten fresh or preserved with salt.

The community was forced to be self-sufficient. There was Mrs. Noseworthy who knew how to bring babies into the world. There was Mrs. Roberts who knew the proper way to prepare a body for burial. Then there was Lillian Burden to whom the neighbors turned for medical problems. Lillian used different kinds of teas and herbal remedies made from local plants to treat various ailments, such as senna for constipation. For an infection, she would use a poultice.

But Lillian's high standing in Woody Point was mainly due to her unique ability to "charm" away toothaches and earaches. She would put her finger on the tooth or ear, recite the Charm, and after a short time the pain would be gone.

Anne Gillman believed firmly in Lillian's amazing power. For two days, Anne's brother had been experiencing pains radiating from his tooth to his ear. The pain had become so excruciating he was curled up on the bed unable to move. In his agony he was begging her, "Lard, tunderin girl, go git dat toot charmer. Me nerves is rubbed right raw."

It was pitch black outside and Anne was afraid to leave the safety of her house. She knew she had to help her brother, but fear of the dark overwhelmed her. She walked on to the bridge – which is what they called the porch in Woody Point. She stood there, counting the steps to Mrs. Burden's in her mind, gauging the length of time it would take to get to the Burden's house and back. She hoped her brother wouldn't know she hadn't actually gone to Mrs. Burden's house. When she quietly crept back into the house she was amazed, and very relieved, to find her brother sleeping soundly. The next morning the toothache was gone!

Few doubted the power of the Charm. The men folk of Woody Point loved to tell the story of Uncle Charlie's finger. One evening, a group of men were out in the woods cutting logs when Charlie's finger was accidently chopped off. As night fell, Charlie was walking back to the main road, his hand wrapped in a torn shirt, when he came across an old man. When the man saw Charlie's blood-spattered coat and the blood from his hand staining the makeshift bandage, he asked Charlie if he believed in the Charm. Charlie said he did not. Ignoring him, the Charmer told Charlie to take off his hat. He put his hand on Charlie's finger, muttered the Charm, and the bleeding immediately stopped. "He were bleedin like a stuck pig", witnesses acclaimed. "Good ting der were a man dar who had de Charm."

Uncle Charlie became a believer and enjoyed showing the children his stubby finger.

○

The children of Woody Point enjoyed many fun activities. When the bay froze over, they could skate from one end of town to the other. In spring, as the ice broke up, they would dare each other to jump between the ice pans. Released from the confines of the one-room school house in summer, they swam in the brook and went hiking in the woods where they might encounter moose, bears, fox or mink. Marigold's brothers were assigned work duties on their father's fishing boat and would often be out to sea for several days. Much as she enjoyed the boisterous bustle of a large family and playing with her friends, nine-year-old Marigold longed for time alone with her mother. Maybe, she thought wistfully, one day, when the boys are away and the older girls are busy with their friends, this might happen.

One fine day her wish came true. Marigold's abiding curiosity was going to be satisfied, and sooner than she had hoped. Every summer she had begged to go with her mother on her harvesting walks deep in the woods. Finally, Lillian had invited her to come with her to search for the plants she used to prepare her remedies. Since it would be just the two of them, Marigold could ask her mother all the questions bubbling in her mind about the nighttime visitors, the Charm, and how her mother made the teas and other medicines. As they walked through the woods, Lillian showed Marigold how to identify the medicinal plants, how to correctly break off the right part of each one, and gently place it in the basket.

Suddenly, Marigold felt something in her eye. "Ma, ders a bug in me eye." Placing a warm, strong hand on either side of Marigold's head, Lillian examined the eye. She gently massaged the eye with her tongue, and spit out the bug. Marigold's eye immediately felt normal again. Marigold had watched her mother use this technique on the other children whenever one of them got something in his or her eye.

When they sat down on the mossy ground to rest, Marigold had her chance. Lillian patiently answered the questions that poured out in a rush.

The Charm was given to Lillian by her father, James Matthews, when they lived in Chimney Cove. It only worked at night, which explained the frequent night time visitors at the Burden home. Marigold was devastated to learn that the Charm was passed down from father to daughter, mother to son. The Charm would never be hers, but would pass on to one of her brothers. To comfort her, Lillian told Marigold she would teach her how to make the teas from the plants they had just gathered. Marigold, partly mollified, kept thinking how unfair it was that her brothers were not at all interested in their mother's abilities, but one of them would be blessed with the Charm. It just wasn't right!

1949

Everyone in Woody Point was talking about this thing called, "Confederation". This fellow, Joey Smallwood, had been on the radio talking about all the good things that would come to Newfoundland when it became part of Canada. Marigold and her friends were excited. Maybe a road would be built so they could get cars and drive around the island.

Marigold's father was worried about what would happen to his fishing rights. Lillian and many of the older folks had secret worries that they didn't talk about.

After Confederation, change slowly crept into Woody Point. Roads were built linking Woody Point to Trout River and Deer Lake, where an airport was built. A medical clinic was built, staffed by a nurse and visiting doctors. Woody Point's designation as a Registered

Heritage District within Gros Morne National Park brought summer tourists. The town's population remained steady at three hundred.

2005

Marigold, now seventy-three years old, lives in the Burden family home with her husband, Charlie. Woody Point remains a picturesque hamlet of friendly people whose naivety charms her grandchildren when they visit. Marigold sometimes worries about her husband's health, as there is no doctor in Woody Point and they must travel to Deer Lake for medical care.

Marigold's nephew telephoned one day. "Auntie, I've been doing some genealogy research on our family and I've discovered we are Mi'kmaq!" This news was a great shock to Marigold but it explained many unanswered questions about her mother. Further family research revealed that Lillian Matthews had been raised in the ways of the Mi'kmaq by her parents, both of whom were Mi'kmaq. Grandpa Matthews lived a simple life, fishing and hunting, always taking only what the family could consume. He was proud of how well he was able to provide for his family. Lillian had never told her children about her Mi'kmaq heritage. When she cooked traditional Mi'kkmaq foods, such as flapjacks and stuffed squid, she simply told the family they were special dishes she had learned from Grandma Matthews.

The Mi'kmaq did not trust government officials. They were afraid their children would be taken away from them and that they would be ridiculed and stigmatized as "Jackatars", a common term for Mi'kmaq on the west coast of Newfoundland. With this newfound knowledge of her family's Mi'kmaq heritage, Marigold could now apply for Indian Status, which provides access to non-insured health benefits such as prescription drugs, dental care, and vision care.

When I call Marigold in Woody Point, she tells me, "Sadly, the Charm has been lost. Not one of my brothers was interested in learning the Charm. None of us knew what my mother said or what the prayer was. I don't know if it was spoken in the Mi'kmaq language, as she never spoke that language to us."

Today, when the gales whip up a stormy sea or winter blizzards cover the roads with ice and snow, any resident of Woody Point experiencing a night-time toothache nostalgically longs for a "Tooth Charmer".

Author's Note

This story came to my attention through Jackie van der Velde and Marsha Traverse, who both work at my dentist's office. Marigold Burden is Marsha's grandmother. She is eighty-two years old and still lives in Woody Point, Newfoundland. Marsha arranged for me to interview Marigold by telephone. Marigold is a charming lady who kindly shared with me memories of her mother, Lillian Matthews. Lillian Matthews was born to Mi'kmaq parents in Chimney Cove, Newfoundland in 1888 and lived to the age of seventy-three.

At the time of Confederation, Newfoundland government officials told the Canadian government that there were no native people living in Newfoundland. In 1972, in response to disturbing government actions, the Mi'kmaq from the entire province came together in an organization called The Federation of Newfoundland Indians, the purpose of which was to achieve recognition by the Federal Government.

In September of 2011, the Government of Canada announced the recognition of Canada's newest Mi'kmaq First Nations Band, the Qalipu First Nations in Newfoundland and Labrador. The number of applications received by the application deadline on November 30, 2012 exceeded 100,000. The deadline was extended to January 31, 2014, and then to February 10, 2014. Its members are recognized as Status Indians, joining other organized Mi'kmaq bands recognized in southeast Canada.

PATHWAYS: THE LIFE, WORKS, AND EPIPHANY OF CAROLINE ARMINGTON

DRYPOINT ARTIST

Bruce Meyer

The guns she'd heard continually as she sketched on the left bank quay were a distant memory now. Through the olive trees came the bleating of goats. A shepherd had passed by earlier in the morning, and she marveled at how white the flock was. In the Holy Land everything was pure.

Frank spent most of his days inside Jerusalem's walls. He had met a group of ex-pat artists who debated the role of colour and shape, and whether things seen with the naked eye needed to be defined by more than splashes of paint. Caroline wanted no part of that. Drypoint, with its minute and exacting details, was her passion. The world was full of details. The artist's job was to show the beholder everything that could be missed.

She checked the time on the heart-shaped locket watch Frank had bought for her at a jeweler's in the Marais. It kept good time, even when it measured bad times. It had, for example, ticked away the death of good friends she and Frank had known in the cafes of the Blvd. St. Michel before the storm had broken in 1914.

Guillaume's shining regimental numbers: why did she remember them? When they had lunched together, his red collar against the bright French blue of his tunic looked so beautiful. She had thought to herself that it would be awful for someone to shoot him and spoil the exquisite craftsmanship of the man and his uniform. His waxed moustache made him look as if he was on his way to a salon rather than the banks of the Marne. And when he returned, one eye almost shut, his head bandaged, he held both hands up to his ears during the one lunch he attempted with her and Frank, and his one good eye wept a single tear. He could barely speak. His hand shook as he passed a letter across the table to them. It said merely, "*Mes ami, au revoir*. Guillaume Apollinaire." It contained the keys to his two-seater blue auto that he treasured so much. They had gone for drives in "Le Petite Auto" on summer afternoons before the war began. She never saw him again. The wound grew worse and worse, until Robert telephoned them to tell them the great poet was dead.

Robert had arrived in Paris at the same as she and Frank, and had been invited to the same luncheons. People still had dreams and adventures then, and Robert summed up that spirit in his poetry. Fresh from New York, a fair, thin man in a banker's three-piece suit, he had sat down opposite them at the table for ten at the Cote D'Or on the Blvd. St. Germain and extended his hand. She expected it to be cold for having been so far north for so long. When she shook it, it was warm.

One day Robert called by to tell them that he had joined the Ambulance Service, because, as he said, "I've got to do my part." He also wanted to show off his khaki uniform with its Red Cross arm band and military hat, badged with the universal symbol for mercy. Robert was a year older than Frank, and tried to twist Frank's arm into coming with him. "Oh," he said through his Glasgow brogue that had not a hint of a Yukon twang in it, "it'll be good work, and what an adventure we'll have to tell."

Caroline had pleaded, "But why? You're old enough to be the father of the boys who are going off." Robert fell silent for a moment. He turned his tea saucer round and round as if it was a wheel of fortune and he was attempting to read it.

"My brother, Albert," he said.

She could see tears starting to well in his eyes.

"I got the telegram after the Somme. I have to go. One of those boys lying out there could be another Albert." He paused, and there was a long silence. The mantle clock's ticking grew louder. He suddenly smiled. "So, hey Frank, you're made of good Canadian stuff. Come along. See the world with me."

Frank's health had never been good. He often joked that he married Caroline not merely because she had been his childhood sweetheart in Brampton, nor because she was the other half of his artistic soul, but because she had been a nurse. During their sojourn in North Africa in 1904, where they sketched Berbers in the narrow passageways of Moroccan towns, he had fallen ill with a fever. That had put an end to their work for several months. When he recovered enough to go out and find a shady place to do their sketches, they met an English doctor. "You need some good, cool, weather," he advised Frank. They returned to the gaiety of Paris, and even a Parisian summer was more welcoming than the shadiest places they had found in the bazaars, courtyards, and orange groves of Casablanca.

When the war broke out, Caroline considered putting her nursing experience to use in the military hospitals of Paris. The wounded were pouring into the city in unheard of numbers from places such as Vimy Ridge, Verdun, and La Chappelle. The thought of death, however, overwhelmed her. She'd seen a lot of it when she nursed in Guelph. The hardest moments were when children passed away. Being around death had made her even more determined to dedicate her life to art. Life was short and she wanted to devote herself to something that could outlive human frailty.

One morning in the spring of 1915, she summoned the courage to visit a small hospital, Ste. Marie des Invalides, on a sidestreet off the Tuilleries Gardens. There she offered her services. As she set foot in the door, the stench of antiseptic, and the sound of men calling out in pain shook her. She turned in a state of confusion and saw a man without hands looking toward her from his cot. She collapsed in the hallway. The doctor who attended her said he had too much to do to look after soldiers and that, owing to her constitution, she should go home. He put her in one of the few taxis still available in Paris that month. Most had been called to ferry the French army to the Marne, and had not returned.

Frank stood over her and handed her a cup of tea. "Well, I guess your nursing days are over."

"I guess they are," she said. "This is an awful business. Just before I dropped, I saw a man in a room off the corridor. He smiled at me and nodded. I'd seen him before. Several years ago when I was on the quay just below Pont Henri IV, he had been painting a scene of the river. I'd wandered over and admired it, and I'd shown him my sketches – including one of the ones I transferred to a copperplate. He'd admired it. I remember him commenting on the fine lines. Today when I saw him, he was in bed. His hands had been blown off and the stumps were bleeding through the bandages. Someone had set a sketch book up in front of him, and with a pencil in his teeth he was trying to draw."

"Maybe that's what I'm supposed to do," Frank said.

"You're not thinking of enlisting are you? No, Frank, no."

"On the contrary. Robert wrote me a letter. It seems they need someone to assist in the hospitals in the north end – Saint-Denis or some place – so I'm going up there tomorrow to do what I can."

"But your health!"

"I'll come home every night. It's just a train ride. You can show me what you've done during the day, and if I get the chance I can show you what I've managed to slip in around my duties."

Frank came home the next evening in the uniform of a hospital orderly. His face was long and he had the black crescents of exhaustion under his eyes. He opened his sketch book to several pages of the wards and of men who asked to be recorded by an artist before they died. Caroline sucked in her breath and began to sob. "This is going to go on a long time," he said.

Now Caroline felt even more determined that she should record the life of the city around her, even when it appeared the city might die. The lights of Pigalle and the electric signs on saloons at the foot of Montmartre were dimmed, and there was even talk of painting the pale white stone of Sacre Coeur black so that its beacon of hope in dark times would not provide a landmark for the Zepplins that came in the night with greater and greater frequency. As Frank slept, depleted by his constant routine of wheeling bodies to the morgue and stripping the bloody and soiled sheets from cots so they could be replaced for the next man who would suffer the same fate as the last, Caroline curled up beside him and held him close. She prayed that something would show them the path to peace.

She went to the window and opened the shutters just as a rain of shells exploded in the streets around them. A building down the avenue from their studio burst in a white flash and collapsed onto the sidewalk while screams echoed through the night. The pane of window glass through which she saw it all, cracked across her reflection. The world was broken, and everyone in it was breaking, and turning to dust.

The war even changed the great optimist of the north. When Robert returned – having survived longer than almost any of the ambulance men who had run into the middle of no-man's land to save dying soldiers – nationality meant nothing to him. A wounded man, be he French, English, German, was a fellow human being in distress.

Caroline and Frank asked Robert and his wife to come for dinner. Frank wanted Robert to see etchings of the old Paris they had known before the war. Not only were the critics back home admiring them, but men of taste and artistic temperament who had passed through Paris while on furlough or their way to the Front had paid generously for them. Frank was now a success.

Robert said little over dinner, which was not like him. Madeline, the wife he had married just after he'd arrived to "set Paris on fire", as he told everyone, was also strangely silent.

When the silence became too much, Robert spoke up. "I tried to write about the war, and I did. I wrote a book, not of poems, but of my experiences going out into No-Man's Land for the wounded."

"He burned it last night," said Madeline. "The whole manuscript. He tossed it onto the fire. It is gone."

Robert explained, "I can't live here any more. I want to go somewhere where there's peace and tranquility. There was one night I went out on the wire. There was one of our chaps there, tangled, shot through several times. I started to cut him loose. 'I'm crucified here,' he said to me. 'Are you going to take me down and wrap me in a shroud?' I whispered to him, 'Nothing of the sort. I'm going to cut you loose and take you back where you belong. 'Tell me a story,' he said. I had no idea what to say. I just wanted to get him out of there and me out of there with him, so I recited 'The Cremation of Sam McGee.' I'd done that often enough, and it was the first thing that came to mind. I don't know why. It just popped in there. 'He said,' I bet you think you're Robert Service or something, don't you?' I was just about to tell him 'No, I've never heard of the guy' when the Germans opened up on us. I scrambled for safety into a shell hole. They put so many rounds in him..." Service paused and began to weep for a moment, and then shook his head. When he recovered enough to stand up and take leave of the Armingtons, he said "You'll have to come and visit us in Normandy. I bought a place right on the coast. You can hear the waves there. I have to hear the sound of God's heart or I'm going to die."

As she sat up that night with the shutters open again and the doors to their lounge spread wide to the April night so full of peace, Caroline understood what Robert had tried to say to them. She had grown too familiar with the sandbags at the intersections of major thoroughfares, the men hobbled and cut down to their knees, pushing their way along the sidewalks in small wooden carts they had built. She remembered the whirr as shells from the railway guns passed overhead just as she saw an avenue or a perspective that looked through time to a tomorrow that might reside at the far end of the passage. And she had wept and clutched her pencil and sketch book as the crashing screamed around her.

Before the war, the Paris she and Frank had sought was the Paris of Degas and delicate ballerinas in flowing chiffon skirts. It was a world where Renoir myopia, that blurring of lines and distinctions where objects and vistas acquired an ethereal, other-worldly air, made even the most commonplace of things beautiful. She had studied the panels of Monet's "Rouen Cathedral" with Frank when they went to visit the almost-blind artist at Giverny, and had stood upon the small Japanese bridge over the lily pond, and watched as golden koi surfaced to feed on breadcrumbs tossed into the reflection of a cloudless sky. The couple had sat together in the square in front of Notre Dame and, inspired by Claude Monet, had done their own renderings of its front while tourists with *Baedecker Guides* wandered past, looking up at the church with the same awe that had inspired Victor Hugo. Their Paris had been a world where the streets were crowded with men and women, arms linked after an evening rain had turned the pavement to gold beneath the street lamps. It had been a city of an unquenchable thirst for life where all the brave faces of brilliant men and women, their late friend Guillaume Apollinaire among them, had laughed and celebrated. Now Guillaume was but a name, freshly inscribed on the wall of the Pantheon.

The next morning as he read his *Herald Tribune* at the breakfast table, Frank said, "You know, I think there's hope yet. All those chaps gathered at Versailles, Wilson in particular, they actually think they can remake the world so there won't be any more wars, at least not with Germany."

Caroline said, "Frank, last night I had a vision. I don't know whether you'd agree or not, but I think there is a path to heaven, and it is where we will find our subject matter."

"You don't mean Turner, bright lights, and dancing angels, do you?" he chortled.

"No. I think it may be where Man saw God in all his glory the last time humankind spoke with Him. We need to go to Jerusalem."

"Dear, Jerusalem is just as bad as anywhere these days. The Turks left it in a mess. The Jews are assassinating British soldiers and Foreign Office men there every week."

"Please. I can't for the life of me explain it, but there is something there I need to find."

Frank sighed and put down his paper. "Well, I guess it can't be worse than anywhere else that's a mess these days, so why not? We'll close up the place here for a few months and see what happens."

The voyage from Marseilles was hot and dirty, as was the ship itself. The streets of Jerusalem were also hot and dirty. In her heart, Caroline questioned why God would choose this place, of all places, for his miracles. One instant the sunlight would bounce off the pale, flesh-coloured walls of the old city, and in the next blink of an eye, they would be wrapped in a shadow as dark as a crypt. The constant dialogue of birth and death that Jerusalem seemed to shout at them was more than Frank could take. It was like being back in North Africa. He never did well in the heat.

But for Caroline, Jerusalem became a riddle she felt she had to solve. She had always been fascinated by corridors, avenues perceived through the perspective of a portal, a vision caught in the corner of the eye as she passed an open door. In one door, an old woman was standing at a raw wooden table, slapping a wet shirt against a pro-truding stone and then soaking it in a wooden bucket. She did not look up to see Caroline. She repeated the movements over and over again until she opened the arms of the shirt as if she held a crucified body before her, and a stream of light passed through the wet cloth and made it glow.

Frank did not protest when she said she was going to the Mount of Olives. She hired a car at their hotel, and for some reason the driver approached the long way from the south. She had left Jerusalem in the darkness just before dawn, and her driver let her off at the Necropolis, the city of the dead at the foot of the south slope. She paused for several minutes as the first light fell upon the doors of the tombs. Was that what resurrection looked like? The light to see by as one awoke from death's sleep? She took that as a sign that the world was coming back to life. She continued on the road up the mount.

As she reached the crest she remembered the passage from Matthew 21 where Jesus could see Jerusalem off in the distance and wept for it. Tears came to her eyes as she tried to sketch the vista. She had wept for Paris, and the Son of God had wept for the world. But it was on her way down the slope, on the north side, that she grew tired and thought, "I can't go on. Lord give me strength, but I can't go on."

She sat down in an olive grove. The shepherd passed with his sheep. They bah-hahed and brushed against each other. One wandered up to her, and she put out her hand to touch it. Its wool was soft, though bramble and thorns were embedded in it. The shepherd nudged it with a long stick, and the straying sheep joined the others of its flock. A warm wind cooled her. The shade of the olive trees and the coins of light they threw down made her sad. If life was short, how could an artist, a dry-point maker turning out likeness after likeness until the plate could not repeat the image any more, make the slightest difference to a world gone beyond madness into the depths of hell? She whispered to herself, "O Father, why have you forsaken us?"

She had seen that hell in the hospital during the day of her failed attempt to volunteer. God did not want her to see the horrors of the war as Frank and Robert had seen them. He wanted her to see an order composed of small, intricate lines and patterns that would rise off the page and be something more than just broken twigs of ink upon a page. Her purpose, she realized at that moment, was not merely to record what she saw, but to speak for life in small images that could be so easily overlooked until one went to look for them. She finally understood. A person cannot be told to see life, but could be persuaded, like an artist, to look for it. The words of Francis Bacon she had seen in a stained glass window at the University of Toronto sprang to mind: "God shewes Himself best in His smallest things."

Her driver found her.

"You have been drawing well today?" he asked.

"Yes, but thinking, too. This is an odd place for God to have chosen to speak to Man."

"But it *is* the place He chose, God be praised. For you, a Christian, it is the place you call Gethsemane. I believe Jesus asked many questions here."

Caroline's eyes filled with tears again. "Yes," she said, "but I guess it is up to us to answer them."

O

Frank more or less gave up etchings after their journey to Jerusalem. He decided to dedicate himself to paintings. John Phillip Sousa liked one of his canvases so much that he purchased the work and hung it in the study of his home where he composed the marches that men heard as they stepped in time together toward death.

Caroline was long considered the lesser talent of the couple because she refused to give up her small, intricate, and complex etchings of doorways and portals. She was finally discovered and acclaimed as a major artist following a show of her tiny etchings in New York in 1925. The critics loved the images of Jerusalem.

The Armingtons continued to travel together. Frank got used to heat because, he said, "Hot places have better light for painters."

Every two years or so, they would return to Paris. Caroline would walk along the boulevards and past cafes they had frequented before the Great War; but the names had been changed. The faces all belonged to strangers now. She would pause in front of her old haunts, and, for an instant, believe that Guillaume was waving her to come in and join him for a coffee or a cognac.

But soon another war began. A bomb fell three doors down the block from their Paris studio one afternoon in the middle of September 1939. The shock of the explosion made Caroline's heart leap from her chest. She dropped on the spot. The city, a work of art made even more beautiful by artists who worked to remember it their way, was declared an open city. The Nazis would be there in a matter of time.

Frank decided to stay behind. He could be useful again in a war. He put Caroline on one of the last American liners to leave Le Harve during the first week of October. Shortly after she arrived in New York to be treated by a heart specialist who also had a collection of her etchings, Caroline Armington died in her sleep on October 25, 1939.

O

Robert Service thought that he had put the world behind him when he opened the patio doors of his home in Normandy one summer afternoon in 1922. The sea air blew in and filled his lungs, and he thought, "We'll be safe here. No more adventure for me." But that was not to be.

In 1940 the Germans charged through Normandy and raced to capture "The Bard of the Yukon" three days before the debacle at Dunkirk. Making a prisoner of the great Robert Service would have been a propaganda coup. Instead, a small fishing boat pulled away from Service's private dock, and on the back of the fishing boat, as a German officer fired his Luger and missed, Robert Service gallantly waved goodbye to his pursuers, a handkerchief in one hand, and four framed etchings of Caroline Armington's "Mount of Olives" series clutched tightly in the other.

Author's Note

As a collector of etchings, I was astonished to find the Canadian couple, Frank (1876-1941) and Caroline Armington (1875-1939), listed as master "dry-point" artists of the twentieth century, and credited with keeping the form of copper plate etching alive. Frank Armington's works command higher prices on the art market, but it was with the works of Caroline Armington that I became fascinated. Her plates display an incredible and powerful intricacy of detail, shadows, and perspectives. Frank Armington's paintings can be found in numerous American galleries, including the Metropolitan Museum of Fine Art in New York. Caroline Armington's works, however, are sadly neglected, especially in Canadian galleries, where she deserves to hold a place of significance as the leading artist of her time in the etching medium. I own six Caroline Armington etchings in my private collection, and they show me something unique and different every time I study them.

GUTEN MORGEN, MEINE HERREN

MONA PARSONS, PRISONER OF THE NAZIS FOR HELPING THE BRITISH IN HOLLAND

Wendi Stewart

Willowy is how I was described when I was young. I was certainly taller than all of the girls in my class and most of the boys by the time I was fifteen. I liked being tall. I stood up straight, kept my neck long, my chin level. I was poised and self-assured.

"You're so tall, dear," my mother whispered, from behind her hand so no one would hear, in case they hadn't noticed my height. She sounded confused, as if she had no idea how she could have created this girl, a daughter who grew to such a height and found her voice early, too early in my mother's opinion. I had always been strong-willed, with a mind of my own, a head full of opinions and ideas, dreams and plans.

"Long and lean," my father said with a smile, the kind of smile that said I pleased him. The Colonel – that's what everyone called my father, even me, after his service time in World War I. The Great War. The War to end all wars. Little did we know.

I am in prison in Vechta, Germany, a prisoner of war a long way from the safety of my beloved Nova Scotia. I grew up there, my family moving from Middleton, Nova Scotia to Acadia Street in Wolfville when I was ten. Acadia Street was beautiful with its mighty elms reaching up from each side of the street and across, their branches entangled as if the trees were dancing, swaying in the breeze. Perhaps that set the tone for my life.

We moved in 1911, the same year The Opera House opened in Wolfville. I call up the images in my mind now to stave off despair and madness on the long dark nights, to block out the wailing and the cold and the hunger. I put my back against the cold stone wall, my arms drawn in around me and I close my eyes and remember.

The Opera House was a magical place. I hear the music and see the actors and dancers, the vaudeville acts that mesmerized me, had me dreaming, sitting on the edge of my seat, my back straight, hands folded at my chin to keep my head from leaping off my shoulders. I remember best the screening of Sarah Bernhardt as Dumas's Camille. She was lovely. I wanted to be on the stage one day; every cell in my body was keen to do so. When I walked I practiced grace and composure, put self-assurance in my stride and formed my thoughts and opinions. Women told my mother I oozed self-confidence and suggested perhaps a life on the stage would be in my future. My mother's reaction was a fearful one.

"Oh dear," she said, her face turned down, undoubtedly worrying I would never find a man willing to marry me, as if being someone's wife was the only definition of a woman.

Women of my mother's era weren't encouraged to stand out, but rather expected to blend in while they served and obeyed their husbands. My mother had mastered this undertaking to perfection, adding a healthy serving of silence and down-turned eyes. She could very well have written the rulebook of obeying and serving. Obedience. My mother learned early on the rules of her day, to be an attentive and diligent wife. A life like that wasn't for me. No thank you.

The world was changed by World War I. Women took up the reins in the absence of men. Women ran businesses, operated farms, made decisions without permission, without waiting to be asked. Women like Cora Pierce Richmond, a strong and independent widow, my voice teacher who opened a music studio in downtown Wolfville when women didn't do such things. Women like Blanche Leigh

McLean, the widow of a Cape Breton physician. She taught expression and voice in Halifax and then accepted a position on the faculty of Acadia University where she became the Dean of Women and a strong advocate of theatre art, a woman who led by example. Both these women shaped the woman I would become.

When the First World War was over I believe men wanted to silence the newfound voices of women, to return things to how they were, but the tides had turned and the world would never be the same again.

I'm not sure my mother could comprehend these changes. This new world must have baffled her, just as my strong will baffled her. What would she think now if she could see me, the hair of my whole body shorn, the Germans wanting to remove any evidence that we were individuals. Most of my hair had fallen out on its own from a diet lacking of anything nutritious. I give willowy a new meaning. My fingers – long and manicured once upon a time when they played the piano, dancing over the keys – are battered now, bruised, the nails broken and blackened with dirt. I am diminished, starving, forgotten.

What would my mother think if she had seen me in Amstelveense Prison where I slept on straw, infested with fleas and lice? Or in Anrath Penitentiary when the Nazis moved me from Holland to Germany and I was forced to share space with those who had committed heinous crimes, those who had murdered their own children. Or when I was loaded on an airless cattle car and moved from prison to prison, as if my humanity could be erased, as if war gave the Germans the right to treat human life as if it had no value at all.

It took only five days for Holland to fall to Germany in May 1940. The Nazis came to Ingleside on the evening of September 29th, 1941; Ingleside, the home Willem and I built together to mark the start of our marriage. We imagined a life of beauty and ease, of celebrating the arts, a life of dance and laughter. Perhaps we took our freedom for granted, but we had no idea how quickly our lives would change.

"Mrs. Leonhardt," the officer at the door said when I responded to his knock, a second uniformed officer of the Gestapo behind him, with a robotic face, the uniform dark and ominous. He looked directly at me, my name not a question, but rather a statement loaded with what was to come.

"Come in, come in," I said, stepping aside, my arm sweeping them in the direction of the drawing room. "May I offer you a drink," I said, lifting the crystal stopper off the Scotch decanter. They shook their heads. "A cigar, then," I said, opening the lid on Willem's small humidor.

"Where is your husband, Mrs. Leonhardt?" the officer in charge asked, drawing deeply on the cigar as he lit it and examining its end as he exhaled the smoke above his head.

"He is fishing in Friesland. I'm not sure of his return. I suppose it will depend on how the fishing is going."

The officer laughed, indicating that he didn't believe me.

"You've had house guests recently. Two British airmen," the second officer said, blowing smoke directly at me.

It was my turn to laugh, an incredulous tone to my voice. "How absurd. If someone had been staying here I think I would have been aware, and I assure you, we've had no such guests."

"We will examine your house," he said.

They searched the entire house, as I followed behind looking calm and indifferent. "You'll find nothing," I said. "But do suit yourselves."

They tromped in their heavy boots from room to room, until they stopped and adjusted the sleeves of their coats, in unison, as if their movements had been choreographed.

"You will come with us to Headquarters in Amsterdam," the taller of the two said.

"What on earth for?"

He didn't offer an answer but took my elbow a bit too firmly.

"I'll need my coat and purse."

They weren't letting me out of their sight and the second officer accompanied me to my room and then helped me into the waiting car with even more force.

I was taken to Weterinschane Prison in Amsterdam. A miserable place with an unpleasant reputation. The marathon of interrogation began. The same questions over and over. I never changed my tone, never showed any sign that they were getting to me. I almost laughed a couple of times watching their frustration. But, I managed to keep my composure. I expected they would turn me loose soon enough.

Willem and I joined the resistance movement almost immediately after Holland succumbed to the Nazis. It was our mission to help downed Allied airmen escape from Holland back to England. It was an obvious choice, to help however we could, not a decision we spent any time considering. We had only managed to help navigator Richard Pape and flight engineer William "Jock" Moir. The fact that the Nazis had their names meant the two airmen had not made it safely back to England.

I was interrogated continuously. Fools. I was an actress. They couldn't slip me up. I had the ability to learn long passages and I gave them the best of my theatrical training, appearing almost bored with the whole proceedings. I yawned, sighed, tipped my head. My abhorrence for authority from my youth was re-awakened and the Nazis' aggressiveness only made me more determined. The interrogating officer exploded in anger at my lack of cooperation and confession. Nothing encouraged my determination more than his rage.

"You will tell us?" he shouted, his fist stabbing the air.

"I know nothing of what you are asking," I said, my voice heavy with calm.

In the end, the same traitors who facilitated my capture assisted in the capture and imprisonment of my husband Willem three months after me. The Nazis felt they had won.

"Ah," the interrogator sighed, pointing his finger at me and nodding his head, a look of evil delight on his face. "We have trapped the mouse," he said, hissed the words through his teeth.

"Did it ever occur to you that you are wrong?" I asked and looked directly at him. He stared back, but was the first to look away.

I stood trial, a trial that was a mockery of justice. My legal defence spoke no English and no Dutch.

"Todesstrafe," I heard the the judge say and my blood ran cold. Death sentence.

The word bounced around the room without settling on me. Death. I held my body erect, tapped my heels together after the sentence was read.

"Gutten morgen, meine herren," I said, with my most confident voice as I left the court room, without a hint of the fear that was raging inside, and with a gentle bow to the judge. It may have been my finest performance.

What would my mother say as I was escorted from the court room and loaded on a train destined for Amstelveense Prison? She would whisper, not in anger but in despair. "Look where your opinions got you."

I loved my mother. Mary Keith. She married my father, Norval Parsons, a man she grew up with, a boy she had admired walking home from school and from church. When he asked her father for her hand I'm sure my mother never entertained any other response but yes, as if she was hardwired to be a wife, to tend to her husband's needs.

I did broach this once, when she was rolling out her pie pastry, checking that the thickness was uniform and precise, the lard blended evenly. "What did you want to be, Mother?" I asked, with my knees pulled up in front of me in the chair across the table from her. She didn't have an immediate answer, as if she didn't quite understand the question.

"It is my duty to love and honour my husband," my mother explained, her voice soft, never raising her eyes from the pastry she fit carefully inside the pie plate, as if this pie like every pie and every cake and every Sunday roast and every starched shirt would be judged for its perfection, scrutinized to see if my mother measured up. She offered no hint of what else she may have longed for.

My mother made certain I attended the Acadia Ladies Seminary, where girls were taught to be genteel and cultured, a skill, it turns out, that may very well have saved my life. It wasn't that I didn't want to be genteel so much as I wanted something more. I wanted my own place in the world, to be my own person. I didn't want being a wife to define me. Nor was I going to let the Nazis take my spirit. The Nazis wouldn't break me. If I had the will to choose my own life, to break the pattern of what was expected of my mother, I could do this, too – a promise to myself. They may have claimed my freedom. They may have taken Willem from me, and my home. But they would not defeat me. *I will not die in this miserable prison*, I chanted over and over in my head.

I appealed the death sentence. At the very least my performance of being cool and calm impressed the judge. So I was given life in prison instead. Life. This was anything but life. Moving from prison to prison, as more and more of those fighting the resistance were captured. Here at Vechta I wear a uniform that the former inmates of this Girls Reform School wore, inmates that were turned loose to make room for the great number of enemies of The Third Reich. We were slave labour, working long hours with little food. I spliced wires for the manufacture of bomb igniters, a mindless task, but one that gave me an opportunity to sabotage the igniters, when I didn't secure the wires, hoping the bomb wouldn't detonate when dropped.

Now I peel potatoes, day after day after day, preparing food for nearby hospitals until my fingers throb. Other than that I recite recipes to my prison-mates. I tell the story of each ingredient and the instructions and what the dishes look like; the wonderful meals my mother made. My deep alto voice carries in the darkness and even those several cells away can hear me. They tell me the recipes help ease their hunger. I recite them with my best dramatics and sometimes we all laugh and I like that best and I hope the Nazis can hear us. The desserts, the soufles, the crème brulee, the coq au vin, the glazed hams.

"But Mona," says Wendelien. "When do we eat?"

Wendelien van Boetzelaer arrived not long ago. She is twenty-two years old. A baroness and a university student. She has escaped twice before and now the Nazis aren't taking any chances. They keep her locked up in solitary confinement. I managed to slip cooked potato to her in a hidden pocket of my uniform. I eventually convinced the prison director to let Wendelien join us.

The prison director tries to make our lives bearable. She was the former matron of the Reform School. She follows orders, but she is a lesbian and doesn't think too highly of Hitler's intent to exterminate all such deviants. How absurd that Hitler considers others deviants. The SS keep a close eye on her, so she must be careful. She ensures we are given water to wash with and a bit of clay soap, but we only have a small bowl of cold water to wash our bodies and our clothes. It is something.

I have organized a method of dividing rations. The oldest gets the largest rations and the youngest the smallest. If one of us is ill we make exceptions. I am ill a lot of the time with my respiratory problems. I am given extra rations in the infirmary because of my status in Holland, having been married to such a wealthy man as Willem. Madness, as if Willem's wealth has any real value, as if it makes me better than those standing next to me. I make sure to share my extra rations with those in need. It is the only way to hang on to my humanity and decency. I'm sure my mother would approve of that. I'm sure she would understand and say, "Well done, Mona. Well done."

We noticed the increase in plane traffic about mid March. It is 1945. I have been in prison for almost four years. I have no idea if Willem is alive or dead. But I don't let those worrisome thoughts create despair. The Nazis respond with anti-aircraft fire, the noise almost constant. Each day there seem to be more and more aircraft. We are all on heightened alert, even the weakest among us.

It is Friday morning, March 24th. We are readying for our workday. I hear the bombers first, but then everyone pauses to listen. At first it sounded like a far off growl, but now it grows closer and louder.

The earth is moving, the prison is trembling almost. Will we be killed by our own Allies? We can see the men's prison from the Reform School. It looks like it has taken a direct hit and has exploded into flames.

"Willem!" I cry out. "Willem."

The prison director runs ahead and throws open the prison gates.

"Run for freedom," she shouts, waving her arms madly, trying to be heard over the explosions. "Or run to the bomb shelter. It's your choice."

Everyone is running for the shelters underground. Wendelien grabs my arm.

"This is our chance," she says, not waiting for me to respond.

We are running, running through the smoke and the gunfire and the chaos. Running without shoes, in nothing more than our thin dark blue uniforms. All I can think of as I run is my mother and her precisely perfect pie pastry.

"What will I be remembered for, Mother?"

Author's Note

Mona Parsons and Wendelien van Boetzelaer did make it to safety, after many weeks of walking and sometimes crawling. They were separated and Mona went on alone, coming upon Clarence Leonard of the North Nova Scotia Highlanders regiment. She wanted to get home to Holland and pushed on, but was picked up by a Polish transport and thought to be a spy. She was taken back to Oldenburg Germany, not far from where she started her walk to freedom. Friends from Wolfville in the Canadian forces heard of her dilemma and verified her identity. Harry Foster was among them.

Willem also survived, though his health was seriously compromised and he never fully recovered. Upon his death in 1956, Mona discovered she could not inherit Willem's wealth and property because she was not a Dutch citizen. She was forced to sell her beautiful home. After some travels she and her piano moved back to Canada to live near Halifax. She was reacquainted with Harry Foster. She and Harry married, but he only lived for five more years. At his death Mona was denied the widow's portion of Harry's military pension, the military offering no reason or explanation.

For further reading I would recommend Andria Hill's *Mona Parsons, From privilege to prison, from Nova Scotia to Nazi Europe* (Nimbus Publishing Limited, 2000).

Mona Parsons died on November 28, 1976 in Wolfville, where she had lived at 444 Main Street. Her grave is in the Wolfville Cemetery, a place I visited when I first moved to Wolfville in 2011. The epitaph on her tombstone says, "Wife of Major General H.W. Foster". I, and many others, find those words unsettling and disrespectful in light of her sacrifices, her vigour for life, her personal journey as a woman with a voice. A movement is underway to have the epitaph changed, or certainly to bring awareness to the life she lived. I fear that Mona would think she died as her mother had lived: silent and forgotten. Surely we won't let that be her legacy.

DR. FARRELL AND THE VACCINE MARATHON

LEONE FARRELL, POLIO VACCINE SCIENTIST

Frances Hern

"The National Foundation for Infantile Paralysis has asked for help," said Dr. Rhodes, the virologist in charge of polio research at Connaught Laboratories.

"What kind of help?" asked Dr. Leone Farrell, who was a senior researcher at the lab.

"Jonas Salk is ready to test his polio vaccine. They want to conduct a huge field trial in the U.S. but it will take them forever to produce enough vaccine."

"And in the meantime ..."

Dr. Rhodes nodded. "Exactly," he said.

The United States had had its worst polio epidemic ever the previous year. Now, in 1953, it was Canada's turn. Hundreds and hundreds of Canadians, many of them seemingly healthy and robust children and young adults, were contracting polio. Approximately one in eighteen of those died. There was no cure. Dr. Farrell was well aware that prevention was the only answer on the horizon and a vaccine was desperately needed.

"You found a way to mass produce bacterial cultures," said Dr. Rhodes. "If anyone can do the same for the polio virus, you can. I'll leave it in your capable hands. Keep me informed."

Back in her second-floor apartment on the corner of Avenue Road and Oriole Parkway, Dr. Farrell lay in bed thinking. She had been at Connaught Medical Research Laboratories for ... she counted up ... eighteen years of working with antitoxins and vaccines. Scientists had come a long way since the first modern vaccine had been designed to combat smallpox in 1796, but there were still many challenges in producing such vaccines. The virus had to be grown and then inactivated so it would stimulate the immune system to produce antibodies without causing symptoms. Unlike bacteria, however, viruses could reproduce only inside living cells. Scientists had made major breakthroughs in recent years. They'd discovered how to grow the virus in test tube tissue cultures instead of in live monkeys, and the team at Connaught Laboratories had formulated a synthetic mixture of over sixty substances they called Medium 199 in which the polio virus would grow, so there was no longer any danger that people might have allergic reactions to the animal proteins as there had been in the sera they used to use. Nevertheless, growing viruses was still a laborious and complicated process.

Dr. Farrell's mind wandered. She was almost glad she didn't have children, that she didn't have to worry about the polio virus attacking motor neurons in their spinal cords and brains. Sometimes unable to breathe, patients were put into iron lungs – expensive steel chambers that encased the body from the neck down and mechanically changed the air pressure inside to pull air in and out of the lungs. Those that survived were left with wasted limbs and damaged nerves that had limited response, if any, to physiotherapy. Dr. Farrell tried to think of more pleasant things, but it was a long time before she fell asleep.

Female Ph.D. students were few and far between, but then Dr. Farrell came from a family of high achievers. Her parents had moved Leone and her five older brothers and sisters from a small farming community outside Ottawa to Toronto, and her older brothers all had university degrees. Perhaps influenced by a brother-in-law who edited and published scientific trade magazines, Dr. Farrell had followed a Ph.D. in Biochemistry at the University of Toronto with two years of working as a chemist with the National Research Council of Canada. Dr. Rhodes, her department head, had good reason to believe that Dr. Farrell would find a way to speed up virus production. Since joining Connaught, she'd studied antibiotics, penicillin, staphylococcus, and had worked on the prevention of bacterial infections that caused cholera, diphtheria, and whooping cough.

The following morning, as Dr. Farrell rode the streetcar south to the University of Toronto's Knox College on Spadina Avenue where the lab was located, her mind was on more practical matters. She gathered her team together and explained their task.

"I'm wondering whether the rocking technique I devised for whooping cough vaccine would work," she said.

"What technique was that?" asked the newest team member.

"I had a machine made that rocked bottles of whooping cough bacteria. It really sped up bacterial growth. Of course polio is a virus, but now that we can grow it in Medium 199 the same procedure might just work."

"It's worth a try if no one else has any suggestions," said another member of the team.

No one had.

The team set to work accumulating equipment. They needed specially designed machines that would hold five-litre, glass, Povitsky bottles full of sterile liquid Medium 199 containing monkey kidney cells for the virus to grow in. The bottles were placed horizontally on shelves that gently rocked them. The machines had to fit inside incubator rooms that kept the bottles at 37 degrees centigrade.

When they had all the equipment they needed, they began to experiment, looking for the optimum time to leave the bottles of monkey kidney cells multiplying before infecting them with the polio virus. They also had to determine how much virus to add and how long it would take the virus to infect and destroy all the cells. The virus then had to be filtered from the medium and tested. To complicate matters, there were three different types of polio virus that ranged in severity. The mildest could be passed on without the carrier even knowing they had it. The most severe caused the dreaded and sometimes deadly paralysis. Contaminates, such as moulds and bacteria, could grow quickly in the nutrient-filled medium kept at body temperature, so strict procedures had to be used to keep the cultures pure.

Staff also had to take great care while handling the polio virus to avoid infecting themselves. They wore long white lab coats made of thick cotton fabric to protect their clothing. Dr. Farrell, the consummate professional, was always smartly dressed, usually in a business suit with a silk blouse, her stockings and sensibly-heeled shoes visible below her mid-calf length lab coat. She kept her curly hair short and neatly styled. Although she enjoyed playing bridge at the university's Women's Club, and was close to her family, she spent much of her spare time thinking of ways to improve the process they were developing at the lab.

As the weeks passed, results began to look promising and, after some months, they had worked out a technique that gave the required results.

"Good work," Dr. Farrell said to her team, "but it's not over yet. Now we've been asked to produce 3,000 litres of polio virus fluids for the field trials as quickly as we can." We'll have to design labs and incubators, and build more rocking machines.

They all realized this was a huge project, but the scientists at Connaught had faced major challenges like this before.

"One more thing," said Dr. Farrell. "Due to its sensitive nature, given the upcoming Federal Election and public demands for a vaccine, we've been asked to keep our involvement a secret. I know I can rely on you all not to tell anyone that we are producing the fluids for the U.S. field trials."

The research team set to work.

Well aware of the interminable days patients endured while isolated from their families in hospitals and encased in the huge, noisy iron lungs, often in pain and unable to sleep, Dr. Farrell made sure the machines rocked twenty-four hours a day to maximize production. Once a week the latest batch of polio virus was carefully packed in ice inside metal dairy pails and driven to pharmaceutical companies in Detroit and Indianapolis. These companies inactivated the virus in a delicate process using formalin to produce a safe polio vaccine.

One Saturday morning, Dr. Farrell was waiting to be served in her local grocer's shop when a mother entered with her daughter. Dr. Farrell guessed the girl was perhaps 7 or 8 years old. She clumped along awkwardly, her right leg strapped into a leg iron and a built-up shoe. Dr. Farrell thought of the many hours she and her childhood friends had spent playing skipping games and tag. How many more children would be permanently disabled before they had a safe polio vaccine?

By April 1954, there was enough stockpiled vaccine to begin the U.S. field trial. Roughly 1,800,000 children took part. Some were injected with the vaccine, some received a placebo, while others were merely monitored. In May, Canada was given the opportunity to take part and, despite the short notice, Alberta, Manitoba, and Halifax did so, with a national trial planned to begin the following April. Everyone anxiously awaited the U.S. trial results and on April 12, 1955, Jonas Salk's vaccine was declared to be between 60-90% effective, depending upon the type of polio virus, in preventing children from contracting polio. Like the rest of North America, the research team at Connaught was thrilled. The vaccine wasn't perfect but it would prevent thousands of cases of debilitating disease. Dr. Rhodes and his researchers were interviewed and photographed for newspaper articles. The delighted director of Connaught, Dr. Robert Defries, read them a letter he'd received from Dr. Salk thanking them for their Herculean task in preparing the virus, and treated them all to a slap up dinner at the fancy Royal York Hotel.

The euphoria didn't last long, however. By the end of the month, seventy-nine children who had been given the polio vaccine, and over one hundred more that they had been in contact with, went down with the disease. Three quarters of these cases were paralytic and a few of the children died. Dismayed that the vaccine wasn't working and had caused the deaths of healthy children, the U.S. Surgeon General cancelled the entire U.S. vaccine program.

Dr. Farrell's team was glum.

"Do you think Paul Martin will call off the Canadian vaccine trials?" one asked.

"Well, he's had polio," said another. "So has his son. They know what families are going through."

"But they can't risk infecting otherwise healthy children," said the first speaker. "Would you allow your son to be vaccinated if you thought the vaccine might give him polio?"

Dr. Farrell thought of her young nieces and nephews. So far they had escaped the dreaded disease. What would she say if her siblings asked her whether the polio vaccine was safe?

When Mr. Martin announced that he had every confidence in Connaught Laboratories and that the trials would proceed, the Connaught staff cheered.

"Apparently," Dr. Farrell told them, "the seventy-nine U.S. children all received vaccine from Cutter Laboratories in California. In its haste, Cutter didn't properly test all of its batches. Some hadn't been fully inactivated. This is exactly why we follow strict protocol."

Everyone nodded.

"All of Cutter's vaccine has been recalled," Dr. Farrell continued. "Let's hope that the Canadian trial will be successful and restore confidence in Jonas Salk's vaccine."

The following year, Dr. Rhodes showed Dr. Farrell and her team a newspaper article reporting Connaught's delivery of 2.3 million doses of Salk vaccine for Canadian children.

"They're calling your rocking technique the Toronto Technique," he told Dr. Farrell. "We're on our way to eliminating polio. Well done."

"They should have called it the Farrell Technique," Hilda, one of the team's technicians, told Dr. Farrell later when the two of them were alone. "I bet if Dr. Rhodes had invented it, it would be called the Rhodes Technique."

She was likely right, thought Dr. Farrell, but knowing she had helped save thousands of children from the horrors of polio was perhaps satisfaction enough.

Dr. Leone Norwood Farrell died on September 24, 1986, at the age of 82. Her grave in Toronto's Park Lawn Cemetery was unmarked until her relatives added her name to the family's headstone and added an inscription detailing her achievements.

Author's Note

I was inspired to write this story because I was probably among the first batches of children in England to receive the Salk vaccine. I can still picture our family doctor in his surgery taking his large metal syringe out of its black case. I also remember, when I was a little older, medical television dramas about people with polio in iron lungs. My first occupation was a laboratory technician in research labs.

AWAKENING AT AJANTA

INDIAN PAINTER, AMRITA SHER-GIL

Richard Van Holst

The young woman, elegantly clothed in a flame-coloured sari, stood transfixed in the middle of one of the caves.

She was not here with any of the Buddhist groups who had climbed the hill, filled with fervour, to pay homage to the great Gautama at the various temples and monasteries which had been carved from the bare rockface centuries ago. Neither had she come with any of the groups of boisterous Indians, there merely because their friends had recommended it and seemingly unable to restrain their restless children from scrambling all over the statues or swarming among the pillars. Nor was she one of those vapid Western tourists who, heroically overcoming their barely disguised aversion to the natives, had come to gawk at some fascinating examples of exotic art from the "Mystic East". She felt as though she were still in the shadows, groping toward her purpose, but her instincts told her that soon it would become very clear.

Despite her outward appearance of tranquility, Amrita was alert. Eventually she began to approach the murals; she had seen them before, but only in Gladstone Solomon's book on Ajanta. The grainy photographs and poor reproductions did not even begin to do justice to the originals. She would take a step or two, gazing up and around; her large brown eyes, ringed with kohl, swooped swallow-like from detail to detail, taking in the features of the frescoes, statues and pillars. The tourists and devotees seemed to respect her desire for privacy.

Miraculously they did not crowd her too much, or peer over her shoulder as she made some sketches.

What Amrita did not realize, as she stared about and then sketched busily, was that Barada Ukil was actually making himself useful for a change by keeping the other visitors at bay. Even though she despised most of the art of the Bengal school which he headed, he himself was not a bad sort, when it came down to it. After a few brief conversations with her, his interest had been sparked and he had officiously appointed himself her escort on this journey. At present, he was preserving what he thought was a discreet silence; she wished only that he would not keep favouring her with these secretive syco-phantic simpers and obsequious smiles. He would probably want to look at her sketches and ask her in that irritatingly self-important man-ner of his what she intended to make of them. She'd never had her sister's talent for flirting with those she didn't really care for. Indu would not only have encouraged Ukil's idiotic ways, she would have had him on the verge of proposing marriage in no time. Amrita, on the contrary, could never dissemble like that. When she liked a man, she was forthright enough to make her feelings known. And when she despised a man the way she did this one, well, she had to restrain her-self from insulting him. The only thing that stopped her now, frankly, was the fact that he might be able to help her find buyers for some of her paintings.

But so annoying he was! Yesterday afternoon, for instance, he'd insisted on taking a photograph of her at the entrance to one of the caves. Fussily, he'd forced her into one of those studied poses which was meant to make her look casually sophisticated; in reality she'd had a hard time maintaining a prettily downcast gaze and a coy little half-smile for him. Her father who, in spite of his absent-minded air, had a much keener eye and better sense of who she was, would have known exactly how to place her so that the lighting would be to her best advantage and so that her eyes would meet the viewer's gaze directly.

All these petty frustrations were ultimately of little importance though, because she was here! Starting from Bombay and winding their way through the south of India, she and Ukil had paused at the caves of Ellora a few days ago; she had been mightily impressed with their solemn silence. However, on arriving at Ajanta, she knew that the previous stop had been but a sort of preamble. She felt as if she were a princess who, accompanied by a lowly footman, had stepped from the ante-chamber of a palace into its throne room.

She still found it hard to believe how far she had come, despite the fact that she was a veteran of voyages. Conceived in the city of Lahore where her parents had met and married, she had, even while in the womb, crossed oceans and continents to be born in her mother's home in the old city of Buda in Hungary. At a young age she had sailed back to India and settled with her family in their home at Simla in the northern state of Himachal Pradesh, only to migrate to Europe once again in order to attend various prestigious art schools.

But she had crossed more than miles and waves; she had bridged worlds and cultures, finally leaving the West and its static art traditions behind to seek her true and lasting homeland. She had returned at last like a prodigal child to Mother India. During the years she'd passed in Simla, Amrita had been cocooned in a world of music, dance and language lessons. But this time, on returning, she had seen the land and its people with adult eyes. And what had stricken her to the heart was the sadness and misery of so many of them. She had ached for them and desired to express her emotions on canvas.

She had always been steered by her emotions, as the sea-winds blow the sails of a ship. She had made her first drawings in response to the stories her mother had told her. Her illustrations, done in coloured pencil, were a child's attempts to retell in brilliant yellows and greens, fairy tales about blonde princesses wandering in the woods, only to happen upon friendly creatures, handsome princes or enchanted castles where their yearnings for an idyllic life would be fulfilled. Later, as she entered puberty, her drawings took on a decidedly more melodramatic and erotic cast. And at l'Ecole des Beaux Arts, with a more expert knowledge of how to portray the female anatomy, she had actually done a portrait of herself as one of Paul Gauguin's Tahitian nudes!

Even Gauguin might have raised an eyebrow at the sheer lasciviousness of the figures before her in the caves of Ajanta. Here, beside exotic lotus-ponds, were narrow-waisted dancing girls, hips frozen in mid-undulation, bestowing alluring glances upon the males in their audience. Those noblemen who were not ogling the performers dallied, bare-chested, with bejewelled ranis who seemed to receive the amorous overtures of their admirers with great complacency and very little resistance. Amrita gazed, entranced, and then continued to sketch.

The rounded lines on the paper before her did not look like much; they were little more than contours, albeit rounded and pendulous ones. But she knew there was a kernel of substance hidden within them. Something of the sensuousness of the painted figures had mysteriously been transferred to the page, although much simplified and pared to bare essentials.

Moving on, she viewed a scene which was set shortly after the enlightenment of the Buddha. Here he was in full view, tranquilly seated with his hands close to his chest, one palm extended out and the other upward in the stylized pose which meant he was preaching to the throng of disciples. Their faces a study in concentration – their dark robes themselves exuding a sense of devotion – they hung breathlessly on his every word, as attentive as St. Francis' birds.

It had not been possible to bring the paints necessary to do justice to the colours which shimmered on the murals. But colour was something that had never daunted Amrita. Flesh tones were old friends from her days in France, where she had blended various paints to match her own complexion or that of her models. In Florence she had revelled with the Italian masters in the profusion of vibrant colours. Here in India she had been drawn to the astonishing variety of skin tones in those around her, which changed it seemed, as she travelled from city to city. And then, of course, there were the fabrics whose luxuriance equalled anything depicted by the Renaissance; the indigos matched the bluest azures of Raphael; the reds rivalled the richest cardinals' robes, and the saffrons outshone the burnished golds of the haloes of Giotto's angels. But the murals of Ajanta were quite a different matter. Her imagination might have been playing tricks, but the colours here – despite the fact that they were quite muted – glowed slightly as if backlit by candle-flame.

Amrita was not by any means an adept of meditation, Buddhist or otherwise. Even the discipline required to recite the rosary was something she had rebelled against in the convent school she'd briefly attended. Yet now she felt her soul distancing itself from its petty concerns and daily problems. As she focussed on the figures of the frescoes, her mind searched avidly for insight as to what it all meant.

For her, it was not the story itself that was of prime importance here. Her father, who had studied many religions, said that temptation resisted and virtue rewarded by revelation were motifs that appeared in many religions. But that was the point! It was the *pattern* that mattered. And this was a lesson she wished she could teach to some of the artists whom Ukil favoured so much; they tried too hard to tell a story, in antiquated, saccharine and disgustingly unsubtle ways.

She began to see how the scenes of the whole mural fit together. The Temptation of Mara, which might have evoked the admiration of Hieronymus Bosch himself, was in stark contrast to the Sermon of the Buddha, yet there were subtle correlations and continuities that flowed between them. For one thing, there were two audiences in contemplation, even though the one was dissipated and the other devout. On a more abstract level, the skin tones of the figures were alike, the forms of the faces similar. Lush flowers and ornamental animals could be found in both scenes. She began to detect patterns in jewelry, folds in robes. Then, ovals and circles began to coalesce in patterned formation. At some point a subtle spark seemed to travel though them. It was almost as if some spell, which had forced them to slumber motionless on the walls, had finally been broken and now they were stretching themselves to recover the circulation in drowsy limbs. Amrita could almost have sworn that they were moving, ever so slowly, in a sedate and measured dance.

It was not as if she were receiving a divine revelation. No deity thundered from the clouds; no ethereal vision smiled from some niche in the cave. No heavenly messenger directed her to recite mysteries or even to depict them on the pad of paper she carried about. And yet, she felt as if an ember, lodged deep within her heart, dormant until that moment, had received a quickening breath and had begun to glow with renewed vigour. She knew that the whole course of her life and her artistic career had been altered somehow. At l'Ecole des Beaux-Arts, Papa Simon, as she called her teacher, had treated her kindly. He had not tried to force her to paint his way, as the teacher in Florence had done. He'd allowed her to develop her talent at her own pace and in her own style. The other students had accepted her and she had even won an award for one of her portraits. Yet, she'd had the sense of being a little different, of not quite fitting. So she had worked hard to prove her worth – to herself as much as to them. She'd been put through her paces like a horse at a show; she'd mastered techniques and genres. As a result she had executed many portraits, landscapes and still lifes which were deserving of notice – and many that were not.

However, she had come home now – home to Mother India. She belonged here, with these people in the caves, with the fruit vendors on the street corners, with the child brides and the women in purdah, with the story tellers in the bazaars, the children, the animals, trees and seascapes. And she would find a way to immortalize their beauty and their essence on her canvas.

Barada Ukil did not know exactly what had happened to her. He had no way of realizing that the scales had fallen from her eyes. It would take some time before she could give adequate expression to the change that had been wrought in her. But even he sensed, in his dim way, that something momentous had taken place. For now, Amrita stepped up to him with a more benevolent expression than she'd ever offered him before. She gave him her pencils and paper to carry, and, smiling, bade him follow her out of the cave into the incandescent afternoon.

Author's Note

I had never heard of the Indian artist Amrita Sher-Gil until she was mentioned to me by Bernadette Rule, who learned of her from her sister Bridget, an artist in her own right. Amrita is not as well known as she should be beyond the borders of her own country – or perhaps that should be countries – for her complexity stems from the fact that she belonged to both East and West and spent much of her life trying to make sense of that.

Born in Hungary to a Sikh father and a Christian mother of Jewish descent, she moved back to India at a young age. Her early attempts at drawing and painting drew the attention of both her family and her teachers, who decided she must go to Europe for training in art. Eventually she ended up in Paris, at L'Ecole des Beaux Arts, where she won an award. However she began to yearn for India, taking it as her mission to find a way of making art that was authentically Indian and to unlearn the training she had received in the West. (Whether she achieved that or not, is another question.) At the same time, she was highly critical of much of what the Indian artists of her own day were doing. Her own oeuvre, considered bizarre by some, was revolutionary. Before long she was a celebrity, winning awards, arranging exhibitions, giving talks and writing articles on Indian art. She married a Hungarian cousin, Victor Egan, who was a medical doctor, and shared much happiness and hardship with him. Tragically, her life was brought to an abrupt close by a sudden illness at the age of twenty-eight.

For more information, I would recommend *Amrita Sher-Gil: A Self-Portrait in Letters and Writings*, a two-volume collection of her written work, supplemented by stunning colour illustrations of her art. The Amrita who emerged from those pages was very conscious of her own limits and talents. She was sensitive, warm, caring, often ironic and sarcastic, but always passionate about life, family and art. It is my hope that this brief fictional sketch reflects something of her vibrant spirit and helps spread her fame outside of India, where she is revered today.

ANOTHER TWIST OF THE DOUBLE HELIX

ROSALIND FRANKLIN, SCIENTIST WHO DISCOVERED
THE SHAPE OF DNA

Ellen S. Jaffe

The scent of chestnut blossoms coming into flower wafted into Rosalind's room as she lay in her hospital bed at the Royal Marsden. She could almost see her dear flat around the corner at Drayton Gardens, and wished she could be there, snug in her own bed if she wasn't well enough to work in her lab. It had been a cold March but April was warming, and the morning sun brightened the white room and cast rainbows on the walls. Through the slightly open window, she could hear the birds.

Rosalind looked at the photograph by her bed: herself, her friend Don Caspar, and their mutual friend Richard in the Alps last summer – was it only last July? She longed to be back there, picnicking in a flowered meadow, looking at the massive, snowy peak of the Matterhorn. She thought of all the mountains she loved to climb: the Alps, the glaciers in Norway, the Rockies.

She and Don had gone climbing in the Rockies, near his home in Colorado, deepening the friendship that had begun when he started working in her lab in London. They had met at the wrong time. The summer of the Rockies, 1956, just two years ago, was the summer the cancer began to make its presence known, an insidious enemy. This enemy was more vicious to her personally than the world war, which had ended eleven years ago and killed so many, destroyed so much.

Notes for an unfinished paper on the polio virus, the project she was working on now, lay on the table beside her bed. She had one more thought, an idea hanging by a thread, but it was such an effort to pick up her pencil. Yet she had to do it. At least she could add a few words to make the concept clearer.

Ironic, she thought, as she lay back down on her pillow. The cells she had studied all her life were now running amok, breaking their orderly patterns, using their secret codes to take over her life. Her ovaries, with eggs that could have grown into an embryo, a fetus, a newborn infant with its own miraculous and specific genetic information, were now filled with cancer cells growing wild – destroying, not creating.

Rosalind closed her eyes, letting the sun's rays warm her face. The same sun would be shining in the windows of her flat, illuminating her new orange cushions. She had signed a three-year renewal of her lease last spring, an affirmation she would get better, whether through medicine or her own will to live. There was so much to look forward to: the Indiana conference on viruses in the summer; perhaps another trip to the Rockies. And her research team had just been given funding to go to a new lab at Cambridge – she belonged there with them, with her good friend and colleague Aaron Klug and all the others.

Just before coming back to the hospital – a week ago? longer? – she'd gone to her parents' house to celebrate her father's sixty-fourth birthday. She had tried to be happy, but shuddered each time her mother looked at her with those tearful eyes. Her parents had always wanted her to stay with them while she was recovering from surgery, or was just too ill to stay at the flat, but she preferred sleeping at her brother Roland's house, playing with his children, having space to herself. That night, however, she'd felt well enough to stay with her parents, enjoying their company, their talk around the kitchen table. The next morning her father had to bring her back here, to the hospital.

She remembered the refugees from Germany, Poland, Lithuania, Hungary who had gathered in her parents' kitchen before the war, the ones who could see what was coming, and had the courage – and the luck – to escape. There were shadows in their eyes when they talked about the people who stayed behind. She remembered one young writer with shaking hands who told her father how fortunate it was that the Franklin family had come to England from Europe when they did, almost two hundred years before, and made a good life here. "And now fate has brought us together."

Then there were the few who came after the war, thin, terrified, with blue numbers like veins on their arms. A malicious code. As a scientist, as well as a human being, she wondered how people could do this – distort reality so much that they killed people who seemed "different," when the underlying genetic material of all homo sapiens was so much the same, just arranged in slightly different patterns. What was the pattern that created Nazis?

At Cambridge, and then later at Kings', she hadn't been killed for being Jewish, nor for being a woman, but her career was certainly threatened by both. Being a woman was worse in that atmosphere, much worse. They still had separate common rooms for men and women at Kings' – the women's much shabbier than the men's. And only a year or so ago, she'd been called "my dear" when applying for yet another grant.

She thought of Maurice Wilkins, assistant director of the lab at King's, who had always seemed to undermine her work. She'd felt disparaged, alone – and then treated as too emotional when she tried to fight back. You couldn't have an honest discussion or argument with him, and that's what science was all about. She liked men with whom she could debate fiercely and still be friends. She knew what Wilkins had called her, "the dark lady of DNA". And she knew that Watson and some of the others called her "Rosy" behind her back. Rosy, indeed! Don had called her Ros – but that was different. They were friends. Interesting that the closest male friends she'd had were Jewish, even though they didn't know it when they first met.

She had worked hard on the x-ray photographs of crystallized DNA – both the A and B forms – trying to find the key, trying to do her best in a lab where she never felt at home. Her student, Gosling, had been a great help. And she was the one who had first seen that the sugar-phosphate molecule had to be on the outside of the DNA structure. Then Crick and Watson, working at the Cavendish lab in Cambridge, had taken the crucial next steps, intuiting the structure of the double-helix, like the railings of a spiral staircase, with matching base pairs lined up between them. A great achievement – but it was almost as if they had seen her photographs, especially that beautiful Number 51 of B-DNA, and developed their model from that. How could that have happened? She'd once thought someone was reading her notebooks. And the photographs were available in the lab. Gosling could have shown them to Wilkins. Could Wilkins have shown them to Watson on one of his visits to London? Maybe that day Watson had popped into her office unexpectedly, upsetting her with his barrage of words...

There had been such competition back then, when they were all working toward the same goal, searching for something close to truth.

That was several years ago, but the memory still hurt. She fell into a spasm of painful coughing.

Well, she had moved on, found a real home in Bernal's lab at Birkbeck College. It was still in London but with a much more welcoming atmosphere and colleagues she valued. There she had done work she loved: the tobacco-mosaic virus, and now polio. Each discovery led to more questions, more discoveries.

Rosalind knew she had accomplished a great deal, even if she could have done much more. She loved the world of cells, molecules, the almost unbelievably small Angstrom units of crystals. She trusted the precision of photography, the testing of hypotheses and finding evidence. Still, she worried about the wider world – people who did not have enough to eat, people who believed that the possibility of victory was reason enough to go to war. Yet the world itself was so beautiful. She remembered all the places she had travelled, alone and with friends. She'd even become friends with Francis Crick and his wife Odile, travelled with them, stayed in their home.

Her greatest sadness now was that she would never go to her laboratory again, never study her beautiful photographs, never think more deeply about their crystalline puzzles, their mysteries, never make more discoveries about their codes. DNA was something like the enigma codes Alan Turing worked on during the last war. His suicide four years ago had shaken her.

Alan's codes were external, while the DNA, RNA, and viruses she was working on were *inside* the body, the secret language that coded and expressed who each person would become. Who knew where this research could go? She wasn't forty yet. If only she had another thirty or forty years to work and learn – or even twenty. Even ten. "If I had only one more year, that would be sufficient," she thought, the words of *Dayenu*, the old Passover song, haunting her. If God had only done this miracle but not that – *"if he had split the sea for us, but not led us through it on dry land, or if He had supplied our needs in the desert for forty years but not fed us manna – it would have been sufficient."* One more year.

But life followed its own chaotic pattern. If – by a miracle – she could live to the year 2000, she would be eighty then, still able to work if she stayed healthy. What amazing things could she accomplish?

What would the world be like in 2000? Maybe, using her own research and that of her colleagues, they could find the cure for cancer, find ways to stop rogue information from taking over the cell's controls. Maybe the world would even be at peace, no more camps and gas chambers, no more atom bombs, no more prejudices, dividing people. People like Alan would not have to suffer for being who they were.

She didn't think that she had become ill directly through her work, the way radium had affected Madame Curie. Rosalind had been fourteen when Marie Curie died, already sure she wanted to be a scientist and old enough to mourn her loss. But now she wondered... she hadn't been too careful with radiation in the Paris laboratory. Or maybe she was born with the genetic material for ovarian cancer already lurking there in her body. She had heard of a few distant relatives, great-aunts and older cousins, who had this cancer, but no one close to her.

Marie Curie had been the first woman to receive the Nobel Prize – not only once, but twice – first in physics, then in chemistry. No English woman had yet won, though Rosalind thought that Dorothy Crowfoot Hodgson, with her expertise in crystallography, certainly had a good chance. When she'd worked in Paris, she found that women scientists and intellectuals were much more respected in France than in England, and treated as equal to men. Maybe that was one reason she had loved her four years there – in addition to Paris itself. The Europeans had such a different attitude to life.

At least this was the twentieth century, not the nineteenth or earlier, when things were even harder for women. She thought of Emilie du Chatelaine, Voltaire's mistress – a physicist and mathematician in her own right. She had never gone to university but through her own studies, and the help of Voltaire, she taught herself math, physics, and other sciences, well enough to translate and critique Leibnitz and Newton. She struggled to finish her translation of Leibnitz, working until just before going into labour with her third child, an unexpected event when she was forty-three, her two older children already grown. Emilie knew that "a woman of forty cannot survive this," and died of infection soon after the child was born. Whatever happened to that baby? Rosalind wondered. Somewhere she had read it was a daughter.

Rosalind herself had wanted to focus on her work, not raise a family. She didn't have that "natural" call to motherhood that most women seemed to have, including her mother, her brother's wives, and some of her friends. She loved all *their* children, enjoyed getting down on the floor and playing with them, taking them for walks, showing them leaves and caterpillars. Wasn't that enough?

Enough thinking! She flung back the blankets in a sudden burst, and her arm jerked, knocking over the glass of water on the table. The glass broke and water puddled on the floor. She scrunched back her tears. If she'd had children and then got cancer, they would be left motherless, like Emilie du Chatelaine's daughter. What purpose would that have served?

As for the Nobel, she worked in science for the love of it – but recognition would be nice, too. She knew they did not award the Nobel posthumously.

On her bedside table, beside the photograph of the Alps, was a notice about a fellowship in Venezuela. She had been so determined to get well, to go there. Perhaps a warmer climate and being away from the familiarity and the tensions of England would help. She had even thought of emigrating to Israel when she had gone there for a conference, but the political climate was too restrictive. Maybe if she had stayed in Paris, her life would have been different.

O

There was a knock on her door, and a figure entered, carrying the scent of Paris with him. Paris. I must be dreaming, she thought. Mering... here?

Jacques Mering, her former boss from the *laboratoire* by the Seine, just after the war. Four of the happiest, richest years in her life, despite the after-war scarcities. For a moment she was back in that lab, analyzing and photographing coal, or cycling by the river, buying *baguettes*, walking in the woods on Sunday mornings to gather morels. For a moment... then she saw him standing by her bed in this white room.

He touched her face gently and kissed her cheek, stirring long-submerged, unspoken feelings. But his touch was tender, like that of one of her brothers. *"Bonjour, mon p'tit."*

She murmured something. French still came easily to her, but her voice was too soft now, too weak for the proper accent and rapid rhythm that she enjoyed. She did not like to see the tears in his dark eyes, usually so sharp and intense. *"Quel dommage."* Silently, he cleared up the broken glass and spilled water, then sat by her bedside, chatting of this and that, until she dozed off. She did not hear him leave.

O

Rosalind woke, hot, sweating, and in pain, when the nice nurse, Felicity, entered with her medicine. Today she did not want to be sedated. She wanted to observe what was happening, what would be happening. She held the blue pill under her tongue instead of swallowing it, then spit it back into her hand when the nurse turned her back to fill the water glass. Pain and nausea almost choked her as she spit.

Then a siren ripped through the air, as if it were right inside her. "The bombs.... Luftwaffe.... have to get to the shelter...." she murmured.

"No, love, that's just the ambulance. Sounds like it's right here in the room with us, it does. Gives me the shivers, too, even though the war's been over for years. I was in my first year of nursing back when the Blitz started. Saw enough to last me a lifetime. I'll never get used to an ambulance siren again. Even if they do make it sound less like the air raids." Felicity's East-End accent was as comforting as a hot cup of tea. She smoothed the sheets around Rosalind's face, stroked her hair gently, and left. Rosalind slipped the blue tablet under the pillow. Her hair needed washing and brushing, she thought, as she pushed it back, out of her eyes.

She could still feel Mering's touch on her face. Had he really been there to see her, just a few moments ago? Had she been in love with him in Paris? Or with anyone? Perhaps Don? She would have liked a relationship like the one Emilie had with Voltaire, studying and working together, building a house in the country for scientific research and pleasure, with visitors coming and going. Just as Emilie worked into the night, by candlelight, to finish her translation before she would die in childbirth, Rosalind reached again for the notebook and pencil on the table by the bed. She started to jot down some notes, then her writing wavered and the pencil dropped from her fingers onto the blanket. She fell back onto the pillow.

Still, she went on thinking, visualizing new experiments, new lines of research, feeling her mind at play. This was when she felt most herself. She had the odd thought-flash that her ideas were her children – the only children she would ever have. She did not want to desert them now. Besides, they would not desert her. They rushed in, helter-skelter at first, then more orderly, like a parade – no, more like mountain climbers, using ropes and climbing equipment to scale a rough, craggy face, finding a new path, exploring uncharted territory, excited and yet careful. She was sorry they were about to be orphaned.

Her Cambridge friend Peggy, now a medical physicist at the Marsden, stopped by to say hello. "Let's open the window a little wider so you can feel the nice spring breeze," she said. "Bet you're looking forward to being outside again." She turned away from Rosalind and walked across the room. Rosalind watched her lift the heavy window-sash and then gaze, for a long moment, at the trees.

Then Peggy returned, offering a glass, a small mouthful. "Here's some ice to suck on." Rosalind sucked obediently. The cold felt good on her lips and tongue. Peggy left, and through the window, Rosalind could hear robins and sparrows and smell the soft air. She closed her eyes again. When she opened them, she saw she was not alone. Her younger sister Jennifer was there, holding her hand. She felt a cool cloth on her forehead, her wrists, inside her elbows.

Jennifer had brought bright yellow and pink tulips to cheer her up. The colours warmed her but they also hurt her heart. She wouldn't go out into the gardens again where the tulips were blooming freely in the earth, in great arrays. Unlike them, these tulips in their vase would fade quickly, droop and die. This touch of colour made her see how white the room was. The tulips opened like hungry mouths, baby birds demanding food, or stars in the sky. What strange thoughts! If she were a poet, like that American woman Sylvia she'd met at a reception at Newnham College a couple of years ago, she could try to write about this feeling. But her writing had always taken another direction; she would write about the patterns of the tulips, the genetics that determined their shapes and colours.

She was cold now, despite the sunshine, a cold that felt as though her body was turning to ice. Water expanded when it froze, she thought randomly. Crystals. The spiralling shapes of the double-helix DNA, and the hollow structure of the tobacco mosaic virus, RNA woven like thread into its protein shell. Elegant but simple, the world creating itself, becoming visible under powerful microscopes, developing inside her photographs. And then there was the world writ large. Amazing, ancient mountains, containing their own secrets. Alpine flowers, the colour of red and yellow dyes. Oceans, coal, hidden fossils. All the things of this world, with her life – each person's life – a minute but vital part of the whole pattern.

The photograph beside her bed beckoned. She felt the thrill of climbing, higher and higher, then finding a place to rest, an aerie in the cliffs. You could wake up at night and see the stars.

She motioned to Jennifer to give her another blanket, and then to put on her sweater, the azure-blue cashmere one she had bought in Paris on her last trip. She sank into its soft warmth.

Author's Note

I first heard about Rosalind Franklin (July 25, 1920–April 16, 1958) several years ago, and became interested in her story: a woman scientist whose crucial work on developing the structure of DNA was not given due recognition at the time, and a woman who died young from ovarian cancer.

She was from an extensive, well-to-do British-Jewish family which encouraged education, and she became a crystallographer, an experimental scientist who used x-ray photography of crystals to explore and make discoveries. She was considered a careful, excellent scientist; her work on various subjects has many contemporary applications.

It is known that one or more of her x-ray photographs of the DNA molecule (number 51 in particular) was shown to James Watson, without her knowledge or permission, by her colleague Maurice Wilkins, with whom she had a difficult professional relationship. This led to Watson and Francis Crick making the intuitive leap to the double-helix structure of DNA, something Rosalind had not done.

I have set the story at the end of Rosalind's life. Most details are drawn from fact (including the hospital visits of Mering and Peggy), with a few exceptions: the nurse "Felicity" is my invention; I don't know if Rosalind had a connection with Alan Turing but I am sure she knew about his work and life; she probably knew about Emilie du Chatelaine; there is no record that she met Sylvia Plath, but Plath and her husband Ted Hughes were at Cambridge for several months in 1956, and since Rosalind did her first degree at Newnham College, Cambridge, a meeting was not impossible. I love Plath's poem "Tulips," ("The tulips are too red in the first place, they hurt me"), published posthumously in 1965, so I added a gift of spring tulips and made this imaginative link.

Rosalind Franklin has never been completely forgotten. James Watson wrote disparagingly of her in his book *The Double Helix,* although he acknowledged the importance of her photographs; he added an epilogue apologizing for his earlier "wrong" perceptions and praising her "superb" scientific work and her "courage and integrity". Her scientific achievements have been increasingly recognized in recent years. There are several excellent biographies, including one by her younger sister, Jennifer, written when Jennifer was 84. In addition, several scientific buildings and institutions in Great Britain have been named for her.

VIOLA IRENE DESMOND

CANADIAN CIVIL RIGHTS ACTIVIST

John Corvese

Injustice anywhere is a threat to justice everywhere.

MARTIN LUTHER KING JR.

The train from Montreal pulled into Grand Central Station in New York City. I recall the air being cool as it was late in the fall of 1963. I had just graduated from McGill University in a general arts program and, as a new reporter for *The Montreal Star,* had been assigned to interview a Canadian lady now residing in New York. I found the immense city overwhelming. A taxi delivered me to the entrance of her apartment building. The building was old and quite small. I took a deep breath. I didn't want to mess up my first major assignment. No doorman appeared to assist me. I pushed the buzzer on the number of the apartment I had been given.

"Is that you Mr. Beaudry?" a sweet elderly voice answered the intercom.

"Yes, it's Robert Beaudry of *The Montreal Star*!"

A short, white-haired, grandmotherly lady answered the door.

"Please come in, Mr. Beaudry. I'm Wanda Robson. My sister is in the parlour and anxious to see you."

Mrs. Robson led me into the room they called the parlour. There wasn't much space in the modest apartment, crowded as it was with furniture. I began to feel a bit claustrophobic. I guess I expected the lady to be living in more luxurious surroundings. Viola Irene Davis

Desmond sat in a straight-backed chair, her elegant posture above reproach. Being a former beautician she had a reputation for dressing impeccably. I noticed her black hair with its streaks of grey had been carefully coiffed. She radiated an air of serenity and humility. I was surprised by how short she was – less than five feet, I figured. She appeared pale and quite fragile, as though the slightest breeze could blow her away. A smile creased her face in welcome.

"I'll go make us some tea to have with my fresh-baked scones," Mrs. Robson said as she ambled off to the kitchen.

"Please sit down, Mr. Beaudry."

"Robert, please."

"And you may call me Viola.

"So what brings you here?"

"I have been sent to interview you because *The Montreal Star* is running a series of articles on extraordinary Canadian women."

"I hardly consider myself extraordinary. Tell me about yourself."

It took me by surprise that the person being interviewed should ask me questions, although my research indicated that it was in the nature of the lady to express an interest in the people around her. I told her about my graduation from McGill, my parents and home, and my desire to become a writer of historical novels. If she was offended to be interviewed by such a junior reporter, she did not express it.

"So you're an only child. I was born in 1914, the fifth child in a family of fifteen children."

"Were your parents farmers?" I asked.

"No! It was common in those days to have large families. My parents had money and made sure we received an education. That was important to them. Of course an education then meant graduating from high school. Few people, including white people, continued on to university."

" I understand you were quite the entrepreneur?"

"There were few opportunities open to black women in Nova Scotia. Being of African descent, I wasn't allowed to train to become a beautician. I left Halifax and went to Montreal, Atlantic City and then New York, where I trained under the guidance of the legendary Madame C. J. Walker, the first African-American female millionaire. I returned to Halifax filled with ambition. I would become the first African-Canadian female millionaire! I opened my beauty salon and a school in Halifax: The Desmond School of Beauty Culture; and I created my own line of cosmetics specifically designed for black women: Vi's Beauty Products. I marketed these myself, driving around Nova Scotia in my own car. I couldn't afford courier service."

I was frantically scribbling down everything she had been telling me. Perhaps I should have brought a tape recorder. Such is the naivety of youth. She obviously noticed my struggle.

"Robert, I will try to speak more slowly. It is just that I get excited when I talk about those days, when I had so much promise ahead of me."

At that moment her sister re-entered the room carrying a tray loaded with delicious smelling scones and tea. She placed the tray on the coffee table and arranged plates, sugar, milk, cups and saucers.

"Vi, I'll let you do the honours. Mr. Beaudry, I expect you to eat several of my scones. They go well with the whipped cream and jam. I'm going to pack some scones and sandwiches for you to take back with you on the train." And with that Mrs. Robson returned to the kitchen.

Viola poured us each a cup of tea. I munched on her sister's mouth-watering, feather-light scones.

"Your sister is very thoughtful and kind," I said.

Viola nodded, cradled her cup of tea, sat back in the chair and reminisced at a slower pace.

"On November 8, 1946, while driving to an appointment, my car broke down in New Glasgow. The mechanic said it would be a few hours before he could finish repairing it, as he needed to get a part. To pass the time I decided to go and watch a movie. I rarely had time to relax as I dashed off here and there on my deliveries and other business matters. I walked over to the Roseland Theatre. I still remember the movie, *Dark Mirror*, starring my favourite actress, Olivia de

Havilland, opposite Lew Ayres. In Halifax people of colour could sit anywhere in the theatre. (You should know that in my lifetime I'd had little exposure to discrimination, as my mother usually did the shopping and attended to family needs.) I asked the young girl in the glass booth for a ticket and paid the money she requested.

"I intended to sit on the ground floor, as it was difficult for me to climb stairs because of my hip. Also, with my poor eyesight I liked to sit close to the screen. I entered the theatre and sat in an aisle seat. I started to relax as the credits rolled; then a female usher nudged me and said I could not sit there as I had a ticket for the balcony. I thought a mistake had been made and went back to the ticket booth prepared to pay for a ground floor ticket. But the clerk refused to sell me a ticket for the ground floor saying, 'I'm not permitted to sell downstairs tickets to you people.' She said, '*You people* have to sit in the balcony.' The offensive and degrading words *not permitted* and *you people* upset my usually placid personality. We were not troublemakers in my family. I realized I had walked into a situation I had never experienced before. Confused and humiliated, I left money on the counter and went back to my seat.

"The manager was called Henry MacNeil, a fussy little man quite full of his self-importance. He was irate and told me the theatre had the right to *refuse admission to any objectionable person*. He then fled the theatre to summon the police.

"Robert, are you alright?"

I had stopped writing, being completely absorbed and somewhat shocked by what I had been hearing. "Was there a sign posted that 'you people' were not allowed to sit on the ground floor?"

"Of course not! Racial segregation in Canada was subtle. Nothing was ever written down and there were no Jim Crow laws, as in the United States. These things were simply understood.

"MacNeil came back with a police officer. They demanded I move. I refused. So they grabbed my arms roughly and dragged me from the seat, further injuring my hip. I weigh about ninety-five pounds. I went limp, as I had no intention of making it easy for them. In the scuffle my purse fell and a shoe was dragged off. When I came to the doorway I put my hands out to hold onto the frame. They pried my fingers off. I wasn't going willingly. I had no intention of going willingly. They had to call a taxi to take me to jail. While we waited for it, a kind woman picked up and handed to me my purse and missing shoe. MacNeil ran off to get an arrest warrant from a judge.

"They put me into a cell. The other cells filled up with male drunks who shouted obscenities at me. I sat throughout the night on the bench, still wearing my white gloves. I filled the time working on my appointment book and organizing my purse. I had to focus on something. I was terribly afraid, but was also determined to maintain my dignity. People thought I wore the white gloves to look elegant and chic. That was part of it, but the truth is my hands were rough from years of handling beautician chemicals.

"They left me in that cell for twelve hours."

"Did they get you a lawyer?" I asked.

Viola shook her head.

"The next day they took me to the court. I was sleep-deprived and disoriented. I didn't know my rights. I could have asked for a postponement, called a lawyer and cross-examined Henry MacNeil and the other witnesses from the theatre who gave evidence. They all said I had purchased an upstairs balcony ticket and then took a seat downstairs. By paying only the cheaper balcony ticket, I had defrauded the provincial government of the difference in the amount of the amusement tax charged. The tax was three cents downstairs, and two cents upstairs. That was their case against me.

"The magistrate asked me, 'Mrs. Desmond, is this true?'

"I gave him my account of what happened, and he said, 'Well, you didn't pay the amusement tax.'

"I said, 'I tried to. I offered. It was refused.'

"He then asked me if I had any questions. I did not realize until later that he meant did I have any questions of the witnesses. So the witnesses were never cross-examined. I was convicted of cheating the province out of one cent, the difference in the tax between a ground floor seat and a balcony seat. No mention was made of racial discrimination. I was sentenced to thirty days in jail, or a twenty dollar fine plus six dollars in court costs. I paid the fine. The six dollars in court costs went to the manager of the theatre, Henry MacNeil, for acting as prosecutor. How ironic! He made money throwing a black woman out of his theatre. Of course I did not receive a refund for the ticket I never used. I was a black woman and was denied the protection I expected from the police, the prosecutors, the judges and the courts. I still carry that conviction with me wherever I go.

"I found out much later that the *Toronto Star* interviewed Henry MacNeil about the incident. MacNeil maintained there was no official stipulation that a black person could not sit on the main floor. The article quoted him as follows: 'It was customary for black persons to sit together on the balcony.'

"Embittered and ashamed I drove back to Halifax and didn't continue my round of deliveries."

"I understand you appealed the conviction to The Supreme Court of Nova Scotia."

"Not right away. The doctor who treated my hip injury and bruises urged me to appeal. He was a skilled black physician, Dr. Alfred E. Waddell. He was from Trinidad and, because of his colour, forbidden to see patients at Victoria General Hospital in Halifax.

"My husband objected to me taking the matter any further. He told me to, 'Take it to the Lord with a prayer.'

"Carrie Best, the founder of The African-Canadian newspaper, *The Clarion,* took a special interest in the case and published what had happened to me. The recently organized Nova Scotia Association for the Advancement of Coloured People took up the cause. My lawyer, Fredrick Bisset, was white, as there were no black lawyers. Mr. Bisset tried his best, but he was out of his depth. We missed the limitation period to appeal the conviction under The Theatres Act. The four judges of the Supreme Court, all white males, upheld the original conviction on the basis of the fact I failed to pay the one-cent tax. The title of the court case, *The King v. Desmond* (1947) reveals the imbalance of power. How could little Viola be expected to fight the King? One judge commented on the theatre's racist policy, but it played no role in the decision. In other words, let's keep our racist policies in the dark. We are racists, but we are not racists is a form of Doublethink. Unlike Canada, the Americans breathed in racism with their Jim Crow laws in its pure form, undiluted by any hypocrisy."

"Abraham Lincoln?"

Viola smiled, "Almost word for word."

"But things did change. You caused things to change," I said.

"Robert, you must realize it was 1946 and our country had just fought and won a terrible war at great cost in lives and money. It took time. My experience brought racism into the light. Members of the responsible white population realized they were engaged in the same behaviour that Canadians had fought against. The culture of discrimination against minorities became unsustainable. By 1954 discrimination in any form in Nova Scotia was made illegal by provincial legislation."

"They call you Canada's Rosa Parks."

I sensed Viola bristle at what I had just said.

"My sister Wanda likes to refer to me in those terms. I'm Viola Desmond and Rosa Parks is who she is. Our experiences are quite different. Her courage is much, much greater than mine. I was never in danger of my life. I could drive my car anywhere in Nova Scotia without a problem. In Alabama I would have been arrested and probably shot as an uppity black female. She refused to give up her seat on the bus to a white person. Her defiant act took place in Montgomery Alabama, the heart and soul of racial discrimination. Under Alabama law her defiance made her subject to arrest and worse. She could have been shot or beaten to a pulp and hanged from a tree in front of a burning cross surrounded by men shrouded in white sheets. You must also realize that the fight against racial discrimination will always be an American story, eclipsing anything done in Canada."

We looked at each other and sat for a few moments in silence. I guess she needed time to arrange her thoughts.

"Why?" I asked, finally.

"Why did I not just go up into the balcony and sit with other black people? That's what you're asking me? Do I look like a martyr? It was the words *you people* that did it. I felt I had been hit in the stomach. I just wanted to sit in the theatre wherever I chose, watch a movie and relax for a couple of hours. In a darkened theatre what difference did the colour of my skin make? I resolved to sit there no matter what and pay the price."

And you paid it, I thought. "You left your businesses and went to Montreal. You never returned to Nova Scotia."

"I attended business school in Montreal and got involved in real estate and other ventures. Recently I came here with thoughts of becoming a theatrical agent. After the court case, I lost the fire in my belly for commerce. My husband left me. I was marked, for having been in jail. Even Wanda looked at me in a different way for awhile. It's like I had brought shame on my family. My goals were crushed. They crushed all my dreams. Now here I am in this tiny, threadbare apartment. It's too late . . .too late. I'm sick, and I'm going to die."

When she started to cry, Mrs. Robson came back in and held her sister. I sensed it was time for me to leave. I got up and headed for the door. Her sister followed me out and handed me my coat and a bag of food.

"Please thank her for me. I'm sorry if I stirred up unpleasant memories. I wanted to ask her why she came to New York."

"She hasn't told me, but I sense it is because she is ashamed of her country."

I left then. The story was never written. The paper sent me to Washington. Viola was right that events in the United States would prove more historically significant than the struggle for civil rights in Canada. Important things were happening there, culminating in the passage on July 2, 1964 of The Civil Rights Act, granting the right to vote to every American.

Viola Irene Desmond died on February 7, 1965 at the age of fifty. She is buried in her native soil at Camp Hill Cemetery in Halifax. I never saw her again.

On April 15, 2010, I attended the ceremony at Government House in Halifax when the Government of Nova Scotia granted Viola Irene Desmond a posthumous royal pardon. As I sat there my thoughts returned to my interview with Viola. I recalled her words about Rosa Parks and realized how the self-effacing Viola Desmond had seriously undervalued her own achievement of defiance. For one thing, her refusal to comply with racist policies predated Rosa Parks' by nine years. Furthermore, unlike the action of Rosa Parks, Viola's refusal to give up her seat and acquiesce to an immoral colour bar was not a pre-planned act; nor did she have the organized support of the black community to commit the act, as Rosa Parks did. For a young woman, who was somewhat innocent of the evils in society, Viola responded spontaneously, alone and with amazing courage. What she did that day, she did for all of us. It took sixty-four years for us to realize this. I wonder if she ever realized it herself.

Author's Note

I found the source material on Viola Irene Desmond to be sparse. What material there is tends to be contradictory and contains errors. I also found a tendency in some of the material to be didactic. I relied principally on Wanda Robson's book titled, *Wanda Robson Sister to Courage*. It contains a single chapter on her sister's experience in New Glasgow. The book was published in 2010, a long time after the events of 1946. Wanda herself admits her memory of events may not have been the best. But Viola was forgotten in Canada until Wanda wrote the book. The catalyst to finally pay her tribute began in 2003 when Wanda, at the age of seventy-three, took an evening course at Cape Breton University to obtain her degree. There she met Dr. Graham Reynolds, professor of history at CBU. By amazing coincidence Dr. Reynolds was lecturing on Viola Desmond. Things now began to move. Together they established at CBU The Viola Desmond Chair in Social Justice. Viola, along with other civil rights activists was the subject of a National Film Board documentary titled, *Journey to Justice*. In 2010 Jody Nyasha Warner published a children's book *Viola Desmond Won't Be Budged* with illustrations by Richard Rudnicki. The book demonstrates the cruelty of discrimination because of race and honours Viola Desmond's achievement.

The $20.00 court fine Viola paid in 1946 would translate into $260.00 in 2014.

On April 15, 2010, Nova Scotia African-Canadian Lieutenant-Governor Mayann Francis invoked the Royal Prerogative and granted Viola Desmond a rare free pardon at a ceremony in Halifax. The Royal Prerogative of Mercy is granted only under the rarest of circumstances and was the first one in Canada to be granted posthumously. The free pardon erased the conviction and claimed her innocent *ab initio* from any alleged wrongdoing at the Roseland Theatre. The pardon was accompanied by a public declaration and apology from Premier Darrell Dexter that Viola's conviction was a miscarriage of justice and charges should never have been laid. In 2012 Canada Post issued a stamp bearing her image. The Government of Nova Scotia commissioned a portrait of Viola Desmond. The portrait from which Viola Desmond stares with pride at the viewer, hangs in Government House in Halifax.

ACROSS THE SEINE FROM NOTRE DAME: FINDING ALINE MOSBY

JOURNALIST

Timothy Christian

I turn up my collar against the rainy wind and walk past the green stalls of the booksellers on the Quai Montecello. I smile at Bastien, the old soldier, and he tips his hat in a salute. My bag is heavy with ingredients for salad niçoise: green beans, small potatoes, six eggs, a fine tuna loin and strips of pungent anchovy, black olives, a baguette, a Provençal Rosé and mellow Bordeaux. My sister, Mary, is coming from California and I want to prepare a light meal to help with her jet lag. Tomorrow she will join me at the Hotel de Ville where the Mayor of Paris will present me with a prize for my dispatches from China. Though I am cynical after all these years as a foreign correspondent, I am secretly thrilled about this honour and excited to see Mary. I walk along Rue Mâitre Albèrt to a black steel-strapped oak door, insert the old brass key and twist it, push open the heavy door, and climb the stone steps to my apartment.

A long-haired cat watches indifferently, until he smells the fish, and then he rubs against my leg. "You are a greedy boy, Ivan, but then you always were. Ever since I rescued you from that ghastly basement in Moscow. You nearly died, poor baby."

In the small kitchen I set the bag on the rough plank table, glancing through the window past the Café Salon de Thé and over the

Seine to the south side of Notre Dame. This is the view that seduced me into buying the place twenty years ago. It was more than I could afford but it's a writer's perch and energy pulses through the window. I have been inspired to write some pretty good stories sitting at this table and staring out the tall window of this 17th century apartment toward the lacy spires of the cathedral. And now, the apartment is worth a small fortune.

I place the rosé in the fridge, wash the beans, peel the potatoes and light the stove. I walk to the bookcase and pick out Whit Bassow's *The Moscow Correspondents*, which just arrived in the post. Flipping to the photo of me, I read the caption:

The first truly professional reporter assigned to Moscow was Aline Mosby, then thirty seven, who worked in the UPI Bureau from 1959 to 1961. An agency veteran with almost twenty years' experience, she was best known for coverage of the Hollywood film industry. A slight, red-haired woman from Missoula Montana, she was a tenacious reporter who, in addition to the usual political fare, wrote superb feature stories about everyday life in Moscow.

That was me twenty years ago, I think, turning to look at myself in a baroque gold mirror, and frowning at the change. Still, not too bad and only a little grey at the edges. I must see Davide soon.

What a paranoid place Moscow was at the height of the cold war. I was so excited to go. I felt I was watching history unfold. Unfortunately, of the two stories that endured from my Moscow days, one was about me. I still feel chagrin, remembering it.

President Nikita Khrushchev walked into the exhibition hall housing the British Fair in Moscow wearing a poorly tailored, boxy beige overcoat matching those worn by his security detail and contrasting with the slim lines of the blue cashmere coat worn by the British Ambassador. Khrushchev raised his hands and clapped as he walked among the displays of British industry – electrical panels equipped with knobs and dials, milling machines and fashionable clothing. He shook hands with proud company representatives. Then he noticed me and waved. I saw his gold tooth glitter. He was a friendly man who liked chatting with members of the press at the embassy receptions. He often smiled at me and more than once put his arms around me in a mock bear hug, growling and whispering "kotik" (kitten) in my ear. I would twirl away and he would smile. I knew the old peasant had a soft spot for me. That is what made the "incident" even more unbearable. It is always bad news when a correspondent becomes the subject of a story.

Khrushchev's son in law, Alexei Azhubei, was the editor of *Izvestia*, the official organ of the Soviet Government, and he didn't like me. I'm not sure why. Perhaps I was too western for his tastes. I was not provocative in my dress or manners but neither did I wear a babushka. At one reception he came up to me and wiped off my eye shadow and lipstick with his handkerchief. I was horrified. Everyone told me to forget it but I never did. He would never have dared to touch a male correspondent.

Azhubei was behind the story and photo that ran on the front page of *Izvestia*, which showed me in a drunk tank with my head rolling to one side and my tongue hanging out. The story said I had been arrested for drunkenness and was a typical American correspondent abusing Russian hospitality. It was all a terrible set-up.

Just after seeing Khrushchev at the British Fair I noticed two handsome young men looking me over. They came up to chat and were friendly.

"What are you doing here? You are bored, no?" the taller one asked.

"I am a journalist and I am covering the fair," I said.

"This is not too interesting," he said. "You should come out for dinner and some intelligent conversation with my comrade and myself."

He had a pronounced Russian accent but his English was very precise. I was intrigued but apprehensive and declined the invitation with a lie about another commitment.

"Then you must join us for lunch tomorrow," he persisted. "Do you know the very fine bistro next to the Hotel Metropole? You must come and we can talk about many most interesting things."

I thought it would be safer in the daylight and I wanted to get the advice of my bureau chief, Henry Shapiro, who was an experienced Russia hand. So I agreed and they left. The next morning I told Henry what had happened. He did not think the men were KGB and suggested I might be able to pick up some useful information about what young people were thinking, since we hardly ever got to talk to ordinary Russians.

I drove my white MG, which always attracted envious glances, parked at the side of the bistro and pushed open the door, which was sealed with red felt to keep out the cold. It also kept in the strong smell of cigarettes which in those days did not trouble me because I smoked.

The two men sat at a booth with overstuffed seats coloured the same red as the felt around the door. Three glasses of amber liquor sparkled on the table. They stood up and greeted me quite formally and then we sat and started chatting about the British Fair and the recent snow storm. The taller one, Dimitri, slid a glass in my direction and motioned for me to pick it up so we could drink a toast. The Russians always want to toast and often with elaborate speeches. I didn't know what was in the glass but it looked like brandy or something strong like that. I sipped it and it was cognac. I told them I drink only champagne and the waiter quickly brought a glass. They kept holding up their glasses and saying, "Mir i druzhba" (peace and friendship) "Mir i druzhba".

They showed me some small icons, which meant to me they were black marketeers for I had been offered such pieces before. I looked at the art pieces and they raised their glasses, "Mir i druzhba," and I finally relented and drank a mouthful of the champagne. Then I got out my dictionary to look up the word for "hoodlum" for that is what I thought they were, but the letters blurred and I could not read and I thought, My God, they poisoned me. I picked up my purse and coat and staggered out of the restaurant weaving between the tables. I managed to get outside and then collapsed on a window ledge. Photographers were waiting and took shots of me. The two men started to pull me down the street and I screamed for help.

A policeman came up and said in Russian, "You're drunk." He called a car and I was taken to a drunk tank. I remember waking up at some point and seeing they had written an identification number on my knee, like they might for some prisoner. Then I must've passed out.

I woke up at about noon the next day and Henry Shapiro was waiting for me with the doctor from the American Embassy. They were relieved to see me alive and told me the police had called the embassy to tell them I was in the drunk tank.

"They slipped me a mickey," I said.

"Yes, that much is obvious," Henry said. He raised his finger to his lips and we said nothing more 'til we got back to the office. By that time the noon edition of *Izvestia* was on the streets and I was notorious.

Henry managed to get me an appointment with the Foreign Ministry where the Press attaché listened sympathetically but did not say much. I was never expelled and though was I not able to find out officially who was behind it, I never doubted it was the work of Alexei Azhubei. It must at least have been his decision to run the front page story, which was designed to make me look like a drunken idiot and discredit me with the Russian people.

I still blush, remembering how humiliated and embarrassed I felt.

I walk back to the kitchen and see the potatoes are ready. As I blanch the beans and heat water for the eggs, I remember how the scoop which came my way a few days later brought me out of the mild depression caused by the *Izvestia* piece.

Someone in the visa section at the American embassy tipped me that an American citizen had turned in his passport, saying he would not need it again as he was going to stay in the Soviet Union. Knowing that had never happened before, I got his name and phoned him at the Metropole Hotel and eventually persuaded him to talk to me. He later told me he had agreed to speak with me because I am a woman and he thought he would get a more sympathetic hearing. His name was Lee Harvey Oswald. After being with him only a short time I could tell he wasn't that bright and that he wouldn't possess the type of information that would really interest the Russians. But he was conceited and thought he would soon be welcomed into the hierarchy and given a big car and dacha and invited to dine with the leadership, including Khrushchev. I listened to his account and took notes for an hour and I filed a story about the defector. My scoop created quite a sensation.

Fourteen years later I was in Paris when news came over the wire that President Kennedy had been shot in Dallas by Lee Harvey Oswald. In the days following the assassination, I was asked to describe my impressions of the man who had killed the President. I told the press that Oswald was extremely superficial and very immature and misinformed. Oswald told me he had decided to leave the United States and go to the Soviet Union after reading books on Marx, but he actually knew very little about communism and couldn't apply what he had read to the actual life of Moscow around him. It was like he was just quoting passages from *Izvestia* and *Pravda* without really knowing what they meant.

As I read the news of the assassination I had the feeling that Oswald was enjoying every minute of his notoriety. There was that same tight-lipped secretive smirk he wore when he described his grandiose, self-imposed mission during our first interview and that same little smile was on his face when he walked out of his cell for the last time to face reporters and photographers, a smile that changed to the grimace of pain and death when he was shot by strip club owner, Jack Ruby.

The notes of my interview were later filed with the Warren Commission investigating the assassination of President Kennedy. And my notes were accurate, thanks to Mrs. Brock's course in Gregg shorthand.

I pick out my copy of the 1939 Missoula County High School yearbook, the *Bitter Root*, which has a cover made of wood and several features written by me. I glance at the photo of Mrs. Brock. My fellow students filled the book with inscriptions to "Hoops", my nickname in those days. Dorothy Mulroney wrote: "Hoops just think, after tomorrow we will all be out of this old place. Won't we be sad? I really am when I think of all the swell times we've had. You have been a swell friend all these years and I surely hope you will always have fun and all sorts of success."

What ever happened to Dot, I wonder as I peel and slice the eggs and arrange the food on two plates. I whisk a vinaigrette from olive oil, dijon, and white wine vinegar and add some pepper and shredded tarragon. I taste it and add a pinch of salt. I hear a car stopping in the street and look out the window to see Mary getting out of Guido's car. The UPI (United Press International) driver agreed to pick up Mary as he had done on her previous trips to Paris. Guido liked Mary and she enjoyed the attention and he certainly appreciated the bottle of fine scotch I slipped him every so often.

I open the door and there stands Mary, looking gorgeous, and certainly not like a mother of four grown children, even though, I can't help but note, she's a little thicker in the hips.

We embrace. "Oh Mary, how lovely to see you," I say. "How was the flight?"

"It's been too long, Ellie. So good to see you. The flight was not too bad, though I could use a hot bath and a large scotch. And look what I found in duty free," she laughs, holding up an eighteen year old Glenlivet. Ivan strolls over to sniff. Finding Mary unobjectionable he returns to the window ledge from which he can observe birds landing on the tree a few feet away.

"That looks most inviting, darling. You come in and we'll take your things to your room and you can luxuriate in the bath while I fix you a nice large one with a few rocks. I'm making a salad niçoise for dinner. It can be ready whenever you are."

Mary rolls her bags into her room and returns and picks up the copy of *Bitter Root*. "I haven't seen this old thing for years," she says, flipping through the pages until a loose paper floats to the floor.

"What's this?" she asks, stooping to pick it up. "It's the telegram Mrs. Ferris sent to you about Jack getting killed in Iwo Jima. I'm sorry, Ellie."

"Don't worry. That was a long time ago," I say.

"Dad really liked Jack," Mary says. "He looked great in his uniform."

"Yes he did," I agree as I pour two large scotches. "Dad liked him because he thought he could take over the radio station. I liked him too, but not enough to marry him. I always felt guilty for spurning him since he died in combat shortly after, but the truth is that he wanted a stay-at-home wife and that is not what I wanted."

"No, you always were an adventurer, Ellie." Mary hoists her scotch and clinks my glass. "You would never have done what I did, getting married and raising four kids. And I don't blame you. Your life has been a thrill and mine has been pretty predictable. Now why don't you come and chat with your older sister as she enjoys her bath?"

"Sure, Sis. I'll be along when you get settled," I say and pick up the telegram and read it again, probably for the hundredth time, before slipping it back into the yearbook and putting it on the shelf. It seems like someone else's life it was so long ago and so much has happened since. I set the table while Mary runs her bath and when she yells she is ready, I join her.

"You still have great breasts," I say. "You always were the pretty one."

"Oh, do you think so?" Mary asks, taking a sip and raising an eyebrow. "You know, I never really understood why you didn't marry. I know there was no shortage of men interested in you. Like the writer in Los Angeles. What was his name? He seemed like a very nice guy."

"No Mary, you were always better looking. Maybe that's why Daddy liked you best. He was never happy with me. He was disappointed I wasn't a boy. He called me Peter till I was almost three – until Granny made him stop. And remember how stingy he was with money? He hardly ever gave us anything. Or Mommy either, even though she worked so hard in the radio station and at home keeping that huge house clean and feeding us." I watch Mary take a big mouthful of scotch and slip under the soap suds to her chin.

"Yeah, that's all ancient history, but why didn't you marry?"

"Well, I always intended to, and to have children," I say, "but I could never find a guy who would allow me to follow my career. I love being a journalist and feeling independent. Part of it comes from watching Mommy. I never wanted to be like her, especially after the divorce. She was a total wreck. I never wanted to be so vulnerable a man could do that to me. I like making my own money. I mean I don't make that much but I'm free to spend it as I please. All the men I met were good and kind – I mean those I had serious relationships with – but they all wanted me to stop working and focus on them and their careers. They wanted me to be a feminine help-mate and that never appealed to me. It's different now, with women's liberation and birth control, but back then it was hard to refuse marriage and stick with a career."

"Yes, but what about that writer? He was good-looking," Mary persists.

"Mary, we can't just talk about me. How are the kids doing?"

"We'll talk all about them later, but don't avoid the question about the writer. I liked him," Mary says.

"He was nice and he was good looking, but he was also narcissistic," I say. "His work came first, and he wanted me to quit. He actually believed he was making me a great offer. I just did not want to be his subordinate. Then there was an older man, a diplomat in Paris I saw for a few years. He was charming and exciting but he wanted me to quit traveling to Moscow and far off places. He wanted me to give up journalism and live the good life with him in an elegant suite in Paris and lovely places in Cannes and New York. I was attracted, but I didn't want to lose what I had fought for."

"I so admire you," Mary says. "Somedays it was so hard putting on a happy face for Reggie's business and then having to look after the kids. I thought I was going crazy a few times. And then I would get a letter from you from some exotic place and wish I could be with you."

"Believe me it was far from glamorous," I say, "but all in all I've had a happy life and I don't have many regrets."

"What regrets?" Mary asks as she began towelling herself.

"Well, I'm still upset that your sorority wouldn't admit me in my first year," I laugh. "And I regret never having been posted to Washington. But that's about it. You get dressed in something warm and I'll sear the tuna."

"It's great to be here with you, Ellie. I really miss you."

"I miss you too, Mary, more than you'll ever know."

I light the grill and oil the pan, and just before it smokes, slide on the tuna loin. As the oil spits and sizzles I open the rosé and pour it into two of the fluted stems which I have inherited, together with the furniture in the flat, from my Father's second wife. I could not hate her despite how miserable her existence made my mother. In fact I grew to love her, and her furniture and other generous gifts were most welcome. Life is complicated, I think, as I return to the tuna and flip it over.

Mary helps serve the salad and we light the candles, sit down to dinner and toast each other.

"Your vinaigrette is delicious. No matter how hard I try I can't seem to get it just like this, so piquant and yet creamy."

"That may be the only thing I can do rather well," I say. "I think it is the quality of the oil here, and the tarragon. It's slightly pungent."

"This is a perfect meal, Ellie. Here's to you," and we clink glasses again.

"What is the award you're receiving tomorrow? I've come all the way here for the ceremony but I don't really know what it's all about."

"Its called the Bernard J. Cabanes Prize and it's given to journalists from press agencies in memory of Bernie, who was killed in June, 1975 in a bomb attack on his home. Tragically, it was a case of mistaken identity. The bombers intended to kill a different Bernard Cabanes who was involved in a bitter labour dispute. I knew Bernie, but not well. He covered North Vietnam during the war and described the aftermath of U.S. missile attacks on Hanoi. He witnessed the shooting down of the plane piloted by John McCain and later reported on the comments made by McCain after he had been tortured. You probably remember when McCain said that the morale of the Vietnamese people was very high and that basically they were going to win the war?"

"Yes, I do remember seeing him and the other POWs on TV. What a terrible war," Mary says. "But why are you getting the prize?"

"It's for the stories I filed about religion in China last year. I loved Beijing. The people were so much warmer than the Russians and the food was much better. They hadn't seen many westerners and they could not get over my red hair. Children followed me in the streets. The idea of religious faith surviving the cultural revolution fascinated me and I interviewed Christians and Buddhists, Hindus and Confucians, and even three Jewish families I found there. I mean descendants of Jews who had moved to China centuries ago, not recent immigrants from some European country. I got a lot of mail on that story."

Mary stands up and pours us each a glass of the bordeaux, which is earthy. "What's the plan for tomorrow?"

"There's a little ceremony at the Hotel de Ville where the Mayor will present the prize, and then a reception, and then my UPI Bureau Chief, Gerry Loughran, has invited us and a couple of colleagues to dinner at Les Deux Anges. It should be fun."

"Who's Gerry?" Mary asks, raising her eyebrows saucily.

"He is a very hard-working man, a fast and stylish writer with high standards and a quick sense of humour. He's a lot younger than me but I like him and I believe he has promise as a journalist if he can get out of management."

"What does he look like?" Mary asks.

"He's not tall but he is solid and cute and at the moment is sporting mutton chops, which make him look a little stern. He's a great colleague and he likes Ivan and what is more important, Ivan likes him, and Gerry doesn't seem to mind looking after Ivan when I have to leave town in a hurry. Gerry's cat, Oliver, is Ivan's pal."

"Do I detect a little romantic interest in Gerry?" Mary asks.

"No. I am eleven years older than him, but I do like him very much."

"I look forward to meeting him. The dinner sounds great. What a career you've had: Hollywood to Moscow, Paris to Beijing, and all those male colleagues. What was Marilyn Monroe like?" Mary asks.

"She was a practical girl." I pause for a long sip of the bordeaux. "I got a tip that the nude photo on a popular calendar called 'Golden Dreams' was of Marilyn and I wrote a story in which I said so. The picture was tame by today's standards but it was risqué then. The studio people were furious because they thought my story would ruin Marilyn's career and they put a lot of pressure on my editor. Marilyn herself was not ashamed about what she had done and granted me an exclusive interview. I found her quite charming. She told me later that when she first read my piece she was alarmed, but after she thought it over she realized it was good for her, which it was of course. She was never mad at me. I wouldn't say she was an intellectual, but she was foxy and cunning."

"You know, while I was attending P.T.A. meetings and talking to other mothers and entertaining Reggie's business friends you got to cover the academy awards and interview Hollywood celebrities. I was a little jealous sometimes."

"You didn't miss much, Mary. That world may seem enchanting to the public, but actors and actresses aren't very interesting people. Their job is to say other peoples' words and when they haven't memorized a script they are no more insightful than the average person. And sometimes the celebrity cult ruins them, and makes them think they really are special when they're not. And some of them are poorly managed and they make bad decisions."

"Yes, I suppose so," Mary says, slightly slurring the "s" on "so" and I realize that the jet lag, scotch, rosé and bordeaux are taking a toll on her. Sweet girl, she'll need to go to bed soon.

"Elvis Presley comes to mind," I say, and Mary's eyes open wide. "He had some talent, no doubt, but his retinue of cousins and uncles from Tennessee surrounded him and kept him from becoming his own man. He once stood me up, you know. We were supposed to do an interview in Las Vegas after the opening of 'Love me Tender', but he decided to go instead to the opening of a Randolph Scott western. I was furious because I'd driven down from L.A. *Billboard* got hold of the story and only slightly exaggerated when they said I screamed out of Las Vegas with blood in my eyes. Elvis, or his manager more likely, realized that was no way to treat a celebrity reporter and Elvis offered me an exclusive interview on the set of 'Jailhouse Rock'. The studio had just surrendered to fan pressure and agreed to let Elvis perform with a brush cut wig instead of cutting off his side burns and bangs. It was the biggest crisis in the movie industry since Lassie was exposed as a he. Elvis told me he was happy with the decision because the fans liked his hair long, and if he didn't please the fans he'd be back driving a truck. He was a country boy who ate mashed potatoes, bacon and sliced tomatoes and drank coke every lunch because it was the closest thing to his Mama's home cooking."

"Take me to bed, Ellie, and tuck me in. I am fading."

I walk her to her to her room, pull back the comforter and fluff her pillow. She climbs in and I pull the comforter up to her chin and kiss her lightly on her forehead.

"Will you ever come home?" Mary asks, her head nestled in the pillow, her curly hair surrounding her face.

"I can't believe how quickly the years have passed," I say. "I tried New York but I found it boring. Paris is much more charming and alive and I love it here. It's not that I forget Montana. No, I return every summer to the cottage Dad built by the lake, and I love it there, too. I always keep it alive in my memory. I hear the robins' evening concert and see the deer chewing their way through the underbrush and the platoon of Canada geese flapping slowly over the lake, which is as smooth and silent as glass. I hear the raucous cry of the loon and realize that the beautiful Notre Dame is merely man-made greatness. Yes, I will come home... someday." I look up and see Mary has drifted off. Poor woman, having to listen to me go on about myself all night. Tomorrow will be her turn.

I clear off the table and find a few scraps of tuna for Ivan who has come to appreciate my vinaigrette over the years. He purrs loudly and arches his back, almost standing on his tippy toes, and rubs against my leg. "All right my darling, try this," and he snatches the fish from my fingers and paws it into his mouth.

I turn on the water and it becomes warm and soothes my chilly hands. When the sink is full of suds I begin washing the dishes. Looking out my window I see people are still eating at the outdoor café across the street and I think what a long way I have come from Missoula. Reflecting on the honour I will receive tomorrow from Jacques Chirac, the Mayor of Paris, I feel pleased, imagining the elegant ceremony. Then a small photo album lodged in Mary's bag catches my eye. As I flip through the pictures of her smiling children I begin feeling sentimental.

Closing the album I breathe in deeply, look out the window across the Seine and know that the choices I made were the right ones for me.

Author's Note

Kate and I were living in Aix-en-Provence and decided to go to Paris for a week. We rented an apartment across the Seine from Notre Dame Cathedral. It was a magical place and, as I leaned out the window looking at Notre Dame, tourists photographed me as if I, myself, formed part of the fabric of Paris.

I began exploring the book shelves and found volumes dedicated to Aline Mosby by Harrison Salisbury and other famous correspondents. Wondering who Aline Mosby might be, I began researching obsessively and read her book about her life as the only female correspondent in Moscow, *The View From No. 13 People's Street* and many of her pieces published in the *New York Times* and *The Globe and Mail*, and her interview with Kathleen Currie for the Washington Press Club Foundation.

Though Aline had been dead since 1998, her apartment sheltered her books and art and her spirit, and I passed through the portal in her bookshelf and found this story.

BRENDA DAVIES
PLAYS KATHARINA

ACTOR AND WIFE OF ROBERTSON DAVIES

Lise Lévesque

I t is late spring in Peterborough, though the drafts that seep through every crevice of the Little Theatre building would like to tell you otherwise. Spotlights have kept the cast members warm enough to ensure fluid movement through a dress rehearsal of *The Taming of the Shrew*. The play is a brave enterprise by Robertson Davies who, up to now, only has three productions under his belt as a playwright and director. And some of these were not well-received due to his finger-pointing at the boorish attitude of certain members of the political corps and the clergy.

Presently, his wife Brenda, who has taken on the lead as Katharina, is waiting for him in the tenth row of the theatre. She is tired and shivering in a revealing chiffon dress that accentuates her cleavage and waist line. The loose sleeves, flowing skirt and small train have been sewn together in shades of peach and red to depict both the feisty and demure attitudes of the character in the final scene.

The short version of the story is that in Padua, Petruchio is looking for a wife with a hefty dowry. He has heard about Katharina. His friends tell him that she could be a match though her more docile sister Bianca might be better suited to the rigors of marriage. Kate is the oldest and must wed first, but she has the reputation of being feisty. Taming this shrew, they warn him, is a task for Hercules.

"But," he tells them, *"I am peremptory as she is proud-minded:*
And where two raging fires meet together;
They do consume the thing that feeds their fury."

Feeling up to the challenge, Petruchio decides to use reverse psychology. He praises the conduct for which Katharina has been chastised and kills her with kindness. With time, he gets her attention and her willingness to become his wife. Yet, he hurts her pride by showing up late for the wedding. The woman is getting back some of her own behaviour and she does not like it. At the celebration, Petruchio and two other husbands wage money to see whose wife is likely to appear first when summoned. To everyone's surprise only Katharina does. Furthermore, she claims to be ashamed of her peers for being antagonistic at a time when they should be grateful.

To better embody Katharina, Brenda has let her brown hair grow and treated it with henna to bring out the copper tones. It is a departure from her short blunt cut and it has become another item on her long list of chores. This afternoon, for example, once her mane was up in curlers, she had to do the ironing of Robertson's and the children's clothes for the Sunday service at their local church. Then, she prepared the family's evening meal and gave a bath to the younger girls.

All the while, she reflects on the role of wives in the late fifteen hundreds. *I may not be a slave,* she thinks as she checks her to-do list before leaving for the theatre, *but things haven't changed that much. All Robertson has to worry about is the play and yet, he is acting as if the weight of the world is on his shoulders. And, why,* she wonders angrily, *did he allow Miranda to join us and sit through the rehearsal?* Miranda is their nine year old daughter. *I had already said no to her repeated pleas. Does he not think of how his decisions affect me? For one, he undermines my authority. Then, I have to lay out a proper outfit for the child, coax her into it and put the other two girls to bed while I get myself ready. It is no wonder,* Brenda surmises, *that Shakespeare used boy actors to represent women in his plays. Even if it had been proper for a woman of the era to be on stage, unless she was fortunate enough to have servants, she would have been too spent to leave the house after catering to her husband and brood without modern appliances.*

However, Brenda Davies is nothing if not efficient. Not only does get things done in time for the rehearsal but she drives the three of them to the theatre and makes sure Miranda is settled before going to her change room. Afterwards, she slips into Katharina's skin while she puts on her costume and appears on stage fresh and feisty to deliver the character's demanding lines without a hiccup.

Robertson Davies is making some last-minute recommendations to the actor who is playing Petruchio; a role for which he felt himself better suited. But as a director, it would have been too demanding to act and oversee the play simultaneously. So, à la Hitchcock, he decided to make a cameo appearance. In fact, when he finally joins Brenda in the tenth row of the theatre, he is still garbed as a tailor, sporting silk stockings, pantaloons, a rust livery trimmed in brown velvet, and a white jabot collar. Their intention is to review the outcome of the rehearsal.

They have been dissecting plays together for years, initially, after attending performances from the likes of Laurence Olivier, Peggy Ashcroft and Alec Guinness in London, England and, later, at the Old Vic Theatre where he took on roles and she worked as a Stage Manager. Fresh out of her native Australia, she did not have his name or their three children then. It was World War II that changed the course of their lives. It made them flee to Canada where they have established new roots and are attempting to instill the love of Theatre into provincial folks.

It has been arduous, at times, what with Robertson's critical views of his environment made public in his journalistic work at *The Examiner*. But, under his direction and with her magic touch, both on stage and as an adviser to the costume and prop makers, the Little Theatre has planted its feet on the theatrical map of Canada. Still, the outcome of this particular production matters more than ever to all involved. Indeed, Shakespeare's *Taming of the Shrew* is the pearl of all plays, sought by most directors and thespians of caliber as a rite of passage into the world of theatre art. In the role of Katharina, Brenda Ethel Davies is seeking to make a name for herself as an actress. There is more to her than being a wife and living in the shadow of a journalist and prolific writer, more to her than being the mother of three smart daughters. She has assets of her own, such as respectable roots, talent and education. She is well-read, well-travelled and has been exposed to the arts. She can read people as well as she can interpret characters. Her goal, in this endeavour, is to make Katharina shine in Canada, as brilliantly as she did in England, in the days when she was introduced to Shakespeare's shrew.

The Davies have planned and rehearsed this production for months. They have had several tête-à-têtes when, line by line, they have sought to understand and correctly interpret Shakespeare's meanings and intentions. They have chosen a reserved blond actress to create a contrast between Katharina and her sister. They have seen to it that Petruchio is played by an actor who can vacillate, seamlessly, between the boasting bachelor and humble seducer facets of his personality. The whole performance is a feat in as much as it employs twenty-seven actors. The Davies hope that a cast of this size will stimulate interest in the community and fill the room at the première. So far, everyone has managed well and, tonight, the dress rehearsal showed promise.

As is her habit, Brenda has had input into the costumes and the props. She has paid particular attention to the design of Petruchio's wedding attire, since his intention is to further humiliate Katharina by dressing as a clown. As to the set design, after consulting with Robertson, she has taken a minimalist approach. Ten years prior to this production, he had researched the entire *Commedia dell'arte* for the British theatrical director, Tyrone Guthrie. Of late, this has been paying off. This form of theatre supports acting on temporary stages and in outdoor productions by relying more on props than backdrops. Not only does it suit the Little Theatre's budget but it will allow the troupe to show off their ability outside of Peterborough. Undeniably, as they sit in front of the stage, the Davies are proud of their combined achievement.

"Did you hear Miranda laugh at Katharina's antics?" Asks Robertson.

Brenda nods, ostensibly pleased.

"I suppose she's not used to seeing her mother in a feisty mood."

"She's seen me. She just hasn't heard me."

Robertson ignores her comment. "By the way, where is she?"

"She left with the Stage Manager. I've promised to turn off the lights and lock up the theatre in exchange for her driving *our daughter* home."

Brenda has stressed the "our daughter" part of the sentence. She is tired of solving the children's problems on her own.

"You should have heard how belligerent she sounded. She ..."

Robertson's mind is focussed on the fact that the props have not been put away.

"Who?" he asks. "The Stage Manager?"

"No. Miranda ... about having to go home before we do. You're too lax with her lately. She balks at everything I ask her to do."

Robertson's mind is elsewhere and Brenda doesn't bother pursuing the argument. *The only thing you care about is that damn play,* she rants internally as she rectifies her posture in the seat.

"The Stage Manager will be back to tidy up in the morning," she announces in an all-business tone. "Does anything else need my attention?"

After their exchange, Brenda wishes to take a few minutes of quiet time to put the final touch on Katharina's soliloquy in Scene five. She has put much thought into this interpretation. In the days of Shakespeare, women were slaves to their husbands. Their only choice, as they accomplished what was expected of them, was to behave in an obliging or disgruntled way. Acting as a shrew could only end badly. Unyielding women would either be beaten into submission or repudiated to a life of prostitution. In Shakespeare's play, it is the gentle coaxing of her husband-to-be that has brought about a change of heart in Katharina. She is willing to be subservient because she has been acknowledged as a person of value. Brenda relates to this. Robertson respects her opinions and capabilities and it brings out the best in her. Yet, at this period of her life, the women's liberation movement is in its infancy. Though she has the freedom to express herself, and some money at her disposal, her choices are limited. It is still up to her to oversee the care of their home and children, and of her husband.

Brenda is not a fool. She knows that by comparison to her peers, she has gained some ground in the relationship. In fact, as Robertson's timekeeper, critic and collaborator, she has managed to tame his impetuousness as much as she has yielded to his personal needs and creativity. As well, she has been pushing the envelope by using all the arrows in her quiver to pursue her self-actualization. But all is not equal and, of late, she sounds a little sour when she tallies up how, unlike her husband, she has hardly any time to express herself intellec-tually. He is well aware of the situation. Yet, he continues to depend on her for his personal needs and only dabbles in the children's lives by encouraging them to sing and telling them stories. Meanwhile, he relies heavily on the conviction that Brenda will cope with it all. In fact, as she steps into the limelight this week, he has no doubt that his wife will deliver a strong performance, that she will manifest a Katharina that is alternately feisty, poised and tender. As well, he is certain that her Australian voice will release the Shakespearian verses as melodiously as an experienced soprano would sing an aria.

Of late, Brenda has been studying The Alexander Technique and, not only has it improved her demeanour, but it has freed her voice. She claims that it is the tone of the final soliloquy that she wants to fine-tune, after their discussion. Robertson has not planned to sit through this part of the rehearsal. His wife is an artist in her own right. She does not need advice for she understands what is required in the delivery of the text. So, as softly as his corpulence allows, he begins to tread towards his change room while Brenda steps on the stage to deliver the famous lines:

"Fie, fie! Unknit that threatening unkind brow,
And dart not scornful glances from those eyes,
To wound thy lord, thy king, thy governor:
It blots thy beauty as frosts do bite the meads..."

Many interpretations have been made of Katharina's discourse on the role of women in marriage. For one thing, after chastising her peers for not showing up when summoned, she rants on the merit of obeying one's husband. This is an absolute reversal of the stance she has taken towards men, prior to meeting Petruchio. That is the attitude Shakespeare intended to convey through Katharina's character. Yet, when the time comes for Brenda to refer to the women's mates as thy lord, thy governor or thy king, she is aware that only a slight change of tone would be needed for her to turn the entire play into a farce. In fact, saying these words with tongue in cheek is so tempting that Brenda Ethel Davies smiles and takes a moment to revel in the power of her position.

Author's Note

The life of Brenda Ethel Davies spanned over nine decades and three continents. Her last photograph, a digital downloadable picture from the internet, hails her as the supporting wife of the literary giant, William Robertson Davies. But, to depict the whole woman, one has to envision a collage of sepia photos revealing a child in front of a country house with a horse and buggy in the foreground, and a debutante on the steps of a Victorian manor in Melbourne, Australia; shiny black and white snaps of a young woman and her beau, chased from a London theatre by menacing German Bombers; coloured polaroid pictures of a wife and mother of three, driving through the snowbanks of Ontario; printed posters of leading ladies of various moods and vintages; and finally, slides of an ageing woman waxing nostalgic while revisiting England. It was the variety of images that remained in my mind's eye after researching Brenda's life and what made me want to portray her as a feminist and possible activist.

HOW BABIES ARE MADE: MARTHA NELSON THOMAS & HER DOLL BABIES

SOFT SCULPTURE ARTIST WHOSE WORK WAS THE STOLEN SOURCE OF CABBAGE PATCH DOLLS

Bernadette Rule

Martha felt carefully the texture and weight of each piece of fabric in her bag of flesh-toned materials before settling on the honey-gold cambric for baby Ilsie's skin. Ilsie was mixed race, with a German-American mother and an African-American father. She was an apple-cheeked little dumpling with a cleft chin and enormous hazel eyes. Her masses of curly black hair topped a wistful expression.

From a drawer filled with baby clothes gathered from garage sales and used clothing stores, Martha fished out a smocked, lilac dress of handkerchief-cloth and a pair of Mary Jane shoes. Perfect. She shook her head, smiling. She could just see her. Ilsie was partial to mashed sweet potatoes with butter, and she loved to play pat-a-cake. She was a little afraid of bees, but she liked imitating their buzzing sounds.

With swift, sure motions, Martha was drawing unbleached lisle thread through the cambric to make Ilsie's right hand when she heard footsteps cross the porch. Then the rusty hinge of the mailbox lid brayed. She just had time to wave a return to George's greeting as he turned toward the Carters' house with a handful of mail for them.

It was September, lovely and warm. Her thimble still on the middle finger of her left hand, she sat down in the porch swing to sort through the mail. She read Ann's letter first. She had written to tell Martha the news from back home in Mayfield, all the way across the state. Her brother Ernie had taken over King's Flowers and both Ann and Mary Ruth were now working there with him. Mom was well. She'd made one of her famous lamb cakes for Ernie's open house. Pat had been able to make it home for the opening. Martha felt a pang at having missed another family milestone. She and Tucker and Seth would be there for Thanksgiving, but that was two months away. Much as she loved her life in Louisville, she often wished she could be in two places at one time. It had been so difficult to uproot from home. Now she had two homes, and it tore at her heart.

Leafing through the rest of the mail, she saw a couple of bills, a pizza flyer, and a number ten envelope with handwriting she didn't recognize. The return address answered her unspoken query. It was from Xavier Roberts, a young man she had met this past summer at the annual art fair put on by the Kentucky Guild of Arists & Craftsmen. He was the head buyer of a gift shop in Georgia, and not only had he bought a Doll Baby – Jeremy – for himself, but he had taken five more on consignment. Her heart soared at the thought of a cheque – maybe one of them had sold.

She slit the envelope open with her finger and a cheque fell out. $100! Two had sold! Elated, she opened the accompanying letter. *Dear Martha Nelson Thomas*, it said, *I am enclosing your payment for two dolls. They sold so fast I want twenty-five more as soon as possible.*

"Twenty-five," Martha murmured out loud. "What does he think I am – a machine? And if they sold so fast, why has he only sent me the money for two of them?"

The letter went on to say that, in his opinion, she had the dolls priced too low. Since they were so popular, she should charge a higher price, which would make more money for her and increase his commission as well.

Something about the tone of Roberts' letter was off. She stood up and went back inside their little "shotgun" house, dropped the mail onto the hall table, and went to check on Seth, who should be stirring from his nap soon.

She found Seth spraddled in his crib, belly down, his cornsilk hair damp with the heat of deep sleep. Martha stood looking at him, overwhelmed with love. Even after a year, she still couldn't quite believe in him. Whether it was the creaking of the floorboards when she entered, or her intense gaze, something woke him up and he scrambled to his feet with a sleepy smile, calling, "Mama!" She lifted him up against her and he settled his head snugly into her shoulder for a long, swaying hug.

When Tucker got home from work she told him about the letter from Roberts. He packed Seth over to where she was chopping vegetables at the tiny scrap of a counter.

"But this is good news, isn't it, darlin'? I mean, he wants to see you make more from your Doll Babies than..."

"It's not about me making more money, Tucker. He's the one who's wanting more money. And he hasn't sent me the full amount that's owing. I have a bad feeling about this guy. I want to keep my dolls affordable. And besides, you know how I feel about them – they're not meant to be seen as just toys. I want them to be as close to real babies as I can make them."

"I know. Like another member of the family. Ain't that right, Seth?" Tucker blew a raspberry into Seth's neck and the baby erupted into giggles.

"I've about decided I'm going to write him back and tell him I'm not raising the price," Martha said, scraping the vegetables from the cutting board into a pot of water. "In fact, I have a good mind not to send him more Doll Babies at all. I don't think I want to do any more business with him."

"Well, you got to go with your gut instinct on this. They're your babies, not his."

○

When Xavier Roberts got Martha's reply, he was not pleased. The Doll Babies had been a big hit at the store, and customers were coming in asking when he would have more of them in stock. He had made confident promises.

These Doll Babies were something new. Each one was unique, hand-made and named. They were life-sized, and soft. She used the term "soft sculpture" for them. Holding one of them felt closer to cuddling a living infant than you felt with most dolls. Each came with a letter telling the new owner all about the doll, it's special likes and dislikes. They wore real baby clothes, slightly worn, which intensified the sense that the doll was almost a real baby – had had a life. It was genius. You weren't just buying a toy – it was as if you were taking little Dusty or Sandy or B.J. into your life. It took the concept of dolls to a new level, and the customers seemed to understand this immediately.

"'Not going to be sending more dolls,'" he muttered, as he rolled a fresh piece of letterhead into the typewriter. "We'll see about that." If she wanted to play hardball with him, she'd find out he could do business in that sport. How smart could she be, cutting off trade with him when he still owed her for three dolls? He'd show her. He wrote *Mrs.* Martha Nelson Thomas a reply, with the words: *I'll sell dolls like yours whether you make them or someone else does.*

After he stamped and sealed the letter and filed it in the out-box, he didn't go back out to the sales floor, but sat on in his tiny office, thinking. That night he took up the Doll Baby he had bought last summer and examined it. He undressed it to probe its secrets. Looked closely at its neck and appendages. Ran a finger over its seams. Slowly stroked its face and felt under the "hair" on its head. Pulled the tender little petal of an ear out to study it. Simple. Every stitch, simple as could be. He took a pair of scissors to the stitches on little Jeremy's neck, snipping them, one by one. Eventually he had the pattern spread flat on the table, the stuffing laid to one side. Having reduced Jeremy from a little fellow in jeans and a plaid shirt to an object, a thing he could rebuild, he called his mother and, with her support and encouragement, worked out a plan. He would quit his job at the gift shop and begin making dolls himself.

○

Martha felt good about her decision. She was simply not prepared to work with people who didn't understand what she was doing. She continued making Doll Babies – one at a time, each one an individual, like its owner. For Christmas that year she made portrait dolls of herself and Tucker. These were a big hit, inspiring requests from many friends and family members. Martha's doll portraits were both amusing and somewhat startling in their ability to capture a person's look and character. From the first decisions about fabrics and clothing, to the last loop of hair sewn onto the doll's head, Martha had an uncanny ability with soft sculpture. It wasn't only because she was good with her hands; it was also because, outside of her large family, this was how she understood and loved people – one at a time.

She prospered, at exactly the pace she was comfortable with. Her Doll Babies sold about as quickly as she could make them. It was adults who bought them, some to give to children, and some to keep for themselves. Celebrities such as Cher and Sally Struthers owned Doll Babies. All kinds of people found themselves charmed to pieces by their sweet faces and huggability. Martha also continued to paint – portraits, still-lifes and landscapes. As a wife and mother, she thrived, having two more babies, Carl and Mara. The little house was crowded, but life was full and good.

Then one day a friend called to say, "Hey! I saw your dolls for sale in the Atlanta Airport. Good for you, Martha! You're really getting them out there."

"What? I don't have any Doll Babies in the Atlanta Airport."

It was the beginning of the nightmare.

O

When she investigated, Martha found out that dolls, looking very much like the ones she made, were being produced by a company called Appalachian Artworks, Inc. They were called "Little People". These dolls had become an overnight sensation. They came with adoption papers. The name Xavier Roberts was written across each baby's bottom.

She was thunderstruck. "Where do you sign a baby?" she asked Tucker. "Why would you sign a baby?"

Martha was a deeply sensitive person who had avoided the spotlight all her life. The sixth of eight children, she was part of a close-knit, creative family. Her seamstress mother and her father – a forester who died when Martha was eight – had raised their children to value qualities such as humility and honesty. They believed that handmade was better than storebought, not only for the one receiving the gift, but for the giver as well. Now it seemed that modern consumer society was challenging Martha's values through the very work of her imagination.

As time went on, Roberts' Little People dolls became more and more prominent. He was interviewed as a creative phenomenon, and claimed that he had specialized in soft sculpture as an art school student. He said that was when he had come up with the idea for the dolls. He opened "Babyland General Hospital" in his hometown of Cleveland, Georgia, where clerks costumed as nurses "delivered" babies to customers from a big cabbage. It became a huge tourist draw.

Martha tried to ignore the insult of this blatant theft. She tried to ignore Xavier Roberts; but he and his Little People seemed to be everywhere. She carried on with her own work, but she was often brought to tears of frustration and quelled rage as she sewed smiles or quirky expressions of innocent questioning onto the faces of her Doll Babies. The last straw came when a patron at one of the art fairs at which she had featured her work for years, accused her of stealing

Roberts' work. "Why, these are just like 'Little People' dolls," the woman said, an expression of indignant disgust on her face. "Are you allowed to just copycat a brand-name toy like that?"

Finally, in 1979, at the insistent prompting of friends, Martha did something she had never imagined she would do. She filed a lawsuit against Xavier Roberts. Unable to afford to hire a lawyer, she sought help through Legal Aid, and found it in the kind-hearted person of Jack Wheat.

"Do you have any proof of copyright, Mrs. Thomas?" Wheat asked at their first meeting.

Martha had never copyrighted her dolls – each one was different. "It would be like copyrighting Seth," she told Mr. Wheat.

He nodded deeply, but encouraged her to copyright the concept of the Doll Babies without further delay. He said he would look into the issue and get back to her.

"I'll be happy to represent you," he told her the following week. "I've done some research, and I believe that, even without a copyright *per se,* we can prove that you've been making and selling your dolls since 1971. Roberts was a high school student then, and had not yet attended college, where he's claiming his brilliant idea came to him."

Though it seemed to be an open-and-shut case of theft of intellectual property, it did not prove to be simple. Roberts had the money to hire a crack legal team. A bank of lawyers faced off against Jack Wheat. The state of Georgia itself threw its support behind Roberts, not wanting to lose this lucrative phenomenon he had brought them. The court case dragged on for six years, each session intimidating and deeply stressful for Martha. She lost. Wheat appealed. With more and more money behind him, Roberts prevailed. But perhaps he knew his lies made him vulnerable, for in 1982 he began mass-producing the dolls with the Coleco toy company. They renamed them Cabbage Patch Kids, and the roof blew off. By the Christmas season of 1983, the toy went "viral" – years before that term became popular. Still, the word seems apt, carrying as it does the idea of disease.

That Christmas, enough people believed they simply *had* to have a Cabbage Patch Doll, that they lined up for hours and turned themselves into a human tsunami when stores opened. Pitched battles raged over the dolls, as supply could not match demand. Martha watched the newscasts with disbelief and dismay. Tears streamed down her face at the travesty Roberts had made of her idea.

Meanwhile, he became a multi-millionaire. He built himself a mansion, which featured such amenities as a slide from which he could sail down to his huge, in-ground pool from his second-storey bedroom. He was the darling of the media, a "lovely young man" who made this sweet toy that delighted young and old alike.

O

The day the protracted lawsuit finally wrapped up, Martha and Tucker stopped by her brother Albert's house to pick up their three children. Albert and Penny had babysat for them. They were eager to hear the results of the trial.

"What happened?" Penny asked, as the children swarmed their parents. "Come in and sit down a minute."

"Well," said Tucker, pulling Carl onto his lap, "we accepted an out-of-court settlement. It's over. It's finally over."

Albert studied Martha warily. She sat on the couch with Seth leaning against her on one side and Mara on her lap. "Are you happy about this, Martha?"

She tried to smile. "I'm happy it's over, that's for sure."

"What about the results?" Albert asked. "How do you feel about the settlement?"

Martha sighed. "My kids will be able to go to college," she said. "And we'll be able move to a bigger house."

"We're sworn to secrecy about the amount," Tucker added, "so we can't talk about the details, but Roberts'll be allowed to go on producing dolls. The most important thing is that he finally admitted he took the idea from Martha, so that goes on the record. Anyway, it's over – we're sure glad about that, aren't we, hon?"

She was quiet.

Tucker continued, "Anyway, as long as Martha's satisfied..."

"*Are* you satisfied, Martha?" asked Albert.

She looked down, her chin trembling. "It was never about the money."

When the tears spilled over, her family moved to encircle her with love.

Epilogue

Martha Nelson Thomas continued to make art, including her dolls, but the Cabbage Patch craze had taken something vital from her. Xavier Roberts had taken something vital from her. She contracted cancer in her fifties, and died in 2013 at the age of 62. For her memorial service, Tucker invited people to bring their Doll Babies, and the church pews filled up with the seemingly infinite variety of her creations.

Author's Note

I have taken liberties with the timeline of the story (Martha met Xavier Roberts in 1976; she sued him in 1979; she did not marry until 1981), but the story itself is true.

Martha Nelson was one of my closest childhood friends. I have never known her, nor any member of her family, to be anything but kind, talented and generous.

We had only one problem in all the years I knew her. I was ten and she was eleven. I had spent the night at her house several times, and I wanted to host her for a sleepover at my house, which was three blocks from hers. She had agreed to come, but only reluctantly, because she was very shy and was tightly bound to her home and family. As the sun started to set, homesickness overwhelmed her. She suddenly broke down crying, apologized to me and ran home.

The next evening, as I sat at the kitchen table having supper with my family, I heard the front door open and close. When I went to see who was there, I found a homemade doll just inside the door, with a piece of paper tucked under her hand. It read, "I'm sorry." With the doll in the crook of my arm, I went out to the sidewalk and looked up the street toward Broadway. Martha had already rounded the corner for home.

To learn more about Martha Nelson Thomas, see "The Secret History of Cabbage Patch Kids" (2015: Vice Media, LLC) https://www.youtube.com/watch?v=tSk84zU1RuM

AUTHOR BIOGRAPHIES

Jean Rae Baxter writes for both adults and young adults. She has written two short story collections, *A Twist of Malice and Scattered Light,* and a literary murder mystery, *Looking For Cardenio.* Increasingly she is writing Canadian historical fiction. *The White Oneida* (2014) is the fourth book in her Forging Canada series.

Timothy Christian is a retired Professor and Dean of Law from the University of Alberta in Edmonton; a former Chief Federal Negotiator who concluded a number of agreements with First Nations' peoples; and a labour arbitrator and mediator. He lives in North Saanich, B.C. with his wife, his dog and his boat.

John Corvese is a graduate of York University and Osgoode Hall Law School. His short stories and poems have received awards and appeared in a number of publications, including: *Existere-Journal of Arts and Literature, Polar Expressions Publishing, The Prairie Journal,* and *The Great Lakes Review.* He lives in Burlington, Ontario with his family.

Ethel Edey was introduced to writing through McMaster's Writing Certificate program. She was published in *In the Wings: Stories of Forgotten Women,* and in *Engraved, Canadian Stories of World War One.* Ethel lives in Burlington, Ontario and winters in Florida. She lived in Newfoundland from 1968 to1970.

B.D. Ferguson (fergusonsforum.weebly.com) is a writer and educator whose work has appeared in *The Peterborough Examiner, Queen's Alumni Review* and several online publications. She has been long fascinated with1800s spiritualism, the public argument about its validity, and the numerous renowned people involved in both. Equally remarkable is that many of the questions posed by the Society for Psychical Research and other thoughtful folks remain unanswered.

Krista Foss is a writer whose first novel *Smoke River* was published by McClelland & Stewart in May 2014. Her short fiction has twice been a finalist for the Journey Prize. She lives and writes in Hamilton, Ontario.

Frances Hern has written three titles for *Amazing Stories*, a series about Canadian history: *Norman Bethune, Arctic Explorers: In Search of the Northwest Passage*, and *Yip Sang and The First Chinese Canadians*. She contributed to the anthology *Engraved: Canadian Stories of World War One*. Hern also writes poetry and children's stories. For more information go to www.franceshern.ca.

Ellen S. Jaffe lives in Hamilton, Ontario. Guernica published her second poetry collection, *Skinny-Dipping with the Muse* in 2014. She has won several literary awards, received grants from the Ontario Arts Council, and teaches creative writing. She has been interested in Rosalind Franklin for several years, and was glad to learn more about her and tell her story.

Montreal-born **Lise Lévesque** worked in the fields of travel, communication, education and mental health. A graduate of McMaster's Writing Program, she thrives on travel, research and writing. Her stories have been published in *Main Street, In the Wings* and *Engraved*. She edited Harland John's *Soft Targets: The Bali Bombings*, and is putting the final touches on a no-name memoir.

Bruce Meyer is the author of forty-five books, the most recent of which is *A Chronicle of Magpies and Other Stories* (Tightrope), and *The Seasons* (Porcupine's Quill). Dr. Meyer's *The Great Books* series on Michael Enright's "This Morning" is the best selling audio series in the history of the CBC. He lives in Barrie, Ontario.

Jane Mulkewich is a lawyer who has long been involved in anti-racism, human rights and Aboriginal issues, and interested in the local history of racialized people, as well as researching her own family genealogy. Jane is a graduate of McMaster University and the University of Western Ontario, and is interested in writing both non-fiction and fiction. This is her first attempt at creative non-fiction.

Katharine O'Flynn is a retired teacher who lives in Montreal. Her work has appeared in numerous print and online journals and, most recently, in Seraphim Editions' anthology, *Engraved: Canadian Stories of World War One.*

Barb Rebelo studied in McMaster's Creative Writing Program. She's been published in *Main Street, In The Dark: Stories from the Supernatural* (Tightrope Books), and in *Engraved.* Her first novel, *The Ghost of Wye Villa,* is a mystery set among her ancestral roots in Somerset England. She lives in Flamborough where she's writing a sequel.

Writer and editor **Bernadette Rule** also hosts an arts-interview radio program on 101.5 The Hawk (archive.org/details/artwaves). She has edited four books, most recently *Engraved: Canadian Stories of World War One* (Seraphim, 2014). Her most recent book is *Earth Day in Leith Churchyard: Poems in Search of Tom Thomson* (Seraphim, 2015).

Wendi Stewart lives in Wolfville, Nova Scotia. Her four daughters are her inspiration. Her first novel, *Meadowlark,* was published by NeWest Press in 2015. Stewart's work has appeared in *Every Second Thursday, The Antigonish Review,* and *The Leaf,* to name a few. She writes a weekly column for *The Fort Frances Times* and blogs at www.wendistewart.wordpress.com

Richard Van Holst is a research assistant and copy editor at Redeemer University College in Ancaster, Ontario. A voracious reader, he also enjoys films, classical music, and of course, writing. This is his second published short story; the first appeared in the collection *In the Wings: Stories of Forgotten Women.*

Michelle Ward-Kantor (michellewardkantor.com) holds a journalism diploma, a Bachelor of Education degree, and a certificate in creative writing. Her poetry, fiction and non-fiction have appeared in print and on-line collections. She has lived in Calgary, England, Australia, Vancouver and Waterdown, Ontario. She currently lives in Edmonton, where she teaches creative writing.

Carol Leigh Wehking has been writing and telling stories since childhood. Many of her stories, written for oral performance, are about real women who chose to lead lives out of the ordinary. A lifelong interest in the Underground Railroad and her own Quaker faith led her to Catharine Coffin. Carol Leigh lives, writes, and performs in Cambridge, Ontario.